Praise for Beth Williamson's *The Reward*

5 Angels and a Recommended Read! *"The Reward* is another magnificent creation from the mind of a brilliant author... Malcolm and Leigh's story is romantic, passion filled and touching... It never fails that when I read a **Beth Williamson** book I find myself submerged in a wide rainbow of emotions and I'm utterly spent by the last word. From laughter at some of the clever dialogue to shedding a tear when the emotional peaks are at their highest, whether it's from something joyful or distressing, this is what storytelling was meant to be. **Ms. Williamson** has the ability to jump into a reader's mind and soul and leave prints that can never be removed. I can't stress enough the pleasure you will miss if you sleep on this author's great work." ~ *Rachelle, Fallen Angel Reviews*

4 ½ Blue Ribbons! "If you haven't been reading Beth Williamson's MALLOY FAMILY series, you've been missing out. Each story has been heartwarming and thrilling to read. The characters are larger than life, bold as brass, and women included fight for what they believe in..." *Chrissy Dionne, Romance Junkies*

"Lovable as an outlaw, Malcolm is scorching hot as Leigh's lover and protector. Leigh's character was strong yet tender and I adored how Malcolm loved her. As the third book of the Malloy Family series, **The Reward** truly delivers. I finished **The Reward** with a happy heart for a story well told." *Talia Ricci, Joyfully Reviewed*

THE REWARD

Beth Williamson

A SAMHAIN PUBLISHING, LTD. publication.

Samhain Publishing, Ltd.
2932 Ross Clark Circle, #384
Dothan, AL 36301
www.samhainpublishing.com

First Samhain Publishing, Ltd. electronic publication: June 2006
First Samhain Publishing, Ltd. print publication: September 2006

DEDICATION

To my mom for always believing in me and for proudly boasting to one and all that her daughter is an author. Thank you for always being there for me.

CHAPTER ONE

He had lived most of his life in the shadows. Being cloaked in semi-darkness suited him, matched his opinion of the world in general. Very few exceptions ever penetrated the gloom. Most people thought he was an outlaw, and a reward for his capture or death existed for him somewhere. Being thought of as a vicious outlaw had its perks, not the least of which people left him alone in his shadows. However, it also had its drawbacks, and the worst was loneliness. He had always been lonely. He'd ridden alone with no one by his side or at his back since becoming Hermano.

Dressed in his standard dark clothes and battered brown duster, he stood with his saddlebags slung over his shoulder in the pre-dawn gloom of the kitchen and looked around slowly. He saw echoes of the love, laughter and play that marked the Calhoun family's house. A house he had no business staying at. Because he couldn't play, laugh or love. Those luxuries had long since been abandoned. It was time to go.

He reached into the pocket of his pants and pulled out a folded piece of paper with "*Roja*" written on it. *Roja* was Nicky Calhoun, the sister of his heart for four years, ever since she saved him from men who wanted to geld him and leave him for the buzzards. He in turn had helped her hide from the law when she was on the run from false murder charges, until Tyler Calhoun, an extraordinary bounty hunter, had found her and married her.

He laid the note on the kitchen table, then turned and strode swiftly out the door without a sound. The note sort of explained why he was leaving, but it was cryptic enough she wouldn't be able to follow him. He headed to the barn to get his horse, Demon, a roan even meaner than he was, and ride the hell out of Wyoming. It was just too frigging cold in this territory. Texas beckoned him back like a grasping mistress.

He entered the barn and went to Demon's stall, staying clear of his sharp teeth. He saddled the stallion, careful not to make any noise. He didn't want anyone to know he was leaving yet. Tyler was just too damned smart and Nicky too nosy by half.

Living amongst the dregs of humanity for so long had given him the skills to be as quiet as the night. He never wore spurs, or anything shiny or jingly. When he led the horse out of the barn, not even a mouse stirred behind him. He secured his saddlebags on the back of his saddle with his bedroll, then swung up with a small creak of leather.

He winced at the noise. Damn, he was getting old.

Hermano turned and headed back into the shadows of his hellish existence.

ભ ભ ભ

Two days later, Tyler caught up with him. In a small copse of trees, Hermano ate his breakfast of jerky and water in front of a pitifully small fire due to a lack of dry wood in this snowy terrain. Unhappily gnawing on his jerky, he saw the horse approaching. After cursing loudly, he mentally prepared himself to meet the ex-bounty hunter head-on. Hell, he was definitely getting old if it only took two days for him to be tracked. Used to be two years.

It was colder than a well digger's ass that morning. If Tyler had been riding all night, he was going to be in a worse mood than usual. His horse churned up the snow as he galloped toward Hermano, great plumes of hot breath shooting from the black horse's snout with each exhalation. He looked like a demon straight out of hell. Hermano stood and watched him approach, lightly resting his hands on his pistols.

Tyler was a big man, well over six feet and two hundred pounds, with hair like a crow's wing and piercing blue eyes that froze lesser men in their tracks. Hermano wasn't quite as big, but they were similar in build and he had dark hair as well, although his was wavy. His eyes were more black than anything, absent of color.

No doubt Nicky had coerced Tyler into following. It seemed married life had its compromises, ones that got Tyler's back up something good. He glared quite convincingly at Hermano as he dismounted from his big, black gelding. Fortunately, his hands were nowhere near the Colts tucked neatly in their holsters. Hermano relaxed his stance and sat back down on the hard rock that served as his seat.

"*Buenos dias*, gringo," he greeted Tyler.

"Yeah, whatever, Hermano. You know you left tracks a five-year-old child could follow."

"Did *Roja* get my note?"

Tyler grunted. "Yeah, fat lot of good that did her. She was *worried* about you. Sent me to find you and give you this."

He thrust a pair of saddlebags at him, stuffed, it seemed, with supplies.

Hermano felt a grin playing around his lips and tried to stop it. He didn't feel like getting pounded to a pulp today by the mountain of a man several years his junior.

"*Gracias.*" He stood and took the saddlebags. Looking inside, he saw biscuits, bread, canned fruit, coffee beans, other trail supplies and even a clean neckerchief. Embarrassingly, he felt a lump forming in his throat. It was the first time in many, many years someone had cared enough to make sure he had what he needed. Plus a little more. So many years since someone loved him, had been worried about him. *So long.*

"Your wife is a generous person," he finally got out. His voice was husky with emotion, dammit.

Tyler stared at him hard. "Your accent's gone again, *amigo.*"

Hermano stared into the saddlebags and tried to ignore the other man. Ignore the fact he'd made yet another mistake in forgetting his borrowed accent, the second time in a few weeks, in front of him. He was tired of living behind a mask, tired of being someone else.

Tyler cleared his throat. "Not gonna say anything, huh?"

Hermano didn't answer, which was, of course, his answer. When he finally met Tyler's eyes, he'd made a decision.

"Tell *Roja* I said *gracias*."

"I promised her I wouldn't ask you and I didn't. Just pointed something out. At least let's make some coffee and have some chow. My ass is numb from riding so hard to catch you."

Hermano nodded. They would have breakfast and then go their separate ways. They were silent as they ate the biscuits stuffed with bacon Nicky had sent and drank the awful coffee Hermano made from the leftover water in his canteen. There wasn't much they had in common, other than Nicky. Hermano wisely decided not to discuss her with Tyler. He looked annoyed enough as it was.

"Going south?" Tyler asked as he stood, brushing the snow from the back of his pants.

"Yup. Going home." He tossed out the coffee dregs, then wiped out the pot with some snow. After stuffing the pot and cups into his saddlebags, he picked up the blanket to start saddling Demon.

"You want to tell me where home is, or does she already know?" Tyler pulled out a bag of oats from his saddlebags and gave each horse a treat for breakfast.

"She doesn't know, but she knows how to reach me."

He picked up his saddle off another rock and sidestepped Demon's nip to put it on his back. He pushed his knee into the stallion's belly to force him to expel air. Son of a bitch horse tried that trick on him once in a while, and Hermano usually ended up on his head when the saddle slipped. Cinching the saddle, he hooked both sets of saddlebags and his bedroll on the back. He glanced up at Tyler to find him watching with his arms crossed over his chest.

"What if *I* need to find you?"

He stared into Tyler's blue eyes. They both loved the same woman, shared in their concern for her and her children. There might come a time when Nicky couldn't, or wouldn't say, what was in the note. Could he live with the consequences?

Probably not.

"Texas. About an hour northeast of Houston, little town named Millerton."

Tyler's eyes narrowed. "I know where it is. I'm from outside Austin myself. You know, it really chaps my ass that we're both from Texas."

Hermano swung up into the saddle. Tyler had not moved. "Do you have a name?"

He hesitated for a full minute before answering, Demon dancing beneath him. "Malcolm. Malcolm Ross y Zarza."

He turned Demon around and rode away before Tyler could pepper him with any more questions. He'd already said too much, more than he'd told anyone in too many years. The cold wind nipped at his face as he galloped.

He was going home. Going home to find the mother he left behind fifteen years ago. Going home to face Malcolm Ross again. The man he could never be, who he thought he'd never have to be again.

Malcolm. God, how he hated the sound of that name. It just didn't fit, like a jacket that was too small and pinched at the shoulders. He had once asked his mother why she had named him Malcolm. With her brogue rolling like a swollen river, she said great kings of Scotland had borne the name Malcolm. He had looked as great as a king when he was born. He stifled a snort at the memory. *King, my ass.* He was peasant stock through and through.

Home. More like the seven layers of hell.

അ അ അ

Tyler stared after the bandito as he rode off into the morning sun. He'd gotten some answers from the elusive man. Surprising ones. *Malcolm Ross?* Damn, that was a Scottish name. He sure as hell didn't look Scottish. And the y Zarza was an old-fashioned Spanish custom for bastards. So Malcolm's Spanish daddy wasn't married to his Scottish mama. There was a hell of a lot more to this story. Nicky was bound to nag him until he found out more, too. He sighed and looked at his horse.

"She's got me wrapped around her little finger. I'll be in trouble when my daughter starts taking after her mother."

He would wire a friend, a U.S. Marshall, in Houston and find out a bit more about Malcolm Ross. And about Zarza.

ଔ ଔ ଔ

Malcolm Ross had a lot of time to think. Way too much time. He thought about his mother. How wonderful she had been to him growing up. How hard his life would have been without her. That just drove the guilt to new heights, poured salt in the wound, and generally made him feel like the shitty bandito he had become. She would be ashamed of him. That cut even deeper.

He tried to remember all the other people from the hacienda he grew up on, Rancho Zarza. Like Diego and Lorena, the foreman and the housekeeper who had treated him like a favorite nephew. And Leigh. Oh, how could he have ever forgotten Leigh? She was as much a part of growing up as anything on the ranch.

A tomboy who was constantly at his side from the time she toddled up on her two feet and started following him. She was three years younger than he, and they had been as tight as ticks on a dog's ass. Wherever Malcolm went, Leigh was sure to follow. When he'd left at eighteen, she had been a very awkward fifteen. Malcolm remembered giving her a kiss in their tree house— how she'd trembled, then pressed her hands to her lips and looked at him with her bright hazel eyes shining behind her glasses. He'd left her behind, too. Never glanced back. He found himself wondering who she had married and where she lived now. He didn't suspect she lived at Rancho Zarza, but perhaps if her father was still the blacksmith, and if she'd never married… Impossible. Leigh was tall, but she was strong, healthy and smarter than most men put together. There was no way she wouldn't be married with a passel of kids at her feet.

The thought was disturbing in some strange way. He frowned at his bacon as he cooked it over the fire. It was time to stop thinking so much. There were too many memories crowding his brain, so he shut them off. He concentrated on staying alive, staying in the shadows, and reaching Texas in one piece.

He didn't want to think about what was or wasn't there waiting for him.

CHAPTER TWO

Leigh Wynne O'Reilly stared at the carcasses of at least a dozen cattle spread around the banks of a small creek on her ranch. She felt the absurd urge to weep. It was another in a long series of mishaps, accidents, and pure bad luck that had plagued her and the ranch for the last two years. Ever since she became a widow. Ever since she told every man in town to keep his dick in his pants and leave her alone. Ever since she thumbed her nose at propriety and took over a ten-thousand-acre cattle ranch. Alone.

Amidst pressure from the ranch hands, half of whom had walked off the job the day after Sean died, and her neighbors, Leigh stood firm. She was smart, strong and capable of running the goddamn ranch. Too bad if she had tits *and* a brain. If they couldn't deal with it, to hell with them.

But then things began to go wrong. Very wrong. This was just the most recent incident. Obviously someone poisoned the water, intending on killing her cattle. She had about two thousand head and what she figured were three hundred new calves, which were very vulnerable to vicious shit like poisoned water. But it looked like only two of the dead cattle were calves, thank God for small favors.

The urge to weep passed and her anger rose to the surface.

"Earl," she shouted.

"Boss?" he responded from somewhere behind her.

"Post a guard here to keep the other cattle away from this creek. Block up both ends and drain it. Then see to burning the carcasses."

Her voice was firm, no hint of a waver or indecision.

"Yes, ma'am."

His voice was full of quiet resentment, but he did what he was told, even though he was an ornery, spiteful old man. Earl shouted to a few of the other hands, giving them tasks based on her orders. Even if she was a woman, the ranch was still afloat. Barely. With all this crap, including losing two hundred head of cattle to rustlers last month, the boat had a hole in it. She could only bail so fast without sinking further down.

Leigh tightened her grip on the reins of her Appaloosa gelding, Ghost. He whinnied and sidestepped.

"Whoa, whoa," she soothed. "Don't mind me. I'm just angry as hell, boy. It's been a hell of a Monday."

She wheeled the horse around and kneed him into a fast gallop back toward the Circle O.

For the millionth time, she wished Malcolm were there. For the first fifteen years of her life, she didn't make a decision without talking to him about it. He had been her best friend, her only friend, her confidant and her first love. When he left so long ago, he took her heart with him. She had no idea where he was, or even if he was alive. She liked to think he got knocked in the head and couldn't remember where he came from. That way, the hurt of knowing he stayed away for fifteen years wasn't quite so razor sharp.

There had not been any more best friends for Leigh. She had been good friends with Sean, but she hadn't loved him. That was all right, because he hadn't loved her either. They had been friends, not truly lovers. Still, it had been a good marriage that lasted ten years. He'd taught her everything she knew about ranching. Sean had been twenty-five years older than she. It hadn't been a conventional relationship by any means. But it had been a comfortable one.

As she headed across the grassy hills toward home, she tried to set aside her worries for the half an hour it was going to take her. Summer was in full bloom in southeastern Texas. The trees were plump with green leaves, the grass full and thick, the wildflowers blooming, and the steady drone of insects echoed through the land.

If only death wasn't stalking her like a shadow. It was clear someone wanted to steal her ranch or wanted her dead. Today, either outcome seemed to be inevitable.

൪ ൪ ൪

Leigh had grown up on a hacienda, Rancho Zarza, daughter of the blacksmith, a widower and absent father. She had practically raised herself, along with the help of Leslie Ross, the cook on the ranch and Malcolm's mother. Leslie had left shortly after Malcolm's departure, so Leigh hadn't seen either Ross in quite some time.

Her father had been Big Lee. For some unknown reason, perhaps he just couldn't think of another name, he named her Leigh. So she was Little Leigh and he was Big Lee. And he lived up to his name. Her dad had been a bear of a man with a huge chest, arms like tree trunks and hands the size of dinner plates. Little Leigh wasn't very little herself. Just shy of six feet tall, she towered over most men. It was something that came in handy as a female ranch owner who just hit thirty.

But it had been torture to be so tall as a child. Teased unmercifully by Damasco Zarza, the heir to the ranch and Malcolm's half-brother, Leigh used to hunch her shoulders over and try to look smaller. To make matters worse, she had to start wearing glasses when she was six. There wasn't much feminine about her until she grew breasts at the age of sixteen. And then of course, they were big by anybody's standards. As if she hadn't endured enough with people staring at her because of her height or her glasses or her plain features, now she had something else for men to ogle.

She was a mishmash of features from her mother and father. Her mother had been tiny but had a big bosom. She died giving birth to Leigh, so her daughter's entire life had been shaped by men. Men outnumbered women ten to one on any ranch, and Rancho Zarza was no exception. That experience gave her the skills and the sheer orneriness to step where most women wouldn't dare. She wasn't most women and she stepped wherever the hell she wanted to.

As she caught sight of the Circle O ranch house in the distance, a certain measure of pride filled her heart. *That's mine. The whole thing is mine.* Sean's will was clear and ironclad. The ranch had gone to Leigh, totally and completely. For that, she would be eternally in his debt. She had never owned anything until she met Sean. He gave her Ghost, her first horse, and other gifts throughout their marriage. He taught her how to accept gifts and to give them. He taught her how to be who she was without being ashamed. To walk tall and to keep her head high. Though Sean had been her husband, he had been more of a father than Big Lee had ever been.

Leigh brought Ghost back to a trot to cool him off about half a mile from the house. He shook his mane as though telling her he wasn't finished galloping yet. She loved her horse. They had bonded the first time she gazed into his big brown eyes. Impulsively, she leaned over his neck to give the gray gelding a hug when she heard a high-pitched whine, then a rifle report.

Holy hell. Someone just shot at me.

She kneed Ghost into a fast gallop, flattening herself to his back as much as possible.

"Come on, boy, move."

That half a mile seemed like a thousand instead. When she finally got to the ranch, she tore into the yard, heading for the barn. One of the regular drovers, Andy Parker, was there, shoeing a horse and looking at her like she had two heads. He was in his thirties, a wiry man with blond hair and green eyes. He'd been kicked by a horse a few days ago and was ranch bound until his leg healed.

"Miz Leigh, you okay?"

Her goddamn hands were shaking. Completely unacceptable. With measured breaths, she forced her heart rate to slow down.

"Fine, Andy, just fine."

There was no frigging way she was going to allow some stranger, some yellow-bellied bastard who fired a bullet at someone from behind a tree, to rule her life. No way. She had to find out who it was and stop them, before they stopped her permanently.

CHAPTER THREE

Malcolm changed his mind three times after arriving in Texas. He went to two different bandito hideouts and one town in Mexico before he decided to truly go home. By then three months had passed and he was tired of kicking his own ass for being such an ass.

He finally reached his destination on a Friday morning on a beautiful summer day. Crystal blue sky, the weather too warm for long sleeves. He had taken off his duster the day he crossed the Texas state line, and he hoped like hell not to use it again for a long time. Ah, there was nothing like the warmth of Texas. Millerton was bigger—though not much—than when he had left. His stomach flip-flopped when he finally rode in sight of it. Whether from fear or excitement, he couldn't tell.

He had decided to get a job at one of the ranches and find out all he could about Rancho Zarza before letting anyone know he was back in town. It was safer that way. Safer for whom, he wasn't going to think about.

He rode up to the saloon at the end of the street. Used to be the Red Rose. Now it had a chipped sign with peeling gold paint spelling out the name Pink Slipper. So, footwear instead of thorny bushes. Probably a wise name change. He'd only stepped foot in it once, on the day he'd left, to drink a whiskey. He'd never talked to anyone but the barkeep, and only to order his drink. That first glass of real hooch had burned all the way down. Now he could drink a whole bottle and not even feel it sliding down his gullet.

Dismounting, Malcolm noticed a few stares by some folks. Two dusty cowboys lounging outside the door eyed him with distrust and a bit of venom.

One steely glance from him had them tripping over their own feet to run away. *Bandejos.*

"Hey, you."

He turned to find a potbellied man with bloodshot eyes, a runny nose, and at least two days' growth on his sagging cheeks. The top of his head barely cleared Malcolm's shoulder. Worst of all, he was wearing a silver star pinned to his dirty chambray shirt. Looked like the sheriff had eaten biscuits and gravy for breakfast, or perhaps last night for supper.

"Yeah, I'm talking to you. You speak English?"

Better to be thought of as a Mexican drifter, a comfortable skin, than a bastard Zarza.

"I speak English," he replied, laying on the accent a little heavily.

The little man came right up close, trapping him against Demon. The sun gleamed off his badge and stung Malcolm's eyes. He blinked and tried to shift his position. The sheriff grabbed his arm.

Oh, hell, no.

With a flinch, he pulled his arm free like a smoky shadow in bright sun and stepped aside a pace.

"What the hell?" the man sputtered. "How'd you do that?"

Malcolm smiled. "I learn from working with cows how to move quickly."

The sheriff looked perplexed, wondering if he'd been insulted or not. "Well, lookee here, we don't want no drifters in Millerton. So you just move along."

Ah, to be back amongst civilized people. Made him want to run back to his hideout, where he could be rude in peace.

"I am no drifter, *señor.* I come to work at Rancho Zarza."

Might as well use the name, even if he had no right to it.

"Zarza, eh? Alejandro or Damasco?" the sheriff said, looking suspicious.

Now *that* was interesting. Why would he ask that? Was there more than one Rancho Zarza?

"Alejandro." He forced himself to unlock his jaw for his father's name.

The lawman nodded, jowls swinging madly. "Good, good. You might want to steer clear of the Pink Slipper then. Damasco's boys like to throw back in there."

Well, well, well. Two groups of hands and they didn't play well together.

"You'll want to go down a piece to the Silver Nickel over yonder. Alejandro's men go there, along with O'Reilly's."

"*Gracias.*"

"Der nader," he replied. "Tell Alex Joe said hello."

The sheriff ambled off down the street, pausing once to glance back at Malcolm.

Malcolm nodded to him then swung up on Demon to head to the Silver Nickel. He'd visit the Pink Slipper later.

ೞ ೞ ೞ

When Malcolm entered the Silver Nickel, a few heads turned. Obviously not too busy yet. He was sure the cowboys would be crawling all over the place tonight though. It was a relatively clean saloon, with a long mahogany bar to the right, rows of bottles lined up on the wall behind it. A well-used brass foot rail was the only ornamentation. A dozen tables with four chairs each were scattered around, one occupied with four men playing poker, and an empty upright piano that had seen better days.

The barkeep was at the end of the bar talking with another customer. He came over when Malcolm approached. He was perhaps twenty-five, with nondescript brown hair and mutton chop sideburns. His blue eyes crinkled in greeting.

"Afternoon, stranger. What can I git fer ya?"

At least he was friendly. Malcolm reached into his pocket and pulled out a fifty-cent piece.

"Whiskey."

"Coming right up."

Taking a clean glass from beneath the bar, he grabbed a bottle of amber liquid and poured without spilling a drop.

"You one of Zarza's new men or are you working for O'Reilly?"

Malcolm didn't answer. He took a small sip of the whiskey. Out of the corner of his eye, he saw the man at the other end of the bar stand and walk toward him.

"He asked you a question, stranger."

The deep voice was so familiar it was all he could do not to jump up and embrace him. Diego Martin. Foreman of Rancho Zarza and the first friend a lonely bastard ever had. Malcolm swallowed the lump that came to his throat. He hadn't realized how much he had missed, and who he had missed, until now. Diego's hand drifted toward the pistol that rode low on his right hip. Malcolm couldn't allow Diego to draw.

"Diego," he said with a rusty voice as he grabbed the other man's hand. He finally looked up into Diego's face. Malcolm saw many more wrinkles and plenty of silver in the older man's close-cropped dark hair. "Is Lorena still making those burritos I love?"

Confusion and anger were replaced with joy and surprise on his old friend's face.

"*Jesu Cristo.*" Diego pulled Malcolm into an embrace and nearly squeezed the breath out of him. He was surprised to find he was at least four inches taller and a good thirty pounds heavier than Diego. A man who had been more of a father to him than Alejandro ever was. A man he'd thought of as the biggest, strongest man in the world. Now Malcolm was bigger and stronger. The world tilted a bit then.

"We thought you were dead. Lorena is going to cry. Mal—"

Malcolm cut him off and said in a low voice, "My friends call me Hermano now."

Diego understood immediately. "Hermano. It's so good to see you."

The barkeep watched with wide eyes. Hell, he was probably out catching frogs when Malcolm left town. Malcolm turned his eyes to the barkeep. He held his stare for a moment before the barkeep stammered an excuse and fled to the other side of the bar.

Diego chuckled. "Still such a friendly boy."

Malcolm smiled for the first time in a long time. "I can't tell you how good it is to see you, *amigo.*"

Diego smiled back. "You don't have to. I am feeling it too. Damn, I can't believe it. Do you want to come back with me?"

Malcolm shook his head. "No, not yet. I need to find out what's going on at Rancho Zarza first, Diego. What's this about two groups of hands?"

Diego opened his mouth to speak when another voice called from the door. "Let's go, Diego. I don't have all goddamned day for you to chat with your Mexican friends."

Diego's gaze hardened and shifted to the speaker. "Be right there, Damasco."

Time froze. The hate, the anger, the absolute fury for his half-brother flowed through Malcolm like a waterfall. He hadn't realized his hands were reaching for his pistols until Diego stopped him. He almost shook with the self-restraint it took not to follow through on his impulse.

With a barely visible shake of his head, Diego strode toward the door.

"About goddamned time. Don't let me have to come looking for you again. Don't need a frigging babysitter anyway." Damasco always had a petulant tone to his voice. Although Damasco was now a man, the child remained.

Malcolm couldn't stop himself. He turned his head to look at the man Damasco had become. When Diego swung through the batwing doors, he saw his half-brother clearly. The image burned into his brain like spots in his eyes when he looked at the sun for too long. Painful.

Damasco was tall, as big as Malcolm. While Malcolm's hair was wavy and had some brown, Damasco's was still black as pitch and straight as a pin. It hung just below his dark gray hat, which sported a snakeskin band and shiny silver conchos inlaid with turquoise. A brown shirt, clean as if it just came off the line, and jeans with brown leather chaps. The chaps were decorated with the same silver conchos as his hat. And they were clean too, unmarked. No horns had marked the tough leather surface. He glanced at Malcolm for a moment. Damasco looked like his mother, Isabella, beautiful and cold with angular features, chocolate-brown eyes, smooth olive-toned skin and full lips. Malcolm was certain Damasco had never wanted for female company.

"Who the hell is that?" Damasco snapped.

"One of O'Reilly's men," Diego said as the doors swung closed behind him.

Damasco's spurs jangled as he stomped down the planked sidewalk. "Frigging Mexicans are everywhere, like fleas."

Damasco's parting words angered Malcolm. Not because he was Mexican—he wasn't—but because it was straight from Isabella's foul mouth. A full-blooded Spanish noblewoman who thought everyone else was beneath her.

"You working for O'Reilly?" Another man from the poker game stood next to him. Malcolm was shocked he hadn't noticed the other man approach.

Malcolm unclenched his fists and turned to the stranger. Vaguely familiar, he had the bowlegged stance of a man who had spent many years on a horse.

"Looking for a job. Heard O'Reilly was hiring extra drovers."

A small lie, but apparently a true one.

"Yup, we are. Leastwise, I think we are. Name's Andy Parker." He stuck out one callused, brown hand and Hermano shook it. "I'm sure O'Reilly would be glad of the help. I hurt my damn leg last week and can't do much. Be happy to bring you out there. It's just past the Zarza Ranch."

Oh, yes, that was perfect.

๑ ๑ ๑

The afternoon sun was hot. Sweat trickled down Malcolm's spine. Blessed warmth. Made him nearly forget the snow in Wyoming.

Andy and Malcolm rode together to the Circle O. He remembered Sean O'Reilly. Good man, good crew. Hopefully it still was.

"Sean still heading up the ranch?" he asked as they galloped side by side.

Andy shook his head. "He died about two years back. Horse got spooked in a thunderstorm and threw him. Got trampled trying to get clear."

That was a painful way to go. He said a quick prayer for the man.

"Leigh O'Reilly took up the reins. And no matter what you heard, Leigh don't take no shit."

He hadn't heard anything about Leigh O'Reilly, but it was probably Sean's son or nephew. Perhaps young, trying to fill his father or uncle's shoes. That was something he had bitter experience with. He hadn't known Sean O'Reilly or his family well. The man had been at least fifteen years older than

Malcolm. He remembered a wife, and thought her name was Katherine, but couldn't remember anything else about the family.

Looking out over the endless stretch of grassy plain with longhorn grazing lazily, his heart twisted. Western Texas with its rocky, arid canyons did not compare to the plains of Texas. He took a deep breath. The Mexican hats were blooming, waving in the slight breeze. God, he actually missed this place. Unbelievable.

When they approached the O'Reilly homestead, two men replacing a corral fence post waved at Andy. Andy waved back. There was a good feeling on this ranch. It wasn't run like a monarchy.

They reined in at a long building Malcolm assumed was the bunkhouse.

"Earl Brady's the foreman. I think he's out with the boss today. Let's get you settled in and then we'll stable the horses."

Andy was almost too nice. Had he ever been that naïve or trusting? Hell, no. From the time he was six years old, life kicked him in the teeth and in the *cojones*. It wasn't too hard to kick back or, sometimes, kick first.

He dismounted and watched Andy gingerly get down, favoring his right leg. Malcolm took both sets of his saddlebags, slinging one over each shoulder, then his bedroll and duster.

"Damn bronc kicked me. I s'pose I should be grateful it wasn't my balls." Andy grinned and walked into the bunkhouse.

The smell was certainly the same as any bunkhouse. The lack of privacy was, too. Cots only a foot apart dotted the big room in three rows of at least fifteen each. Not too bad. He'd seen some with doubled up bunks to sleep twice as many. Circle O wasn't that big of a ranch, fortunately. He didn't relish sleeping under someone who couldn't control his bodily functions.

Andy pointed to an empty cot in the middle of the room. "That one's empty."

Of course. From there, he could hear, see and smell the lot of them. This job was important though. He swallowed his pride and put his things on the bunk. A quick glance didn't reveal enough, or perhaps too much, of his neighbors' bunks. Dirty shirts, crusty-looking under drawers, lots of tobacco stains and a smell that would knock a horse to its knees. Andy gestured for him to follow him out the door, still smiling.

"I'll give you a tour while we wait on supper. Ol' Moses rings the triangle when it's ready. I reckon we've got about an hour."

Malcolm repeated his reasons for staying in his head. Then repeated them again. They were good reasons. Solid reasons. But, *Madre de Dios*, this boy seemed to be made of sunshine and puppies. Malcolm felt like kicking Andy's bad leg just to make him stop smiling.

"Your leg. Tell me the story, *amigo*," Malcolm prompted as they walked back outside. Good trick. Talking about his injury turned off the sunshine for a bit.

Thank God.

ଔ ଔ ଔ

Malcolm and Andy met up with Earl Brady outside the barn half an hour later.

Earl was a tall, rangy man about fifty, with thinning salt and pepper hair and a craggy face that had seen too much sun. His mouth seemed etched in a perpetual scowl. His first reaction upon seeing Malcolm with Andy was to touch the pistol nestled in its holster. His mud-brown eyes narrowed and his shoulders stiffened.

Andy, seemingly unaware, spoke first. "Hey, Earl, this here's Hermano. He's a drover looking for work. Friend of Diego Martin's so I brought him back to the Circle O."

Earl spit a stream of tobacco at the ground near Malcolm's feet. "Friend of Diego's, eh? How do you know him?"

Malcolm kept his face blank with effort. If he didn't, he might have to teach this foul man a lesson in manners. The hard way.

"Old friends," was his response.

Earl snorted. "Andy, you get on in there and repair that tack on the bench. Might as well get some work outta you."

Andy nodded. "Sure thing. I got those parts for the well pump in town. They're in my saddlebag. I'll bring 'em by later." He shook Malcolm's hand again. "Good to have you here, Hermano. See ya."

He limped his way into the darkened barn.

"Now that the boy is gone, why don't you and me get a few things clear. I'll leave the final decision to keep you up to the boss. But as far as I'm concerned, you even scratch your ass the wrong way and you're on your way. You get me, *Hermano*?" His voice rang hard and curt.

Malcolm bared his teeth. Oh, yes, he understood. He was about to open his mouth and likely lose his job when he heard a horse stop behind him. Earl looked up at the rider.

"Another new drover. Name's Hermano," he grunted. "Andy brought him. Says he's a friend of Diego's. You're the boss so it's your choice, a' course. I say send him on his way. He can go fight it out with the Zarzas."

With that, he turned his back and walked toward the bunkhouse. Earl was damn lucky Malcolm had never back shot a man. It was mighty damn tempting.

He heard the rider behind him dismount so he turned to face him. Determined to be polite and respectful to the boss of the Circle O. Or at least try to.

It wasn't often Malcolm was surprised, even more rare that he was shocked, and he had never been rendered speechless.

Until now.

Holy shit. O'Reilly was definitely not a man.

Staring at him with the ever-present spectacles perched on her nose was Leigh Wynne. The little girl who learned to ride astride, to the shock of her father and the entire Zarza ranch. The little girl who could shoot out a chipmunk's eye at a hundred yards. The little girl who stuck to him like a cocklebur for fifteen years. The little girl who hadn't cried when she broke her leg trying to jump the canyon on the edge of town. His first and best friend.

She'd been fifteen when he lit out, never looking back at those he left behind. Now she must be thirty. And she damn sure wasn't a little girl anymore. She was tall, close to his height, a black hat sitting on light brown hair shorn like a man's, cut above her ears. She wore men's clothes—brown pants, well-used chaps, and a blue chambray shirt with a yellow neckerchief tied around a slender neck—she and *Roja* could be great friends. One pistol rode low on her right hip. She was dusty and dirty from whatever work she'd been doing. But all woman, all over. Her breasts would more than fill his hands, her hips curved so sweetly, and her lips were pouty enough to urge him to nibble on them.

When the hell did Leigh get those tits?

She was his boss.

Worse, she knew who he really was. He saw it in the depths of those shrewd hazel eyes. He should have known. Should have guessed somehow. He could engrave "Should Have" on his tombstone. He assumed Leigh O'Reilly, the owner of the Circle O Ranch, was a man. And he certainly made an ass of himself by assuming.

"Hermano, huh?"

"*Señora* O'Reilly, *sí?* My name is Hermano."

"Horseshit. If you think I wouldn't recognize you, Malcolm Ross, you are dumber than a bag of hammers." She tugged off her gloves and stuck them in her back pocket, then bracketed her hips with her hands.

Okay, so that wouldn't work. He cursed heartily in English, then Spanish, in his head as she regarded him with an unblinking stare. How the hell was he supposed to spy on his father's ranch unnoticed if the one person who recognized him ran the neighboring ranch?

Damn, damn, damn.

"Want to talk inside...*Hermano?*" she offered as she passed by him on her way to the huge sprawling ranch house.

It wasn't really a question, or even a request. It was a command. And he had no choice. He turned and followed her, trying not to focus on her gently swaying hips, hips he'd like to grab hold of and not let go.

Damn. Leigh Wynne O'Reilly just put a major kink in his life. Somehow he had to convince her to straighten that kink out and pretend she never saw him.

CHAPTER FOUR

Leigh could barely control the knocking of her knees, not to mention the rest of her body that was jumping like an ant on a hot rock.

Malcolm Ross was back, more dangerous, handsome and devastating than ever.

Holy hell.

Her legs shook, her heart slammed into her ribs like a stampede of longhorns, and sweat poured down her back. She tightened her hands into fists, nearly drawing blood, willing away the emotions. She had to be hard. She needed to be hard. Life kicked you in the balls, theoretically speaking of course, if you didn't have any. She had to wear armor plating.

Turning down the hallway, she went into the office. Although officially her office, Sean's presence remained. It still smelled like him, and sitting in his chair reminded her of him, but he was gone. Gone two years now. It seemed she was due to be emotional and sentimental today. She stomped into the room like a firing squad was dogging her steps. The bookcase along the right wall was stuffed with books on animal husbandry, several years' worth of ledgers, and a few Montgomery Ward catalogs. The big rough-hewn desk was covered in a pile of papers requiring her attention. When she'd opened the door, some of them had blown up like leaves in a storm and settled somewhere other than where they should have been. The brown leather chair behind the desk was her destination. She plopped down into it and glared at her guest.

Malcolm had followed her in. She had known he would. She gestured to the straight back chair on the other side of the desk. It wasn't a pretty piece of furniture, couldn't get much plainer, but it was sturdy, made with Sean's big hands.

"Sit."

He raised one eyebrow, then swept off his hat and sat.

That was probably a mistake. Sitting in this little office, he almost filled the room. Malcolm had never been small, but now he was big, really big, and not just in height. His presence was huge. No, beyond huge—it was stifling. She wished now they could talk outside where there was fresh air.

He was dressed in browns and blues, with faded dark brown pants that had seen better days, as had those pitiful excuses for boots. She noticed he still didn't wear spurs. That she respected. No horse worth its mettle needed to be gouged to work. His hair was too long, a dark brown, nearly black, with a little bit of wave. Reminded her of his mother Leslie's hair. Leslie Ross was the mother Leigh had never had, until Leslie left soon after Malcolm did. Leigh wasn't even supposed to know Malcolm had left, and not died as the story was told, but eavesdropping had been one of her vices. She had heard Diego and Lorena talking.

Malcolm's eyes were truly unsettling, though, still fathomless pools of absolute blackness. She had always had trouble reading his eyes, except when he was angry. Then they practically burned. But now they were completely indecipherable. She pushed up the glasses on her nose and folded her hands together on the desk.

What the hell was he doing here?

"Did you know that most people around here think you're dead?"

"It doesn't surprise me," was his terse response. And, oh Lordy, his voice had not changed, except perhaps to get deeper, rougher, like an untamed mustang.

"Your mother spread that story around, with Diego's help."

He stared at her. "You didn't believe it." It wasn't a question. "Were you listening at doors again, little Leigh?"

She kicked up one corner of her mouth in a smirk. "In case you didn't notice, I'm not exactly little anymore, Malcolm. There isn't a woman in four counties who's taller than me, and that probably includes half the men."

"I noticed."

She had to restrain the shiver from running up and down her traitorous spine.

"What the hell are you doing back? And who is Hermano?"

His gaze never wavered from hers, damn the man.

"I see you have worked on your manners, *niña*."

She stood and paced to the small window behind the desk.

"I'm thirty years old, Malcolm. I'm not little, not a *niña*. I'm a widow and a rancher, hanging on to what I've got with everything I've got." She turned to look at him again. "I'm going to ask you one more time, and if you don't answer, you're going to leave the Circle O in about five minutes. If you're lucky, your ass will still be in one piece." She paused and leaned over the desk to glare at him. "What are you doing here and who is Hermano?"

ભ ભ ભ

Malcolm may have looked calm on the outside, but inside a twister had taken up residence in his stomach. Goddamn her. Leigh had been the only friend he'd had growing up, more like a pesky little sister, but a steadfast presence in his life. Now she was a stranger, demanding answers he wasn't ready to give her.

Her hazel eyes were hard. That saddened him. Life had probably not been kind to a motherless girl who looked and acted more like a boy. He wondered what she'd been doing and how she'd ended up married to a man at least twenty years her senior. She obviously ran the Circle O outfit with a tight fist. The foreman even looked to her before he hired someone. That told him a lot about how much she was respected, and how hard she worked. This was not a woman's world. It was a man's world with no room for softness.

"Time's a wastin', Malcolm. In case you forgot how to count, it's about four minutes now."

Her sharp words brought him back into the here and now. How much did he trust her? How much did she know about Rancho Zarza?

"I am Hermano. It's a name I took as my own after I left here."

She finally sat back down in the cracked leather chair. She rested her elbows on the arms of the chair and steepled her long fingers together. Waiting. Watching.

"I am here because I want to find my mother."

It wasn't exactly all the reasons he was here, but it was definitely the most truthful. She looked in his eyes for a full minute before nodding.

"Obviously you aren't the letter writing type or you'd know where she was. I think there's more to your story. How much, I can't rightly tell, but it's there. I don't know where she is now, but I'll tell you what I do know. She left about a year after you did. It was strange. She left one day and didn't come back." Leigh rubbed her finger along a stain on the grain of the wood desk. His eyes followed its movement. "I think she just wanted to get away from your father and the memories. Without you here, she didn't have anything to keep her."

There was the smallest hitch in her voice. Very little, but he heard it. His life had depended on hearing and seeing everything around him, every subtle movement or inflection.

"You missed her."

She clenched her hands into fists. "You're damn right I missed her. I was fifteen years old, with no mother but yours. I resented like hell that you left without saying goodbye. When she left, it near about killed me."

She was trying hard to hide her emotions, but her eyes were suspiciously wet. He averted his gaze to the bookcase. Damn. He hadn't thought about Leigh and what she'd go through when he left. He had been in such a blinding rage and excruciating pain nothing had intruded. But now? God, to think his mother had left and Leigh had been alone. He snapped his gaze back to hers.

"Why did you marry Sean O'Reilly?"

That was definitely the wrong thing to say. Fire flared in her eyes and her jaw clenched so hard, he thought he heard teeth breaking.

"None of your goddamn business."

He nodded. "*Lo siento.* Shouldn't have asked. Forget I said anything."

She pursed her lips and stared at him. He sighed and twirled his hat in his hands. "I didn't come here to fight with you, *amiga.* I didn't even know you were O'Reilly until about ten minutes ago."

She looked surprised and another unnamed emotion flitted through her eyes. "So why are you here instead of at Rancho Zarza?"

How much should he trust Leigh? She had been closest to him besides his mother throughout his childhood. Hell, she had grown up in *his* shadow. Did he risk bringing her back into it? Did he have a choice?

"The offer still stands. You've got about one minute left, Malcolm."

He had no doubt she would make good on her word and throw him off the ranch. And where would that leave him? Out of a job, a place to sleep, and most importantly, out of friends. Seeing her reminded him of how much he needed one.

Malcolm crossed his legs at the ankles. Resting his hat on his boots, he laced his fingers together and placed them on his stomach. He sighed deeply and looked up at Leigh.

"I left because if I hadn't, I would have killed Damasco eventually. My mother knew it, that's why she forced me to go."

Leigh sat back in the creaky leather chair. "She forced you? Malcolm, you outweighed her by sixty pounds."

He almost smiled. "She didn't tie a rope around me and drag me out the door, little Leigh. She convinced me it was the best thing. She didn't want to see me dead, and it was certain Isabella would kill me, if not Alejandro, for killing the heir."

She leaned forward, warming to the conversation. "True. Isabella is a world class bitch."

This time he did smile. "You always did have a flair for cursing."

She smiled. *Madre de Dios.* When she smiled, she looked pretty, like a girl. He used to forget she was female the way she acted, but not anymore. He couldn't forget with the proof of her womanhood staring him in the face.

"I learned from the best, Mal."

The years they'd been apart seemed to fly away like fall leaves in a brisk breeze. As if suddenly they were together again and no time had passed. He had missed Leigh. She was truly of his heart, his family.

"Can you fill me in on the last fifteen years at least?" Leigh grinned.

"*Sí*, I can, but I think we need to have some dinner to have so much conversation."

"Good idea. I'll tell Mrs. Hanson to set up two plates in the kitchen for us. No need to eat in the cookhouse with the men. They don't need to know your business."

With that, she left the room with a little grace, but more of a man's swagger. Leigh had grown up, but was she happy? How in the hell had she ended up married to Sean O'Reilly? And why did the thought she had been someone's wife bother the hell out of him?

ଓ ଓ ଓ

Leigh needed a brief reprieve. She had to get away from him for a few moments—the sheer intensity of being in the same room with Malcolm made her heart beat like a jackrabbit's.

For God's sake, it's Malcolm. Not the goddamn King of England.

That was the whole problem. It was *Malcolm.* As she headed toward the bright yellow kitchen to talk to Mrs. Hanson, she tried to put thoughts of her childhood romantic fantasies behind her.

Leigh had thought he'd come back to see her. A little flame of hope had lit in her breast oh so briefly until he'd snuffed it out with one swipe of a tanned hand. He had come looking for his mother. About fifteen years too late in her opinion, but at least he was here. But why did he not just knock on the door at Rancho Zarza?

After Leslie told everyone Malcolm was dead, Alejandro, Damasco and Isabella believed it. They had no reason to think she was lying. Malcolm couldn't just be resurrected without another Easter holiday being declared. Well, damn, now she was having blasphemous thoughts. She shook her head and entered the kitchen.

Mrs. Hanson was pulling a pan of cornbread out of the oven. The housekeeper was a middle-aged woman with mousy-brown hair wound forever in a tight little bun. Though short and squat, she had a long reach. Sean had hired her right before he died. Leigh had never been fond of the woman and it wasn't only because she was rude, big-mouthed and foul-tempered. Hell, Leigh herself was all of that and more. Mrs. Hanson, however, was just plain mean. Leigh had seen her kick chickens, almost pull the ears off Andy, and belittle Old Moses—the man who cooked for the hands and did odd jobs around the ranch—so much she nearly made him cry. Leigh didn't know why she kept Mrs. Hanson around, probably because hiring another cook and housekeeper was a task she avoided. She knew more about longhorns and horses than running a house. Even if her housekeeper was a witch, at least she didn't have to deal with running a house all by herself.

"'Bout time you got here, missy. This cornbread is nearly burnt and the chili is starting to stick to the pot." She slammed the oven door closed and dropped the pan on the top. "Be lucky if it's edible by now."

"Mrs. Hanson, I'm only ten minutes late. I was talking to the new drover in my office."

She turned and glared at Leigh. "You mean Sean's office."

Leigh straightened up and thrust her shoulders back. "No, I mean *my* office. Sean's been gone two years. I think it's time you accepted me as the boss of this ranch."

Mrs. Hanson snorted. "When pigs fly, missy. Now sit yourself down and—"

A deep, deadly voice sliced through her words. "You would be wise to speak respectfully to *Señora* O'Reilly, *bruja*."

Malcolm stood in the doorway, the hat on his head shielding his black eyes. The menace in his stance and his cold words hung in the air.

Mrs. Hanson apparently was too stupid to notice. "Oh, and are you giving me orders now, you filthy Mex?"

He stepped into the room and practically glided to the woman. Being over six feet tall, Malcolm towered above her.

"My name is Hermano."

Before she could clap a hand over her mouth, Mrs. Hanson let loose a gasp. Malcolm smiled, revealing rows of shiny white teeth that resembled a wolf's snarl.

"You know me, eh? *Bueno.* Remember my name. If I ever hear you talk like that to the *patrona*, you will answer to me. *Comprende?*"

Mrs. Hanson nodded and with one last dirty look at Leigh, she stomped out of the kitchen and up the stairs.

"I think she forgot her broom," Malcolm said.

Leigh glanced at him in surprise. "Broom?"

"Don't all witches use them?"

She grinned. Malcolm was home. *Malcolm was home.*

After grabbing two bowls from the shelf, she ladled hot chili into them and placed them on the table. She realized Malcolm was standing and watching her. Self-consciously, she wiped her hands on her pants.

"What?"

He shook his head. "I was memorizing Leigh actually in a kitchen with her hands near a stove. A rare sight if I remember right."

She stuck her tongue out at him and turned back to the stove to get the cornbread. After sticking a knife in the center of the loaf, Leigh picked up the pan with the dishcloth since it was still piping hot, and went back to the table.

"I'll get some of this cornbread for us. Can you pour some coffee? The mugs are right up above the sink."

After a moment's hesitation, she heard his booted feet approach the stove. The clink of the pot on the tin mug followed. Unsure of what to do with the cornbread, she simply sliced it, however crookedly, and left it in the pan. Sitting down, she realized there were no spoons on the table. Sighing at her own ineptitude, she started to rise, when Malcolm's hand rested on her shoulder. The heat from it was almost as hot as the cornbread. She glanced up at him and forgot what she was going to say. His dark eyes were a mere foot from hers. He held two mugs with a spoon stuck in each in his left hand. Her breath caught in her throat and words crowded in there like water behind a beaver dam.

"It would be better to eat with a spoon, no?"

Feeling more foolish by the second, she simply stared. He stared back. She didn't take a mug and he didn't move.

"Leigh?"

She snapped back into herself. What in God's name was she doing? Taking the mug from him, she averted her eyes and set it next to her bowl, willing him to take a seat across from her at the table and to let go of her shoulder. The table was relatively small; it only sat four people comfortably, so he wouldn't be too far away, but he'd be farther away than her shoulder.

Taking the spoon from the coffee, she stuck it in her mouth to get the taste of coffee off it. And still he stood next to her.

Sit down, dammit.

She glanced back up and felt herself start at the fierceness in his gaze. At this moment, she was very nearly afraid of him—she, who feared almost nothing. His black gaze fell to her mouth and the spoon clunked in the mug in his hand, as if he were trembling. She licked her lips nervously and tasted coffee.

"Malcolm?"

He closed his eyes and took a breath. Sliding sideways, he finally plopped into the chair across from her. The mug landed on the table with a smack and some of the coffee splashed on his hand. He looked at his hand, but didn't react to the scalding hot brew.

What just happened?

Her life experience with men was limited to Sean and ranch hands. Any romance she'd experienced, even with Sean, could fit in a thimble— something she didn't think she owned anyway. Whatever had just happened was beyond her meager experience, but she knew it had something to do with men and women.

He couldn't possibly find her attractive. She was a big woman, almost as tall as he, with round hips and big breasts that constantly got in the way. At round-up time, she bound them so she could work unfettered. She must weigh nearly one hundred fifty pounds or better. She knew she was no raving beauty. She was very plain and blind as a bat without her spectacles. What did she have to excite a man? Not much, and she had that from the horse's mouth, so to speak—from her husband. Then again, her marriage to Sean had been a most atypical union.

Leigh knew she needed to get on solid ground again.

"You'd better eat up before it gets cold. I can't vouch for the taste, but it's filling."

She dove into the chili. Grabbing a piece of cornbread, she dipped it in the chili and took a big bite. Malcolm hadn't moved. She glanced up at him and he smiled, the tension melting from his face. He took his spoon from his mug and licked off the coffee. The sight of his tongue was enough to make her heart flip. All of her love, her longing and her foolish dreams congealed like gristle in her stomach. All he was would never be hers.

Giving herself a mental pinch, she again dipped her spoon in the chili and, head down, proceeded to consume the rest of her dinner. Whether or not she tasted it was another matter.

She wiped her mouth across her sleeve—*hell, I forgot the damn napkins, too*—and laid her spoon on the table when she was finished.

"Okay, now how about you tell me everything." She stared at him until he looked up from his own dinner with those black eyes. "Now."

CHAPTER FIVE

She had a backbone and was used to ordering people around, that was for damn sure. Malcolm didn't appreciate being told what to do and had to restrain himself from standing up and leaving the room.

"Did no one ever tell you that you can catch more flies with honey than vinegar?" Malcolm's jaw tightened and he silently counted to ten.

He thought he saw her blush, just the barest hint of rose under her tanned skin.

"Look, Malcolm, I want to help you. I can't do that unless I know what the hell is going on. If you don't want to tell me, there's the door."

Leigh stood and took her dishes to the sink. They clattered as she tossed them. She never paused in her stride and kept right on walking, right out the door. Malcolm stared after her, wondering if he could tell her enough of the truth to appease her. He wasn't ready to tell everything.

He walked outside in search of Leigh. He didn't have to go far. She sat on the steps of the back porch, looking out into the deepening darkness. She appeared so alone at the moment, watching the endless sky, he was tempted to put his arms around her. He knew what loneliness was.

Whoa! Pulling back on his own reins, he shoved that thought into the wind where it belonged. What the hell would he do with his arms around *Leigh?* She was almost his little sister, wasn't she? Shaking off his strange thoughts, he sat down and stretched out next to her.

Leigh broke the silence. "Pretty night."

He opened his mouth to reply when she spoke again.

"Sorry I was such a pushy bitch. I...I don't seem to be able to be anything but that lately."

Well, that was certainly the last thing he expected to come out of her mouth. Leigh didn't know the meaning of the word bitch. He smiled a little into the night.

"You are no bitch, *amiga*. Believe me, I know many, and you aren't even in the same room with them."

She pushed her spectacles up onto her forehead and rubbed her eyes with the heels of her hands. "Yeah, I am. I'm used to having to fight for everything. The last two years have left me no time for anything but daily battles and bloody skirmishes."

The glasses dropped back on the bridge of her nose when she took her hands away. She pushed them up with her finger.

Malcolm sat up and listened very carefully. "What about the last two years?"

She shook her head. "Ever since Sean died, things have just gone *wrong*. Cattle missing, coyote in the hen house, a fire in the barn, milch cow with an infected udder, the damn root cellar flooded, and...I could talk until I'm blue in the face, Mal. Fact is, I'm tired of fighting."

Her shoulders drooped as she leaned forward to rest her elbows on her knees. He took her hand and laced his fingers with hers.

"*Pobrecita*. Tonight we will not fight. We will talk about happy times and be friends again."

She sighed, long and hard. Malcolm vowed right then he'd find out exactly whom she'd been fighting. And stop them. Or kill them. She tried to gently extract her hand, but he wouldn't let go.

"Do you remember the tree house?" He watched her face as a smile spread across it.

"Yup. My favorite place in the whole hacienda. That big old fig tree and our tree house. It was more like a bunch of scraggly boards nailed together wrong."

He squeezed her hand. "But it was ours. Our special place. We would sneak my mama's churros up there and eat until we thought we'd burst."

This time she laughed. "I think one time I did. All over your shoes."

Malcolm remembered it well. She had been ten and he was about thirteen. He had been furious she'd ruined his one pair of boots. She surprised him the next day with another pair. Didn't know where she got them or how, he hadn't asked. He took them as a gift from a friend.

"How about the time we took the pie?" Malcolm asked.

"Ha! I thought your mother was going to pull your britches down and whoop you in front of the whole crew."

He smiled at the memory, although at the time he'd been terrified that's what she would do. A ten-year-old boy does not want his bare ass hanging out for the world to see. Especially in front of his seven-year-old friend, who happened to be a girl.

"I miss her."

"So do I, *amiga*, so do I."

They were quiet for a few moments. Reliving memories buried beneath the day-to-day problems. Memories that brought laughter, joy, tears and perhaps a bit of sadness. They had shared so much together. How could he have stayed away and ignored her for so long? She had been his friend, his only friend, in a world of hate and ugliness.

"Malcolm? Did you ever get hitched?"

Taken aback by the question, he laughed, a rusty, croaky sound. "No, I didn't. No little bastards for the bastard either."

"That's not what I meant," she said, sounding embarrassed, and tugged on her hand again.

"I know. I was just teasing, Leigh."

"Not funny."

He shrugged. "If I don't laugh at myself, others laugh at me."

She turned and looked at him in the deepening darkness. "That's a big difference between you and me, Mal. You're an eagle, talons raised, not afraid of your prey. I'm a turtle, in my shell, keeping everyone out. Hiding."

He squeezed her hand, then reached out to brush his knuckles on her cheek, which was as soft as satin. It was something that shouldn't, but did, surprise him. The lights from the house reflected on her spectacles, turning her eyes into flaming mirrors.

Dios. Leigh *was* beautiful.

"Ah, *amante*, we are more alike than you think. Maybe I am an eagle and fly away. But you, you are no turtle. You are more like a wolf. Ready to fight, to protect, to survive."

She turned her gaze to the road leading to the ranch house.

"Rider."

They watched the approaching horse. When he got about a hundred yards away, Leigh scrambled to her feet.

"Damn. Go inside now." She pulled on his arm and tried to drag him up. Unsuccessfully. Malcolm was not a small man and if he didn't want to move, he didn't.

"Come on, you big galoot. Move it."

"Not until you tell me why. Is this your sweetheart?"

She rolled her eyes. "No. It's…it's business. Now *andale*."

He stared at her until she threw up her hands in disgust and stomped down the steps to the yard.

"Fine with me. Maybe you ought to say howdy to Damasco. I'm sure he'd be glad to know you're back."

ରେ ରେ ରେ

When Leigh glanced behind her, Malcolm was gone. He'd disappeared without a sound to give him away. That was a little spooky. The man moved like a shadow.

Turning back, she watched Damasco Zarza ride in on his big black stallion. He really was a fine-looking man. He and Malcolm had the same build. Big, broad shoulders, wide chest, long, muscular legs. And they both rode a horse like they were born with one between their legs. Damasco rode like a king surveying his realm. Malcolm rode like a natural extension of the horse.

"Ah, Mrs. O'Reilly, what a pleasant surprise."

She let out a very unladylike snort. "Oh, for God's sake, Damasco. For one thing you just rode up to my front porch. Not much of a surprise to actually find me here. Second, we were in nappies together. 'Mrs.' just doesn't cut the muster."

He looked a little taken aback by her, but quickly recovered. He smiled his gorgeous smile and swung off the horse fluidly. The man was so graceful, he couldn't fall down if he tried. Leigh had always envied that about both Damasco and Malcolm.

"Why are you here, Damasco?"

She knew Malcolm was listening with his ear pressed against the door. Serve him right if he got a splinter.

Damasco secured his horse to the hitching rail and stepped up to the porch, his shiny spurs jangling. He seemed to be dressed to go to a church social with pressed black pants, a crisp, white shirt, and a leather string tie sporting a big turquoise center. He swept off his hat and held it to his chest.

"You wound me, *querida*. I have come to see you. To court you properly. You know I want to marry you."

She folded her arms across her chest and narrowed her gaze.

"I've told you before. There's no courting between me and you, and damn sure no marriage. And don't call me *querida*."

"Not *querida*, not Mrs. O'Reilly. Then what should I call you—my queen?" He reached toward her and she stepped back, banging her boots on the bottom step of the porch.

"You're being ridiculous. I'm no one's queen or sweetheart. How about you call me Leigh? It's a small word. I'm sure you can manage it."

Leigh thought she saw a flash of annoyance in his chocolate eyes, but it vanished quickly behind a screen of false sincerity.

"You make me forget myself. I only wish to show you how I feel."

Faster than a snake, he was on her, wrapping his arms around her back, slamming her into his chest. He squashed the breath out of her and her arms were trapped beneath his. When he leaned in and started kissing her ear, her temper flared.

"Let go," she growled.

"We don't have to fight it anymore, *querida*. I know you have longed for my touch. Even as I watched you blossom as a woman and a wife, I knew one day we'd be together again."

Leigh tried to laugh at that. "Are you kidding? I can barely tolerate the sight of you, Damasco. Let me go."

Beth Williamson

He kissed down her neck with practiced precision.

"Let me love you. Let me show you how a Spaniard can make a woman scream with passion."

She tried to take a deep breath but all she smelled was his bay rum. Apparently he bathed in it. She heard the screen door rattle and knew Malcolm was back there watching in the dark, like a brewing storm.

"Let go, Damasco, or so help me God, you're going to be sorry."

When he squeezed her behind with one big hand, she imagined his funeral, down to the damn daisies on his grave.

With no more warning, she brought her right leg up and kneed him as hard as she could in the balls. When he let loose a screech—it couldn't be called anything else—and his arms fell away, she brought up her fist and laid him flat out with an uppercut to his jaw. He landed on the ground in a cloud of dust certain to mess up his pretty clothes.

"That's what an Irishman teaches his wife." With throbbing knuckles, she picked up his hat and threw it at him. "And if you ever touch me again, Damasco, you won't get kicked in the balls; I'll blow 'em clean off. Now get off my land."

Leigh was sure Damasco would pick himself up, at least after he stopped puking, and go home. She spun on her heel and nearly ruined it all when she tripped up the first stair. Regaining her balance, she pulled a muscle in her back. With a grunt of pain, she yanked open the screen door and went inside.

It was almost pitch black in the room. A remote shadowy world of sound and touch.

"I was about to kick his sorry ass, but I see you took care of that already, my wolf," came Malcolm's voice.

Leigh slammed the kitchen door closed behind her, shutting out Damasco and the rest of the world.

"If you Zarza men don't leave me alone soon, I swear I'll—"

He hissed in the darkness. "Do *not* call me a Zarza."

She turned away from him and started to leave the kitchen. Enough was enough. His warm hand touched her arm.

"I'm sorry, Leigh. I don't mean to snap at you."

"I know you don't, but you don't trust me either. And I can't trust anyone."

He sighed as his thumb caressed her inner wrist. The roughness of his calluses gently scraped on the tender skin. The friction sent skitters racing up her arm straight to her chest. Her nipples hardened and puckered, pushing against her undershirt. Now that was startling.

She wanted to pull her wrist out of his grasp, but was immobile. The sensations caused by that one touch were so foreign, so unsettling, she had no clue what to do.

"I want to trust you. And I want you to trust me." His deep voice was rough and scratchy, revealing how upset he was.

"What's wrong?"

His hold tightened on her arm. "He touched you."

"It's okay. I don't think he'll do it again." Amazingly, she felt herself grin. Oh yeah. Damasco would be cursing her name all the way home. Bouncing up and down. On that hard saddle.

"If he touches you again, I may have to kill him."

She had no doubt he meant every word.

"Why?"

"Because he touched what does not belong to him."

"Belong?" She wasn't following his thoughts. "My ass doesn't belong to anyone but me."

"Wrong."

Before she could even take a breath to answer, she was in his arms and his lips slammed down on hers.

He was hard. *So hard.* From top to bottom. Especially the part of his anatomy that was initially soft. It was hard now and knocking on her belly.

And his lips. Rough and demanding, they ruthlessly plundered her own. She felt like she was in the middle of a twister. Whirling head, lurching stomach, pulsing between her legs. His whiskers scraped her chin, her cheeks. It was exhilarating; it was exciting. It was *terrifying.*

She grabbed onto his shoulders to ground herself. She was getting dizzy. Probably because she wasn't breathing. As quickly as it began, it ended. With a last gentle kiss, he pulled away.

She took a shuddering breath and clasped her hand to her stomach.

"What the hell just happened?"

Was that her voice? She nearly turned to look behind her to find the woman who just spoke with a sexy, sultry sound.

"I just proved you wrong." His tone was deeper, if that were even possible.

"Wrong? About what?" Her mind just damn well refused to focus.

"About your ass."

"My ass?"

She felt him smile in the semi-darkness. "I'm going to check to make sure we're not in a canyon, because there is an echo in here."

She shook her head to try to clear it. Stepping away from him, she felt the loss of heat as keenly as if he were a bonfire. Okay, just forget the kissing. Ha!

"Look, Malcolm. This isn't going any further until you tell me the truth. All of it. You have one day. By tomorrow night you're spilling the beans or you're packing your shit."

She walked, or at least pretended to walk since she was shaking so much she couldn't feel her feet, out of the kitchen.

"*Amante.*"

She stopped. That was the second time he'd called her sweetheart.

"What?" she snapped.

"Trust is a valuable thing, no? Once I give it to you, you cannot give it back."

CHAPTER SIX

Malcolm lowered himself into the kitchen chair carefully. He dropped his head into his hands.

Jesu Cristo.

What the hell had just happened? When Damasco grabbed her, Malcolm's pistol jumped into his hand like a snarling dog. He wanted to put a bullet between his brother's eyes for even thinking of touching Leigh. He wasn't prepared for the surge of pure jealousy that roared through him.

Damasco had treated Leigh like a servant's daughter growing up. Now he wanted to marry her? Malcolm couldn't contain the bark of laughter. What Damasco wanted was the Circle O. Malcolm was certain of that, but he didn't know why. Yet.

Malcolm avoided thinking about that kiss, but he couldn't avoid the throbbing hard-on in his pants. Just the memory of her breasts rubbing his chest and the feel of her petal soft lips kept the erection howling. God, who knew?

One thought kept pounding through his head.

Mine.

It was all he could think.

Mine.

But why? He hadn't seen her in fifteen years. He had known the girl, but the woman, ah, she was a mystery.

Mine.

He was driven, consumed by one thought. Brand her. She is *mine.*

CR CR CR

Saturday dawned clear with the barest hint of heat in the air. Malcolm heard the other hands rising and talking. He had barely gotten any sleep between the smells, the snores, the farts and the talking.

Ah, but today he was a new *hombre*. The first paying job he'd ever had. Very ironic. At thirty-three, he finally had a job that paid honest money. If you could call forty dollars a month honest.

"Mornin', Hermano."

Chipper Andy was on again today. Malcolm resisted the urge to grab the man's bad leg and throw him under a pillow.

"Earl sent me to fetch ya. He wants you to replace fence posts out in the north pasture."

Malcolm bit his tongue. He had expected Earl did not like him. He hadn't known how much, though.

Fence posts. *Madre de Dios.*

CR CR CR

After a filling, though somewhat tasteless breakfast served by an ancient-looking black man named Moses—quite possibly the original—Malcolm went in search of the wagon to load supplies.

Earl came out of the barn with a post digger and a smirk. Malcolm wanted to shove the post digger up Earl's ass.

"Hey there, Mex. The wagon is around the side by the wood pile yonder."

He shoved the post digger into Malcolm's hands, trying to knock him off-balance. Unfortunately for Earl, he underestimated Malcolm's strength. Malcolm didn't move a blessed inch.

A grunt of surprise popped out of Earl's mouth. "Ah'll just follow ya out to where you'll be working today."

More likely stand over him with a big stick and a smile of malice.

"*Sí.*" Malcolm turned to go toward "yonder" when Earl grabbed his arm. Dropping the post digger, Malcolm forced Earl into a headlock. The satisfaction tasted tangy on his tongue.

"Do not ever touch me, old man."

Earl sputtered and squeaked until Malcolm released him.

Earl touched his throat gently and massaged the bruised, wrinkly skin. His muddy eyes spoke of retribution. His hat had fallen off and wisps of steel-gray hair fluttered in the morning breeze.

Malcolm stood, hands at his sides, eyeing the old bastard, waiting for him to go for the ancient-looking pistol on his hip. No doubt left over from the war. Earl likely fought for his cause on the losing side.

"You're fired, Mex."

Malcolm grinned. "You need to talk to the *patrona* before you fire me, *viejo.*"

Earl spit at Malcolm's feet. "I don't need a pair of tits to tell me what to do."

The contempt in his voice for Leigh made the hackles on the back of Malcolm's neck rise. He leaned toward the other man, pleased to see him back up a step.

"You are wrong. Not only did she hire me, but Leigh is my friend. *Mi amiga.* I stay."

Malcolm picked up the post digger and left Earl standing there. After a moment, Malcolm heard him start after him. Digging fence post holes with Earl standing over him, it was sure to be a shitty day.

ભ ભ ભ

Leigh hadn't seen Malcolm all day. She entered the kitchen that evening to find Mrs. Hanson emptying a pan of biscuits into a ceramic bowl. A pot of stew bubbled on the stove. Leigh tried to be friendly to the sour old witch.

"Smells good." A compliment couldn't hurt.

Mrs. Hanson slammed the empty pan down on the stove and turned to glare at her.

"What is this I hear about you turning down a marriage proposal from Damasco Zarza?"

Her vehemence was surprising. How did she know about it? And why would she be angry?

"That's not your business."

"Oh, yes it is, Miss High and Mighty. You need a man. A good man. Damasco is a good, rich man. You can't do any better than him."

Leigh sat and stared.

"What do you mean?"

Mrs. Hanson ladled stew into a bowl, plopped two biscuits on top and dropped it in front of Leigh.

"I'm not telling you something you don't already know. You're too old for babies, not much to look at, and your ranch is about to go under. What would possess you to turn him down?"

Her beady colorless eyes danced with indignation and the waddle on her neck quivered.

Leigh shook with anger.

"Get out of my sight, Mrs. Hanson, before I knock you into next week."

Her blood thrummed through her veins, hot with anger, hurt, and sadness. Mrs. Hanson might be correct about her, but she had no goddamn right to throw it in Leigh's face.

"What?"

Leigh stood, towering over her, and felt as if she could truly do this awful woman harm. Her hands were tight fists, snapping to connect with this crazy woman's jaw.

"Now."

"Well, I never," said Mrs. Hanson as she scurried out of the room.

Blowing out a breath and unclenching her fists, Leigh looked down at the steaming bowl of stew, then at the empty chair across from it. She needed Malcolm here.

How or why she came to that conclusion, she didn't even care. She only knew she needed him. Turning, she strode out the back door to look for him.

ରେ ରେ ରେ

Malcolm was unloading broken and worn fence posts from the back of the wagon behind the barn. He was dirty, sweaty, and the sight of him made her heart skip a beat.

He'd taken his shirt off and that chest was enough to make her knees turn to jam. Covered in tan skin with ribbons of muscle and whorls of curly black hair. Drops of sweat traveled down those nooks and crannies, meandering a path she wanted to follow with her hands. Or perhaps her tongue.

What a beautiful specimen of a man. Damn, Malcolm sure had filled out since he was eighteen. Leigh resisted the urge to reach out and touch.

Then he turned to face the wagon and she saw his back. She must have gasped or croaked or something because he whirled to face her. Gloved hands fisted, sweat streaming down his face, black eyes snapping. When he saw Leigh, he relaxed.

"*Amante*, my wolf, you should not sneak up on me like that."

Her mouth was as dry as the Texas wind. His back. *Oh, Jesus help me.*

"I am not fit for a lady's company yet. After I finish, I need to go down to the creek and wash."

She nodded. "I...I...okay sure."

His eyebrows drew together. "Are you okay, *amiga?*"

"I, uh, came to tell you... That is, to ask you. See, there's plenty of stew and biscuits..."

He smiled. A brilliant white slash in the dark, beautiful face.

"Ah, *sí*, a supper invitation. *Bueno*. I will be there in fifteen minutes."

He turned and grabbed another load of wood from the wagon, presenting her with his back again.

Stomach churning, she fled back to the house. She almost fell into the kitchen and ended up smacking her head on the doorjamb.

Leigh pulled off her glasses and slammed them in her shirt pocket. After furiously pumping the handle in the kitchen sink, she grabbed a wash rag and held it under the stream, soaking it in cool water. Great, gasping breaths jumped out of her like grasshoppers in a brush fire. Out of control and frantic.

She wrung out the excess water and pressed the wet cloth to her face, then slumped to the floor.

Get a hold of yourself.

It wasn't working. Lord, it was *not* working.

Leigh knew something had happened between Malcolm and Damasco, and Malcolm had been punished. It was the reason he left. Now she knew what his punishment had been. And she wished she didn't.

Malcolm's back was covered with scars from a whip from his shoulders to his waist. Every square inch of skin had been flayed from his young back. The sheer brutality of anyone doing that to another human being made her heart hurt. To think it was done to her dear Malcolm made her heart weep.

She didn't know how long she sat there, with the cloth pressed to her face.

"*Amante.*"

He was there, crouched on the floor next to her, and she hadn't even heard him come in. He pulled the cloth away from her face and cupped her cheek with tender fingers. His black eyes were full of concern, his wavy hair sprinkled with drops of water. The tips brushed his shoulders leaving what looked like tears on his clean brown shirt. Lord, she had never stopped loving him.

"What is wrong?"

Leigh had never been one to mince words. "Your back. I'd never seen it before."

His eyes hardened. "It's not pretty, *sí?* Ah, well, the señoritas in the cantina don't mind."

Behind his flippant words, she heard ancient pain. *Oh, Malcolm.*

"I'm not usually such a sissy," she said wearily, clambering to her feet. He rose from a crouch like a panther with a fluid grace.

"You are no sissy, *amiga.*"

She shook her head. "Sissy."

He smiled. A real smile so blinding, she nearly wept.

Sissy.

"No sissy. A woman."

With that pronouncement, he cupped her other cheek and lowered his lips to hers. At the first touch, she nearly jumped out of her skin. After a few gentle, nibbling kisses that made even her feet jitter, he let go and stepped back.

"Let us eat, *amante*."

෧ ෧ ෧

Leigh hadn't put her spectacles back on. Malcolm was having trouble eating his stew when all he wanted to do was study those beautiful hazel eyes. He hadn't realized what lurked behind the glass—a deep pond of woman he was drawn to. There was so much about Leigh he didn't know, but he found himself wanting to know more. Wanting to be with her, to touch her, to spend as much time as he could finding out all he could.

Dios, ayúdame.

They had been close. Very close. Children of servants. A bond that remained strong. Misfits who saw in each other what no one else bothered to see. A person.

They were seated across from each other again. Malcolm leaned back in his chair, one booted foot resting on the opposite knee. He tried to keep a bit of space between them without getting too far away from her. The urge to be near her was as strong as the urge to run.

Leigh used her spoon to toy with a bit of potato. She hadn't eaten much, which was very unlike her. That was something he had always liked about her. She had an appetite and wasn't afraid to show it. Not like Isabella who would have died of starvation long ago if she only ate what she picked at during meals.

"What's wrong?" Malcolm asked.

Startled, her hand jerked on the spoon and the potato soared through the air, landing on his lap. He jumped up and brushed it off with a napkin. Good thing he was wearing brown pants.

He glanced at her face. She looked resigned.

"Sorry, Mal. My middle name sure isn't Grace."

Malcolm smiled. "And mine is surely not Saint. So we are even."

Beth Williamson

She smiled back. This he was glad to see. The smiling Leigh of his childhood had turned into a somber, serious Leigh. She needed to smile more often.

"So what troubles you?" He reached out and laid his hand on hers. She hesitated, then relaxed her hand in his.

"You."

Malcolm couldn't say he was surprised. He waited for her to continue.

"You were gone for so long and now you're here. Everything is so topsy turvy. I'm confused and frustrated and at the same time..." She stopped and swallowed hard. "At the same time, I keep hoping you'll kiss me again. Or more."

She met his gaze square on. Leigh, his fearless wolf. Howling at the moon for the world to hear. He hadn't let himself imagine more, but now she'd opened that particular door. He couldn't help but walk in.

Malcolm raised her hand to his lips. Her hands weren't soft or dainty, but rather strong with long, slender fingers that knew what work was.

He briefly imagined them wrapped around his cock and nearly forgot where he was.

Focusing on her hand again, he kissed each fingertip, then gently sucked each one, whirling his tongue over and under, finishing with a soft bite. When he looked up at her face, she was aroused. Her pupils were wide, her breathing shallow, her cheeks slightly flushed. And, much to his delight, her nipples were hard, straining against her shirt. Calling him. Shouting his name.

"That is what I want to do to your whole body."

A shudder rocked through her. She snatched her hand away and stood, knocking the chair over with a bang. She turned and stumbled to the doorway that led to the stairs. Disappointment whipped through him until she looked back at him.

"Coming?"

Malcolm launched out of his chair before his next breath. He took her hand in his again and kissed the back of it.

"*Amante.*"

Her wide eyes held some fear along with a tantalizing dose of excitement, curiosity and determination. Qualities he would always associate with Leigh.

She pulled him into the darkened hallway toward the stairs.

CR CR CR

Leigh was ready, or at least that's what she told herself. Malcolm grabbed her arm and stopped her.

"Malcolm?"

"I want to so badly my teeth are erect," he said tightly. His hand trembled slightly on her arm. "I want you to trust me before I make love to you."

"Make love? I never asked for that. I just wanted a good fuck."

"Don't lie to me." His breath was warm on her cheek in the semi-darkness.

Her body screamed for her to climb him like a tree and to hell with his conscience. Her heart was beating so fast, her pulse thundered in her ears. But her head, the ever-practical noggin, slammed the door on her lust with a thud.

Damn, why couldn't they talk after they tussled in the sheets?

Malcolm let go of her arm and returned to the kitchen. Leigh bent down and put her hands on her knees. Taking a few deep breaths, she sought to regain her composure before facing him again.

"Okay, he's noble as well as sexy," she groused under her breath as she straightened and followed him.

CR CR CR

Malcolm sat on the front porch steps, smoking a thin cigarillo. The sounds of the night—crickets, a horse's whinny and the soft low of cows—greeted her ears. Night had nearly fallen—it was twilight time. As he puffed on the cigarillo, the tip illuminated his eyes in an orange glow. Deep, enticing, bottomless eyes. A shudder made its way from her head to her toes.

"I came back for two reasons," he began.

Leigh sat heavily next to him, jarring her back and smacking her ankle on the step below her. She knew she was acting like a child denied a lemon drop, but dammit, she wanted the candy. Now.

"What are the two reasons?" she asked when he remained silent, waiting for her tantrum to pass.

"I made one good friend since I left here. Nicky reminded me what family was. What you would do for the people you love. I had forgotten what that even meant."

"Where is he now?"

He chuckled softly. "She's in Wyoming."

Nicky was a woman? A dark rip of jealousy grabbed her stomach.

"In love with her husband, newborn twins and an adopted son."

A rain of relief washed through her. She allowed herself a grin. His teeth flashed white in the blue darkness.

"She made me realize how I missed family. My mother, Diego, Lorena…and you."

Her heart certainly did *not* pitty-pat.

"I am ashamed to admit it had been fifteen years since I'd been gone. And not once," his voice caught, "not once did I contact my mother. Not once."

Leigh reached out and took his hand. He puffed on his cigarillo then flicked it into the yard.

"What kind of son does that?"

Leigh didn't answer him. He already knew the answer. One who was running from a painful past by never thinking of anything but the here and now. One who shut himself and his emotions off.

"What's the second reason?" she asked.

He chuckled but there was no humor in it. "I ran into a *bandejo* named Alejandro."

His hand tightened on hers. She stifled a wince of pain.

"My past was suddenly there in my ear. Whispering, grasping at me. I knew it would only haunt me until I came back. Here. Home. I didn't expect my mother not to be here."

He rose and looked up at the stars, twinkling like tiny lanterns in a black sky.

"I need your help, Leigh. I need to find her but I don't know if I can go over there...face him...face them." His voice was hoarse as if forcing out the unfamiliar words.

Leigh stood and turned to face him.

"I'll help. Just tell me what you need me to do."

He drew her into his arms. This time there was no pulse-jumping, stomach-clenching lust. It was the old Malcolm. The boy who held her when she broke her leg. The boy who shared her secrets and dreams. He was right. The past was whispering in her ear, too.

CHAPTER SEVEN

Leigh opened her eyes the next morning and her first thought was she wished Malcolm was there next to her. Stroking, licking, kissing, groping, and everything in between. It had been so long since she'd even had a hug, much less sex. Malcolm's talented mouth had unleashed a monster named Insatiable Leigh.

No use wishing. If wishes were horses, beggars would ride. She forced herself to get out of bed. She'd shared that bed for ten years with Sean. Now two years later, it was as lonely as a coyote's howl and just as annoying.

The old cotton nightgown was the only thing she wore to bed. Pulling it off, she walked naked to the washstand in the corner. Splashing some cool water into the basin, she soaped up a washrag and got to work. As she cleaned herself, she tried not to remember Malcolm's hands or his mouth. Her nipples certainly remembered. They were begging for him. She was acting like a love-struck fool.

Love struck?

Leigh hadn't realized she said that out loud until she heard her voice echoing back. Snorting, she finished washing and dried off. She slipped on a clean pair of drawers, a chemise, jeans and a cotton shirt.

After pulling on her boots, she tucked her jeans in and grabbed her black hat. She was surprised Malcolm hadn't recognized that damn hat since it had belonged to him before he'd disappeared. Leigh had found it under his bed at Rancho Zarza and had taken very good care of the treasured hat since then. The black brim had some wear and tear, but overall was a good hat. And up until two days ago, her only tangible link to Malcolm.

She went downstairs and found Mrs. Hanson drinking coffee and eating a biscuit. Her look could have frozen the Rio Grande. In July.

"Morning." Leigh tried to be civil.

A grunt was her only response.

"I'm going over to see Alex Zarza this afternoon. Can you bake up a pie to take?"

Mrs. Hanson turned on like a sunrise on the prairie. Blinding.

"Of course. I still have some of those dried apples. I'll bake up one of the sweetest pies. Perhaps Damasco might be there."

Her attempt at a subtle hint was more like a blacksmith's hammer on an anvil and almost as loud.

Grabbing a mug of coffee and a biscuit, Leigh made her escape out the back door before Mrs. Hanson started picking her wedding bouquet.

ଔ ଔ ଔ

That afternoon, Leigh headed for the barn with a basket, Mrs. Hanson's apple pie snugly tucked inside. She had to admit it smelled delicious even if was made by a conniving, witchy housekeeper.

She entered the barn to saddle Ghost and went straight to his stall only to find Malcolm waiting for her. He was petting Ghost's long equine neck and murmuring to him. The gelding looked well pleased. She would too if Malcolm were petting *her*.

Stop mooning over him. He made it clear what he wants and it isn't you.

"What are you doing here?" she demanded.

He turned his head to look at her. His gaze traveled from the black hat to her dusty brown boots and back to her eyes. The shiver that danced across her skin was not from cold. Rather, she felt hot. Very hot.

"Do you ever wear a woman's clothes, *amante?*"

The hackles on her neck rose like an army regiment. She refused to listen to that kind of shit from him, too.

"These are clothes. I am a woman. I seem to repeat myself a lot around you, Mal. What are you doing here?"

He patted Ghost's neck one more time, then grabbed a blanket on the stall door and started saddling him.

Leigh realized all her tack was there already. Malcolm must have been waiting for her. To help her. The thought struck her as almost funny. No one had ever offered to help an Amazon daughter of a blacksmith, widow of a rancher more than twice her age. She guessed people figured with her size and strength, she could take care of herself. That she didn't need help. However, it didn't mean she didn't want help. And here was Mal, doing for her without asking. It seemed like a simple thing, but God knows it wasn't. The gesture was so huge, it almost overwhelmed her. The lump in her throat was a testament to how deeply Malcolm's consideration affected her.

She gripped the handle of the basket so tightly, little bits of straw lodged in her fingers.

"Thank you," she murmured as he took the basket and tied it to her saddle with a bit of rope.

"I will ride with you." He handed her the reins.

"Do you know where I'm going?"

Malcolm pulled his horse, already saddled, out of the next stall. As he led the horse out of the barn into the sun, he turned to her.

"You are going to see my father."

ↃↃↃ

Malcolm had decided he needed to protect her. He had talked with Andy Parker at length the night before. The tales that boy told about the bad luck on the Circle O were enough to make him clench his jaw so hard his head ached. He was certain now Sean's death was no accident.

Someone was trying to sink her. Hard. So she'd never come up for air. The logical conclusion was that someone wanted the land very badly and the only thing stopping them was a stubborn Welsh girl who had a shadow at her back.

He intended to be with her as much as possible. Although he'd be hard pressed to admit it, he was very worried about her. Like a rusty wheel, his emotions were creaking to life. He blamed *Roja* and her damned happiness. If only he hadn't gone to Wyoming. If only she hadn't cared about him. If only he hadn't returned to Texas.

Done was done. His feelings were dusty and, right now, making him feel like a dog at a cat party. Out of place, itchy, with an overwhelming urge to bay at the moon.

Whoever was behind the attacks would try to kill Leigh again. Soon. He was damn sure not going to let that happen. No one would get past him without a few more holes in their hide.

They mounted up and headed west toward Rancho Zarza. It was another beautiful day. A clear blue sky with scattered skinny white clouds and bright, shining sunlight.

"Are you going to come with me all the way?"

"*Sí*. I will wait in the stables until you are done."

The very thought of the stables made his entire body tighten. Those frigging stables loaded with prime Zarza horseflesh.

"Are you sure?"

Hell, no. But he was going to do it anyway.

"Yes."

His terse response wasn't really fair to her. Her shoulders stiffened.

"Okay, I'm not sure I even want to go, but I *am* sure you are not going alone."

She seemed to accept his answer without comment. Together they galloped across the miles to the Zarza hacienda. The closer they got, the more cramped his stomach got. A big knot of pain gripping harder and harder.

"Go back, Malcolm."

She looked at him, concern in her hazel eyes.

"No. I'm not leaving you alone."

"But you look like shit. In fact, I thought maybe you were going to bring up your lunch."

If it hadn't been Leigh, he would have been offended. As children, they had always told each other everything. Leigh must have still felt the need to be honest with him, even if it scraped like rusty nails.

"I have to come."

She shrugged and threw one hand up in the air. "Why bother?"

Malcolm wasn't about to answer.

cs cs cs

Two armed sentries by the gate allowed Leigh and Malcolm to pass. Their sharp eyes followed them in, but Leigh was well known. Malcolm hid in his own skin.

Rancho Zarza hadn't really changed. The sprawling adobe house was well kept. A fancy new fountain with a three-tiered birdbath of sorts sat in front of the house like a trophy. Beautiful flowers and vines bloomed, their scent and color thick in the air. Somewhere a dog barked and a few chickens squawked.

Inside, Malcolm was a frightened eighteen-year-old boy, seeing his only home for the last time.

He was unprepared for the sadness, the grief that snuck up on him seeing his home again. His life had been shaped by everything here. The *vaqueros*, the horses, the wealth, and the vicious cold that permeated everything. It was always about money and power.

They reached the house and Leigh dismounted. She looked up at him and frowned. "Get down," she mouthed.

He mentally slapped himself. What the hell was he doing? Calling undue attention to himself like an ass. He dismounted and took the reins of her gelding. She untied the basket and stepped back.

"Be careful," he said under his breath.

"You too." She turned to go into the house. He was momentarily captured by the sway of her hips in those trousers. Damn. He was never distracted by Nicky in her jeans. What the hell was it about Leigh?

Stomach jumping like tumbleweed in a windstorm, he stood with the horses in the sun. He knew he should go to the stables, give the horses some water, but he couldn't move. Sensations, intense and paralyzing, gripped him tightly in their claws.

cs cs cs

Leigh knocked on the door. It was huge, made of hickory with black strips running the full length of the six-foot width.

Lorena Martin opened the door. Lorena had been a fixture at Rancho Zarza ever since Leigh could remember. She was of Mexican descent, with wavy black hair in a bun, twinkling brown eyes and a plump, if short, matronly figure. Leigh had looked down at her since she was thirteen years old. But in truth, she looked up to Lorena. The housekeeper was a smart, kind, tolerant woman who tried to see the best in everyone. She had also been Malcolm's mother's best friend.

"Little Leigh. How good to see you, *hija*. What have you brought for us?"

Lorena embraced Leigh briefly. Leigh bent down, inhaling a unique scent that always floated around Lorena. A scent of home, of belonging.

Leigh held out the basket. "Apple pie. I heard Alex wasn't feeling well so I thought I'd be neighborly."

"You are so sweet, *niña*. Apple is his favorite."

As Lorena reached for the basket, Leigh asked, "Lorena, do you know what happened to Leslie Ross?"

Lorena nearly lost her grip on the basket. Her normally olive skin flushed a sickly shade and her eyes widened.

"Leslie? Why would you ask me that after all these years?"

Lorena was scared. That much was obvious, but of what? Or who?

"Do we have a guest, Lorena?"

Isabella's cold, sharp words behind Leigh were like a bramble bush raking bare skin. Her voice was just as painful and unwanted, leaving behind welts and scratches.

Leigh took off her hat and turned to greet Mrs. Zarza. Isabella's was a classic beauty that had not faded an inch over time. Her straight black hair was swept into an elegant knot at the back of her delicate head. She regarded Leigh with liquid brown eyes framed by long, thick lashes, accented by prominent cheekbones and full, ruby lips. Isabella was perfect on the outside and as rotten as spoiled meat on the inside. Cold and vicious, she was known for treating anyone who wasn't Spanish nobility as a peasant.

"Oh, it's only Mrs. O'Reilly." Her gaze raked Leigh's appearance up and down. One perfect black eyebrow rose. "I see that dresses are still scarce on the Circle O."

What was she supposed to say to that?

"I've come to see Alex."

"She brought a pie," Lorena interjected.

Isabella cut her gaze to her housekeeper. "You may bring that to the kitchen."

Lorena nodded and darted away with her shoulders slightly bowed. Isabella's icy stare returned to Leigh.

"He's not feeling well so you can't stay long."

Isabella turned sharply and went down the hall. Leigh followed.

Alejandro Zarza had been a big man, not just in looks, but also in life. He took what he wanted without excuses or apologies and built his own little empire where he reigned as king. Until now. The king was dying slowly, by excruciating degrees. His was a wasting sickness that stole his strength, his breath, his thunder. Alex used to eat life in great, grasping bites; now life was eating him.

When Leigh walked into his room, she was hard-pressed not to let the shock show on her face.

His black hair, liberally sprinkled with silver, lay lax and flat on his head. The skin stretched taut across his gaunt cheeks, his dark eyes sunken in his face. His lips were bloodless and cracked. He was dressed in a loose white shirt that hung on his emaciated frame making him look like a little boy playing dress-up. Literally, he was half the man he used to be.

Alex rested in a large wingback chair by the window, a colorful red and yellow quilt tucked around his waist and legs. The sun shone on his sallow complexion, giving false life to his dying self. A nurse was busy setting a tray with a silver tea service on the small table next to him.

When he caught sight of Leigh, he managed to smile broadly, a twinkle of life shining from his tired eyes.

"Little Leigh Wynne."

"You're looking better, Alex," Leigh said.

He cocked one eyebrow. "From you, I always expect the truth. I could always count on your father for that, too."

Leigh sat in the chair next to him and looked Alex in the eye. She smiled. "Okay, then you look like you've been ridden hard and put up wet."

He threw back his head and laughed. Leigh remembered the sound of his booming laugh. Alex had the kind of laugh that made everyone want to smile. This time, however, it ended with a wheezing, frantic cough that rattled his thin frame.

"You'd do better to guard your tongue, Mrs. O'Reilly. Alejandro must conserve his strength," came Isabella's sharp rebuke.

Leigh had forgotten she was there. Amazing. Too bad.

"Leave her alone, Bella. Leigh is a burst of fresh air for an old man."

He winked one bleary brown eye.

"How are you?"

Leigh shrugged. "I'm still alive." She bit her tongue to keep from telling him Malcolm was back. The sharpness in Alex's gaze had not faded, regardless of his physical condition.

"It hasn't been going well, eh?"

She shook her head. "No. Last week someone poisoned the creek out by the south pasture. Lost about a dozen more head."

Alex frowned. "You sure it was poison?"

She nodded. "No doubt about it. I don't need to tell you what a longhorn's belly looks like after it's been drinking poisoned water."

"I told you I would send some of my *vaqueros* over to help you."

"And I told you no. I need to do this on my own, Alex."

He reached out and patted her hand. "*Sí*, I know you do. But I worry like I am your *tío*, your uncle. If you need help, really need help, you will ask?"

Leigh didn't want to say yes, but she knew he wouldn't accept anything less. "Yes."

"Promise?"

"I promise."

That seemed to satisfy him. He sipped at his tea, then shakily set the cup back in its saucer.

"Who do you think it is that is poisoning your cattle?"

"Someone local. Someone who knows where I keep my cattle to graze in the spring and summer. Someone who wants the Circle O to fail."

Alex looked at her sharply. "It's not just the poisoned cattle, is it?"

She squirmed a bit on the seat, unwilling to load her troubles onto his frail shoulders. Unaccountably, she was rescued by Isabella.

"You are tiring quickly, Alejandro," she said as she appeared at Leigh's elbow. "I think this visit is over."

With brutal efficiency, Leigh was herded—no other word for it—out of the room in minutes. After a quick peck on Alex's papery cheek and a whispered "I'll be back soon", she was suddenly standing by the front door, Isabella's claws practically gouging her arm.

She stared down at the woman's petite face, then glanced at her arm. "I haven't needed help walking in about thirty years."

Isabella's teeth shone in a feral snarl. "I didn't want you to lose your way to the door."

Leigh couldn't contain her snort. "Since I grew up not ten feet from this door, I don't think I'd lose my way in the dark, blindfolded."

The teeth appeared sharper. "Let us hope that situation never arises. Lorena."

Lorena appeared with the now empty basket. She handed it to Leigh and gave her a quick hug.

"*Vaya con Dios.*"

"*Y tú,*" Leigh responded. Glancing back at Isabella, she could not suppress the shivers of dread that marched up her spine at the expression in her eyes. Isabella was the coldest person she'd ever known. She'd always treated both Leigh and her father, Big Lee, like commoners in a medieval castle. Before, she had only been haughty or dismissive. Now, this particular look was evil. It was the only word that fit. Leigh had to find Malcolm and get the hell out of here.

જી જી જી

Malcolm had stared at the open stable door for at least five minutes. Ghost yanked on his reins, impatient for water and oats. Demon started chewing on Malcolm's ass instead.

"Ouch! *Caballo de Diablo*. Stupid horse."

He stepped out of reach of the horse's big teeth, rubbing his sore butt. A snicker behind him brought his gun up, pointing straight at the heart of a boy.

He was about thirteen, with chunky brown hair, clear blue eyes and a lanky build that held the promise of filling out into a big man. He wore brown pants and suspenders and a formerly blue shirt; his bare feet were dirty. His eyes widened at the sight of the gun, but Malcolm saw no fear, only flatness. The boy leaned against a pitchfork, sweaty, with bits of hay stuck in his unruly hair.

Malcolm slowly put the gun away, silently promising his horse revenge. Before he realized what he was doing, he entered the stable and glared at the boy.

"You should do your job instead of laughing at strangers, *hijo*."

Handing the boy the reins of the ornery horse, he carefully watched the boy's expression.

"I ain't no one's son."

He snatched the reins and led the horse deeper into the gloom. As Malcolm's eyes adjusted, he found the boy rubbing Demon down, the horse's big stupid head buried in a trough drinking noisily. Ghost pulled ahead, nostrils flaring at the scent of the water. Without missing a beat, the boy took the Appaloosa's reins and led him to the next trough.

Malcolm was impressed; the boy knew horses.

"*Como se llama?*"

"I don't speak no Spanish."

Malcolm suppressed the smile that wanted to rise.

"You do not speak English either, eh?"

The boy's expression was disgusted and guarded. He didn't get the joke.

"What is your name? How did you come to work here at Rancho Zarza?"

The boy stalked off to another stall, pitchfork in hand. Malcolm's fear and apprehension over being in the hated stable was replaced by curiosity over the boy, so he followed him. He found the boy working in the fourth stall, the biggest in the stable, filling a wheelbarrow with manure-encrusted straw.

"There was a huge black stallion named Rey that used to be in this stall. He was a big, arrogant horse who used to try to step on my foot every time I had to curry him."

The boy turned his head and looked at him suspiciously. "You worked here when Rey was here?"

"Worked? Yes, I suppose it was work. I didn't get paid though."

The boy stopped and leaned an arm on the pitchfork again, his expression still guarded.

"Was you a slave?"

Malcolm shook his head. "No, *chico*, just the son of a servant. My pay was food and a bed."

"Me, too."

Now he was really intrigued. "Who is your mama?"

The blue eyes finally showed emotion. Anger.

"The cook. She's the cook."

Turning, the boy went back to work. Malcolm grabbed the stall door to keep from falling down. The boy was not him, but how was it possible? It was like twenty years had melted away in an instant. He had to know.

"Who is your papa?"

He almost hoped the boy would not answer.

"You ain't been around in a while, have you? My pa ain't married to my ma, y'know. So's I'm a bastard."

Bastard. The slur hit him in the head like a rock. God, how he hated the sound of it.

"Don't use that word."

"Why not? It's what I am."

He snagged the boy's arm and swung him around. The young arm was as brittle as a twig, easily broken.

"No. It's not what you are. Or who you are. Only you decide that. It does not matter if your parents did not marry. You do not have to pay for that for the rest of your life."

He'd give the boy marks for bravery. He tried to wrestle his arm free, but Malcolm held firm.

"Let go, you son of a bitch."

"Nice mouth. Does your mama hear you talk like that?"

"Leave her outta this." He twisted harder, squirming to get out of Malcolm's grip.

"I would never disrespect your mama, boy. My mama was the cook, too."

The boy ceased his struggles and stared up at Malcolm. "Who was your papa?"

"Alejandro." Malcolm nearly choked on the name.

All the fight went out of the boy. He slumped his shoulders and simply stared, confusion evident in his eyes.

"You're my uncle?"

Uncle? This was Damasco's boy? Dirty, skinny and working in the stable barefoot? Like father, like son. Malcolm tried his damnedest to hide his anger, but something must have shown in his eyes because the boy backed up a step.

"Malcolm?" came Leigh's voice.

"Yes?" Both he and the boy answered.

It was worse than he thought. Damasco was using his own child to exact some kind of twisted revenge on Malcolm.

Leigh appeared in the stable with the now empty basket. When she spotted the boy, she smiled.

"I see you met Hermano, Malcolm," she said to the boy.

The boy's hard expression softened a bit. "Is he really my uncle?"

Leigh's gaze snapped to Malcolm's. "Who told you that?"

The boy jerked a thumb at Malcolm.

"You are mistaken, *chico.* I said my papa was Alejandro. I never said Zarza."

The boy eyed him suspiciously but didn't argue.

"Are you ready to go?" Leigh asked Malcolm. She looked like a spring wound too tightly, ready to snap.

"*Sí. Vamanos.*"

While Leigh thanked the boy for taking care of Ghost, Malcolm led Demon out of the barn. His hands shook with anger. He was absolutely furious.

And there wasn't a damn thing he could do about it.

ରେ ରେ ରେ

They rode home in near silence, both lost in their own thoughts.

"Why didn't you tell me?" Malcolm asked.

"Tell you what?"

"About that boy."

She turned toward him, confused. "He's the stable boy, Mal. Most big ranches have at least one."

Malcolm yanked back on Demon's reins. She reeled Ghost around to face him.

"That's not what I'm talking about!" he shouted angrily.

"Malcolm, what *are* you talking about?"

He stared at her, black eyes glittering with what she thought was fury. "Damasco made that boy. Made a bastard then named him Malcolm."

Leigh was shocked. Damasco was the boy's father? She had always chalked up his name to coincidence.

"How do you know?"

"He told me he was a bastard. *Madre de Dios*, Leigh, his mother is the fucking cook."

Suddenly she understood Damasco's game. Only it wasn't a game. It was a boy, an innocent child, created to live out some twisted desire.

"You did not know." Malcolm's tone made it clear he wasn't asking a question.

"No, Mal, I didn't. I got married when Louise was pregnant. She and I were friends. But I…I never asked her who the father was. I didn't know. How could he?"

Malcolm's face was now an emotionless mask. But his eyes still shone like fiery coals.

"Maybe if I talk to Alex."

"No. He already knows, I'm sure." His lips curled into a sneer. "Throwaways are something he's familiar with."

Leigh was upset to see such hatred from a son to a father. From one friend to another. She dangled between them, caught in the web woven so long ago.

"Did you ask?"

"About your mother? Yes, I asked Lorena, but that bitch Isabella yanked me around like a lost calf."

"Did Lorena say anything? Know anything?"

Leigh shook her head. "I don't think so."

Malcolm gazed into the horizon toward Rancho Zarza.

"Someone knows. I need to find out who."

ର ର ର

When they reached the Circle O, Malcolm was a little calmer, but not much. He didn't want to Leigh to bear the brunt of his anger, but it was hard to keep it in since it festered and screeched to be let loose.

"I'm sorry for snapping at you."

She looked surprised. "There's nothing to apologize for. You were angry. I understand that feeling."

"Things are getting deeper and deeper, Leigh. Are you sure you want to be next to me?"

She grinned. "No other place I'd rather be."

"Even if Sean were alive?"

The smile fell off her face. "I told you before. That's not your business. Leave it the hell alone."

She galloped ahead to the barn, dismounted and grabbed Ghost's reins. Malcolm quickly followed.

"I think it is my business," he said when he'd caught up to her in the barn.

She glared at him and walked Ghost into his stall. He put Demon in a stall and unsaddled him. After a brief rubdown, he made sure the biting beast had water and oats. He returned to Ghost's stall in time to see Leigh shove a piece of paper in her pocket.

"*Amante.*"

She put the empty basket on a nail in the post by the door, then started rubbing Ghost down as the big gelding noisily slurped from a water bucket.

"When I was eighteen, my father died from a horse kick to the head." Pain echoed in her voice.

"I'm sorry."

She waved her hand to brush away his sympathy. "It's okay. You knew my father. We were from two different places in our hearts. After he died, Damasco started sniffing after me. Caught me alone once or twice. I packed my saddlebags and left one night. I walked to the Circle O."

She grabbed a curry brush and stroked the Appaloosa, who seemed to sigh with pleasure.

Malcolm wondered what Damasco had done when he had caught her alone.

"Sean's wife had died a few years back from consumption. He offered to marry me for protection and for a companion. He needed someone to play checkers with."

"What? You married a man because he wanted to play checkers with you? Are you *loca?*"

She threw the curry brush at him. It bounced painfully on his shoulder then continued rolling behind him.

"I was alone, goddammit! You'd been gone three years and certainly didn't give a shit. Don't you dare judge me."

Malcolm made a grab for her hands, but she snatched them back and bumped into Ghost. The horse whinnied his displeasure.

"Don't pull away from me. I would never hurt you," he said in a low voice.

Her hands clenched into fists. "Sean was my friend. Just when I needed one most. Don't you understand? I was alone. I had *no* one."

She stalked away, grabbing the basket as she went by.

Malcolm let her go, filled with self-loathing. He'd only been concerned about himself as usual. He left behind his best friend, his first love, all without a backward glance. The first girl he'd kissed, hugged, held hands with, dreamed with.

And then he'd thrown her away.

Like father, like son.

CHAPTER EIGHT

When Leigh got to the house, she'd already been stopped four times. Andy wanted to show her how the well pump was fixed and didn't stick anymore. Earl let her know three dozen head were missing. Jerry wanted her opinion on a mustang they'd caught. And Mrs. Hanson gave her a list of supplies they needed.

After all that had happened already, Leigh was exhausted. She folded the list and went to put it in her pocket. Something else was already there. It was the paper that had been stuck in the bottom of the basket. She unfolded it. It simply read "MacAdams Farm, Leslie" in Lorena's handwriting.

Leigh's heart picked up its pace.

Lorena knew where Leslie Ross was. She had no idea where the MacAdams Farm was, but next time she was in town, she'd ask Burt Green to look into it. Burt was the only attorney in Millerton, and strangely enough, also the undertaker. But he'd help her find out what he could. He was a good sleuth.

Leigh tucked the papers in her hand and climbed the stairs. It was only just after five, but she needed a bath. Time to be by herself and think. Fortunately Sean had had a fancy tub with running water installed five years ago. Hot water was stored in a cistern outside. Somehow it all came together with cold well water and filled her tub.

Leigh stopped in her room to grab clean clothes, then headed straight for the bathing room.

क्ष क्ष क्ष

Malcolm couldn't find Leigh. She wasn't outside anywhere, nor was she in the kitchen or the office. When he'd come inside, Mrs. Hanson gave him a dirty look, mumbled something about stew on the stove, then slammed out the door.

He didn't trust that woman as far as he could throw her. Truth be told, not far at all.

After looking downstairs, he figured Leigh must be upstairs. As he climbed the staircase, he heard humming that sounded more like a screeching bird than a human. She always was as tone deaf as a cast iron skillet. There were four doors upstairs and two were closed. One was a guest room, the other empty. That left the two closed doors. He followed the humming, biting back a grin at how awful she sounded.

She was behind the last door. He raised his hand and knocked lightly.

"Is that you, Mrs. Hanson? Come in." Her voice rang out.

And so he did, even if he wasn't Mrs. Hanson.

Then he forgot what his name was as his dick rose hard and fast.

She was naked. Not only naked, but wet. Just stepping out of the tub. He absorbed every inch of her like a dry sponge long without water.

Poised with one leg on the floor and one leg still in the tub, her legs were slightly parted. Her wet hair slowly dripped sparkles of moisture that snaked down her perfect honey-toned skin.

Her breasts were incredible. Large round globes with dark nipples puckered tightly, rose buds in the first blush of spring. Her nest of curls, mahogany brown kinky hair, glistened with bath water. He saw a hint of pink flesh between those curls and had to hold the door to remain upright.

She was sleek and muscled like a thoroughbred mare, but round in all the right places.

Madre de Dios. She was a goddess.

Her hazel eyes widened with shock. After a few moments of resembling a surprised rabbit, she made a quick dive for the towel on the floor next to the tub. She clumsily covered herself then began to blush the same color as her incredible nipples.

"I…I thought you were Mrs. Hanson."

He spread his left arm out. "As you can see, I'm not."

Her gaze fastened on the tree growing in his very tight trousers, which caused it to grow a few more inches.

"*Amante*, I don't have enough words to tell you how beautiful you are."

Leigh screwed up her face and snorted. "Don't even try to wiggle your way out of this one. Just hightail it back downstairs."

He closed and locked the door and took a step toward her. She frowned.

Malcolm took two more steps, then another, stopping mere inches from her. The smell of her freshly scrubbed skin caressed his senses. He ran his hand down her wet shoulder.

"I would not lie to you. Just looking at you and I am as hard as a stone."

He placed both hands on her shoulders and squeezed gently.

"Let me love you."

గ్రు గ్రు గ్రు

Sweet Jesus.

Malcolm caught her naked. Not only that, but he was still there. Watching her. Those black eyes had an intensity that shook her to her core. As his gaze touched her skin, it raised goose bumps and sent shivers skipping all over her. Her pulse thumped in her veins as arousal crept in on all fours.

"You want *me*?"

He closed his eyes and Leigh would swear she felt him shudder.

"Want is not a strong enough word."

"Not strong enough?" Damn, she wished she had at least something witty to say. She felt like a mare penned in with a stud—a stud who made her heart race and her entire body hum.

"Burn." The word burst from his mouth.

"Burn?" She hated the fact that she squeaked the word.

"We must be back in the canyon again. The echo is strong in here."

She tried to smile but all she could concentrate on were his hands—strong and callused, caressing her skin. His thumbs were dangerously close to her breasts. That thought made her clench deep inside.

"I burn for you, *amante*."

He leaned forward and kissed her. His lips were gentle, making little sucks on her lips. Slowly traveling back and forth across. Kiss. Suck. Kiss. Suck.

More.

She dropped the towel, wrapped her arms around his neck and pushed her body up against him. Lord, Jesus, the man was as hard as granite. Everywhere. His cock felt like a hammer knocking on her door. Come on in.

She kissed him back, pushing her tongue into his mouth and lapping at him slowly, deliberately. His mouth felt like a fire and his tongue, a branding iron. Hissing, steaming heat. Like a big cat, he licked her mouth, her teeth, her tongue. Leigh moaned when he tickled the roof of her mouth. Her nipples scraped against his shirt, screaming for attention.

"Touch me," she whispered against his lips.

Malcolm's hands danced across her skin. Those long fingers ran up and down her spine, then caressed her round derriere, dipping lower to tantalize, tease and stroke. One finger made lazy circles near her other hole. If she got any hotter, she might explode before he even took his clothes off.

"I need to touch you." She started yanking on his shirt and buttons flew every which way, pinging on the floor, tub and walls. "Jesus, Malcolm. Help me. I need you."

As he slipped his shirt off, he bent down and sucked one pebbled nipple into his hot mouth. Oh, damn, that tongue. It swirled, licked and nudged her nipple until she thought she'd go mad. Then he bit it. She yelped and grabbed his now naked shoulder. The iron muscles bunched under her hand and she had the crazy notion to nibble on them.

"My God, you are so hard," she blurted.

Malcolm chuckled and straightened. Leigh realized he had somehow slipped his pants off and was as naked as she was.

She stared at his incredible body. It was bronze toned, with tufts of black hair on his chest that made her palms itch to feel. Like an arrow, a line of hair led straight down past a sexy navel to his cock. The huge member jutted out from a nest of curls cupping his large balls. He was thick and throbbing, with a moist tip that signaled his readiness and begged for her tongue.

"It won't fit." Leigh blurted. She'd never seen a member so large before, not that her experience was extensive. He was magnificently made.

"*Sí, amante,* it will fit. You will be so wet and so ready for me, it will slide right in."

Malcolm's hands cupped her breast and her mound. His finger slipped into her pussy and slid back and forth, rubbing and stroking. He lapped at her nipple with a grin on his wicked mouth.

More.

He tweaked and pinched her nipple to a peak it had never reached before, while he nibbled on the other. The sensations were about to drive her over the edge. An orgasm built inside her and her breath was short and choppy. She didn't want it to be over before she had a chance to have him nestled inside her.

"Malcolm." She sounded husky, and dammit, needy.

"Miz O'Reilly?"

Mrs. Hanson's voice outside the bathing room door was not a welcome sound. The throbbing in Leigh's pussy matched the stroking of his fingers and tongue. Blood pulsed through her like a river of lava she was helpless to stop. Dammit, she was going to come.

"Yes?" she managed to say.

And still he didn't stop. Stroking, pinching, licking. Oh, Jesus, so close.

"Everything all right? I thought I heard you yell."

"Just slipped on the water. I'm…"

His mouth captured the other nipple with an audible slurp and he stuck two fingers up her pussy.

"I'm fine," she croaked. Oh, no, she wasn't fine. She was about to have the orgasm of a lifetime.

"Okay then. Supper's on the stove waiting."

Over the roaring in her ears, she heard Mrs. Hanson's footsteps fade down the hallway.

"Now come for me, *amante.* Come." He bit her nipple and Leigh came in his hand so hard she saw stars behind her eyes. She jerked and clawed at him as his fingers continued to fuck her and he suckled her nipple deep into his mouth. Oh, God, so *good.*

More.

"Malcolm, please." She needed to feel him inside her. Now.

His eyes were onyx pools of heat.

"Yesssss…"

His tongue dueled with hers while he backed her up to the wall. Pushing her against the plaster, he pulled her legs up to wrap around his waist.

His hardened cock nudged her pussy and she held her breath as he slid in. All the way in. Like a key in a well-oiled lock. She had never felt anything so perfect in her life. He filled her completely.

"You are so tight, *amante*. So fucking tight. *Dios*."

When he began to move, she changed her mind. He fit. All of him. He thrust in and out as his mouth reclaimed her nipples. Stroke after stroke. Faster and faster. Her body clenched with need, with hunger, with pleasure. She was going to come again, a nearly impossible feat until that day. With his big, hard cock pushing inside over and over.

"Mal, I'm going to come. Jesus, you're going to make me come again."

He let loose her nipple and looked into her eyes. With a wicked grin, he reached between them and stroked her hot button.

"I want to see you."

He pounded into her again and again, surrounding her with heat and passion until her world exploded. A cascade of stars sparkled behind her eyes, and she stifled the scream of ecstasy by biting her lips. She pulled him deeper into her body as the pleasure washed over her. Her breath caught in her throat and her blood zinged through her.

"Ay, *Dios*, you are beautiful, *amante*. Now you bring me with you," Malcolm whispered.

Leigh looked into his eyes as he reached his own peak. Slamming home, he thrust into her so hard, she was sure her shoulders made a dent in the wall. He gripped her ass and held on as he groaned low and deep in his throat like the predator he was. After a seemingly endless minute, he stopped moving.

Leigh shook like a newborn calf. Hell, even her toes were shaking. And he was still inside her. Hard and pulsing. Her body grasped him hungrily, muscles tight with pleasure.

Nothing had prepared her for this. Not that first painful, horrible experience in a horse stall. Not any of the dozen times in her marriage Sean had fumbled beneath her nightshirt. Not any of the times she eased her own aches in the dark of night. Or that crazy night in Houston after Sean's death when she spent the night with a stranger. None of it even came close.

She took a deep shuddering breath echoed by Malcolm. He slowly withdrew and set her back on her feet. The floorboards felt cool against her heated skin.

They didn't speak. Malcolm walked over to his clothes, slipped them on, then stepped out of the room, closing the door behind him.

CHAPTER NINE

Malcolm changed his shirt without talking to anyone in the bunkhouse. Andy tried to talk to him, but he just ignored the boy and left as quickly as he came.

He went to the barn and saddled Demon like a madman. He had to get out of there fast. It was the only coherent thought he had.

Run. Get out. Disappear.

He was cinching the saddle when he realized his damn hands were trembling.

Santa Maria.

He needed a drink. A lot of them. After he led Demon out of the barn, he threw himself onto the horse and took off like the hounds of hell were snapping at his heels. The ride into Millerton was a blur in the fading sunset. His body still hummed and his balls tingled.

It had been incredible. No, more than that. It was the single most significant event in his life since that fateful day fifteen years ago when he hit Damasco and his entire life changed for the worse.

Life had just taken another drastic turn in the bathing room of the Circle O ranch house. Malcolm didn't understand what was going on with Leigh and it scared the piss out of him.

Ayúdame, Dios.

When he'd seen her naked, he'd lost all ability to reason. All he could do was hang on while his body took over. He had never, ever lost complete control with a woman. And this woman wasn't just any woman. It was *Leigh*.

What the hell happened?

He didn't know and didn't think he was going to figure it out while he was still lightheaded from coming his brains out.

Malcolm headed right for the Pink Slipper. It was time to let Damasco know who stood in the shadows. He was sure his brother was behind the attacks on Leigh and the Circle O. He would not allow her to be hurt any more. It was time for the fox to flush out the hound.

CR CR CR

Malcolm sat in the back of the room, nursing a bad whiskey, waiting for Damasco to appear. He used to be so patient, able to wait like a spider in its web. But tonight he felt antsy.

Maybe you shouldn't have left her naked with your seed dripping down her leg.

He chose to ignore his inner demons' taunts and focused on the door. One moment it was empty. The next, Damasco appeared and Malcolm's fury leapt at the sight.

Damasco walked in like a king greeting his subjects. Three men followed him in, guarding his back, looking as smart as a trio of rats. Malcolm itched to grab the knife strapped to his back.

"*Buenas noches,*" Damasco boomed.

A few half-hearted replies greeted him. He pushed an old man out of his chair at a table near the bar. His rats chortled merrily.

"Move it, *abuelo.*"

The old man skittered out of the way and left the bar in a hurry.

A barmaid hesitantly approached them after they sat at the now empty table. She was a young redhead with a sweet body and apple-sized breasts. Her blue eyes watched Damasco. She obviously knew his tricks because she wouldn't get within three feet of him.

"Whiskey, *chica. Rápido,*" he shouted.

The girl jumped and scurried back behind the bar. Damasco and the rodent brothers laughed and pounded their thighs like they'd never seen anything so funny.

"Soon, *amigos,* it will all be mine, and I will buy this shithole. All the girls will wear smaller clothes and sit on your lap while they serve you."

He made a swipe for the barmaid when she came back to the table with the whiskey. She yelped and fell back on her ass, dropping the tray. The whiskey-filled glasses shattered on the floor.

No one moved. The silence was broken by the sound of the girl whimpering. Damasco and his rats started howling with laughter.

"Bring me another, *chica*, and next time don't drop it."

More knee slapping and general stupidity. If given a choice, Malcolm would never admit this miscreant was his brother. He watched the girl, shaking and crying, at the bar. When he turned his attention back to Damasco, Malcolm heard what he'd been waiting all night for.

"I tell you, once the old man kicks off and I can get that cold bitch to spread her thighs for me, I will buy this whole town."

"Didn't she knee you in the balls last time?" asked one of the rat brothers.

Damasco's face flushed red. "Next time she won't get the chance. That *puta*—"

Malcolm stood abruptly, knocking over his chair, which clattered noisily in the suddenly silent saloon.

"You need to watch your mouth, Damasco."

Damasco turned his head to look at him. He appeared so cocksure and full of himself.

"Who the hell are you, *cabron*, to speak to me like that? Don't you know who I am?"

Yup, he knew who he was, all right. If Damasco had been a little bit smarter, he would have noticed Malcolm called him by his first name.

Malcolm walked over to Damasco slowly, and his half-brother didn't even bother to rise from his chair. He just sneered.

The three prairie dogs rose to back him like a wall of muscle and flesh. The quiet was pregnant with anticipation and fear. Malcolm heard the barkeep and the girl dive behind the bar. A few smart people ducked out the batwing doors.

When he finally reached Damasco, all the hate and loathing he had for this scrap of humanity filled him up to his eyes. With his right hand resting on a pistol, he pushed his hat back and stared into the deep brown eyes of his brother.

"*Hola, hermano*. Miss me?"

He counted three seconds before the recognition hit him. Damasco's eyes widened and Malcolm saw fear and disbelief in their shallow depths.

"Y-you're dead. You can't be here. You're d-dead, dammit. Mama told me so." Damasco's voice shook like a young boy's.

For a moment, it was fifteen years ago, and he heard the childish taunts spewing from the young Damasco as Malcolm was punished. Damasco watched it. He'd watched every damn lash fall down on Malcolm's back.

Malcolm had to grab onto his hatred like a snarling dog before he killed Damasco in front of twenty witnesses and got his neck stretched within the hour.

"As you can see, your bitch of a mother was wrong. I am very much alive."

Damasco finally stood, pointing a finger at Malcolm.

"At least my mother was not a *puta*."

His hands gripped both pistols in a heartbeat without even thinking about it, so great was his anger. His blood was running so hot it scalded his brain. He wanted to kill Damasco so badly, Malcolm could actually run his tongue on his lips and taste it. The three rats all had their hands full of steel and were pointing them straight at Malcolm's heart.

"I just wanted to say hello, little brother."

The word brother rippled through the saloon like a breeze across a field of wheat.

"You are not my brother."

Malcolm threw back his head and laughed with all the bitterness in his heart.

"If only that were true. Believe me, I'd rather not be brother to such a stupid dog like you."

He stepped forward to leave the saloon, more than conscious of the dozens of eyes and three pistols pointed at his back.

He turned to point at Damasco. Like trained rats, the three walls of muscle shifted to stand behind Damasco again. They were like a portable shield.

"Take my advice, Damasco. Leave Leigh O'Reilly and the Circle O alone. She has my protection now. And I don't show mercy to anyone who harms me or mine."

"So you cracked those dusty thighs, eh? I heard even Old Sean couldn't stand the stench."

Malcolm barely held onto his rage as it pumped through him like fire. All he wanted was to see the *bandejo* die.

"You've been warned, little brother."

He turned to leave when someone called out, "Who the hell is that?"

Malcolm stopped and looked around the saloon. "Malcolm. Malcolm Ross y Zarza."

A few gasps and one or two exclamations of "I'll be damned!" and "Goddamn!" met his proclamation.

He stepped out into the darkness. He didn't think his warning would stop Damasco, but maybe force his hand to act quickly. And people in a hurry made mistakes.

As he stepped off the wooden planked sidewalk toward Demon, he heard the whistle of wood right before it slammed into his back. Two sets of hands grabbed him and pulled him into the alley. Malcolm began to fight for his life.

CHAPTER TEN

Dawn was just painting the eastern sky when Leigh saddled Ghost in the barn. She was headed to town to do some errands. And trying not to notice Malcolm's horse was gone. Still gone. She didn't have the *cojones* to ask if his saddlebags were missing from the bunkhouse. She was afraid she'd go *loco* if he had left for good. Again. Without saying goodbye. Again.

After Malcolm had walked out of the bathroom last night, she had climbed back into the tepid water until it was cold. She dried off, dressed, then went downstairs.

Gnawing on a piece of bread, she sat on the front porch, staring into the night sky. It took her hours to accept the fact that not only was she still deeply in love with Malcolm, but that she could never lie with another man again. What she found with him was so absolutely unexpected, amazing…and she wanted more. A lot more.

She had crazy, erotic dreams all night she couldn't remember. But she woke up wet and throbbing. The quick relief found with her hand didn't come close to quenching her hunger for Malcolm. He hadn't returned the ranch during the night, and she was afraid he never would.

Leigh led Ghost out of the barn, mounted and headed into town, praying Malcolm would be at the Circle O when she got back.

છ છ છ

Leigh was halfway back from town when she saw Malcolm's horse, Demon, under a cottonwood tree, riderless.

Her stomach flip-flopped and she had to force herself to trot slowly toward the stallion. He was not a friendly horse. He pricked his ears and watched her approach. The roan's nostrils flared, but he didn't run.

She dismounted, knowing Ghost would stay put. She walked carefully toward Demon, grabbing a sugar cube from her jacket pocket, grateful she always had a supply handy for her sweet-toothed horse.

"Easy, boy, easy."

She held out her hand, palm up with the sugar cube in the middle. She hoped like hell the damn horse didn't take a chunk of her hand, too. Surprisingly, he delicately nipped the treat without any flesh accompanying it.

Leigh leaned over and blew softly into the horse's nostrils, allowing him to get used to her scent. She was rewarded with a whicker and a small nudge on her shoulder from his great head.

"Good boy."

She ran her hand down his powerful neck, kneading his tensed muscles.

"Good boy," she repeated.

Leigh picked up the dangling reins with deliberate movements, murmuring soothing words to the horse. When she stepped closer, she saw the blood.

She reached out and dabbed her finger in it. It was on the saddle and the saddle horn, nearly dry, and tacky. There was a lot of it, not enough to indicate Malcolm was dead, but he was damn sure hurting.

Her throat tightened at the sight of his blood. Instead of blubbering about it, she squared her shoulders and walked back to Ghost. Demon docilely followed her as she tugged on his reins.

Mounting quickly, she surveyed the immediate area, but saw nothing unusual. The dew was still slick on the grass and she followed the meandering hoof prints of the hungry stallion.

Where the hell are you, Malcolm?

Leigh looked for nearly two hours. By that time, the sun had burned off the dew and she'd lost the trail. Cold fingers of panic clawed at her mind. God only knew how long he'd been out here, bleeding and alone. It was at least fourteen hours since she saw him. Or at least his half-buttoned ass leaving her bathroom.

Stop it!

She grabbed the saddle horn until her knuckles blanched white and the hard leather bit into her hands. The pain dragged her back from the edge of an idiotic panic.

Think like Malcolm. Where would he go if he were hurt? Water. Even if he was disoriented, water usually led to people. People led to help. *Look for water.*

She forced herself to slow her breathing, she sounded like a bellows, for Chrissakes. Slow and easy. After a minute or two, she could finally hear over the blood rushing past her ears and she focused on the sounds in the woods. Birds, squirrels, a woodpecker, and…there. Over to the right came the faint sound of water.

Leigh had to physically restrain herself from breaking into a hard gallop. She could trample him before realizing he was even there. She kneed Ghost into a walk and kept her eyes moving back and forth, scanning the tall grass and tree shadows and behind the small bushes. Even so, if Demon hadn't yanked on the reins and whickered, she might have missed him.

Malcolm was lying on his side, under some brush. His brown clothes blended in with the bush and the surrounding bed of leaves.

Leigh forced herself to dismount normally when all she wanted to do was scramble off and run.

ଓ ଓ ଓ

Malcolm opened his eyes slowly and tried to focus on the brown thing an inch in front of his eyes. A leaf. It was a leaf. So he was on the ground somewhere. He heard water trickling nearby, probably a creek. It was damp beneath him, so he must have landed there after the dew. His brain felt muzzy.

He heard the crunch of a leaf and he struggled to turn and draw his gun with his free hand. But his movements were as slow as his mind.

"Malcolm?"

Leigh's voice stopped his struggles. He blew out a breath, rustling the leaf by his nose.

"*Amante.*" His voice was crusty and rough.

He felt her hand on his shoulder, rolling him over gently. A groan worked its way up his throat. There wasn't much of his body that wasn't cursing at him. Loudly. Those rats sure knew how to throw a punch.

Cool fingers touched his swollen face. Her hazel eyes were concerned, brows puckered over them.

"Looks like you got the shit kicked out of you."

If he could have laughed, he would. Leigh was nothing if not honest.

"Can you sit up?"

With her help, he rose to a sitting position. Grunting and screaming wounds made themselves known.

"*Dios!*" he yelled.

"Easy. You don't need to bust a bronc or anything. Just use your ass. I'm sure you know how to do that."

He wasn't sure if she was trying to piss him off or not. If she was, it was working.

Her strength supported his pitiful shaking self. He couldn't remember the last time he had gotten such a beating. It had been at least five years or more. He was getting too damn old for any of it and was tired of his life. That realization hit him as hard as one of the fists of the damn sneaky sons of bitches who blindsided him last night.

He was tired of living in the shadows. Tired of being a no-name pretend bandito known as Hermano. He wanted to be Malcolm Ross again. He had thrown down the gauntlet to Damasco the night before, the first step in becoming Malcolm. In acknowledging Malcolm's existence and reclaiming his life. Even if he had been beaten for it, he was glad he'd done it.

"Are you planning on setting up camp here?" Leigh's voice intruded on his startling thoughts. "Because if you are, I'll tie up your damn horse and ride back to the Circle O."

She knelt next to him in the leaves and grass, looking annoyed and worried at the same time, wearing her customary shirt, vest and pants. The black hat was perched back on her head.

Damn, that was *his* hat.

He recognized it as the one he had left behind at Rancho Zarza the day he left.

He didn't need to ask why she'd kept it. He knew. Deep down in his heart, he knew. They had been together for the first half of their lives, a bond that went deeper than mere friendship. It crossed over into love.

He choked on that word and she started slapping his back with enough force to steal his breath. He grabbed her arm to try to stop her, waving his other hand to catch her attention.

"I not only look...like shit...I feel like...shit... So stop beating on me." He took a quick breath between words, trying to ignore the pain in his ribs with each huff.

She immediately stopped, a horrified expression in her eyes.

"Oh my God, I'm so sorry Mal. I didn't mean to—"

He cupped the back of her neck and brought her lips to his.

Oh, *yes*. That was exactly it. She was a perfect fit, in size, shape, personality, temperament, *in life*. God, why didn't his heart remember sooner?

He kissed her hard. Branding her. Marking her. She kissed back hard. Branding him. Marking him.

When he tried to open his mouth to deepen the kiss, his lip split open with a vengeance.

"Dammit!"

Blood started streaming down his chin. Leigh plopped down on her ass. Her pupils dilated, a sheen of sweat sat on her upper lip, and her hat had fallen off. The breeze ruffled her light brown hair, sparkling golden in the dappled sunlight coming through the trees.

Malcolm pressed his hand to his lip to try to staunch the bleeding while his cock rose to attention like a good soldier the second his lips touched hers. He commanded it to relax, but the damn thing didn't want to listen though, and grew another inch when her gaze flicked down to his crotch.

Leigh glanced back up into his eyes. He saw raw desire in them. God, how big could he get before his pants busted open?

Dios mio.

She rubbed her hands on her thighs, slapped the hat back on her head, and stood.

"Can you ride?"

It wasn't a question of can; it was a question of must.

ల ల ల

Leigh was shaken. She thought she understood everything that had happened, understood how she felt about Malcolm and the incredible sex they'd shared. She was wrong.

Finding him hurt made her own chest hurt. The depth of her feelings for Malcolm scared her. Leigh floated in a sea of confusion, arousal and love for which she was not prepared. Before she could even sort anything out, he kissed her.

There weren't any words she could think of to describe that kiss. It was a fierce mating of two animals, each trying to claim the other. Maybe she really was a wolf.

Kissing him again was like being dunked in an ice-cold mountain stream. It woke her up and left her shivering. Shivering in heat for more. When she saw how his pants bulged, she had to hold herself back from ripping their clothes off and jumping on him to find out just how big he could get.

But it went way beyond that. She was not only in heat, she was in love. What he felt was anybody's guess. His black eyes never revealed anything other than the shine of the sun.

Leigh was proud of the way she helped him stand and mount his horse. So what if her hand slipped on his ass and accidentally fell a little lower? He did jump a bit, so apparently he noticed but he didn't say anything. What she really wanted to do was mount him, not the frigging horse.

But she got on Ghost and slowly made her way to the Circle O with a bruised, bloodied man who she knew now she couldn't live without. Her heart was going to cease beating altogether when he packed up his gear and rode away.

Leigh decided on the ride back that no matter what happened, she was going to make love with him as much as possible until he left. It was too good…too *astonishing* an experience to only have one taste. She wanted more.

CHAPTER ELEVEN

Damasco rode his horse like there was a prairie fire behind him. It was worse, though.

Malcolm was still alive.

Damasco felt sick to his stomach. He just couldn't believe it. How the hell had Malcolm come back to life after fifteen years?

Madre de Dios!

There was no mistaking him either. He looked exactly like their father. Or like Alejandro used to look, anyway. A painting hung in the salon of Alejandro and a two-year-old Damasco. The hair was longer, and the eyes colder. But Malcolm was the spitting image of Alejandro.

Damasco rode into the courtyard at Rancho Zarza and headed for the house. He leapt off the stallion's back and left him, confident one of the hands would take care of him.

His spurs echoed on the cobblestones as he trotted up the steps and burst through the door.

"Mama."

Lorena came running from the kitchen in a flurry of flour and apron. "Damasco. What is the matter?"

He ignored the stupid cow and continued down the hallway.

"Mama."

Damasco found her in the salon, sipping tea. She sat perched on the edge of a damask sofa, wearing a dark blue dress perfectly fitted to her form, with a hint of lace at the sleeves and neck.

The bone china teacup was slowly lifted to her mouth. She took a sip, then replaced the cup in its saucer.

"You will stop shouting, Damasco. It is not the mark of a gentleman."

"But Mama."

She held up a hand to silence him. "Like a gentleman, Damasco."

Duly chastised, he forced himself to take a deep breath. His insides still felt like a churning pit of vipers.

"Excuse me, Mama."

Damasco waited for her. She indicated the velvet settee for him to sit. He sat quickly and waited some more. Mama insisted on the most particular manners. He hated them. Sometimes he nearly hated her.

"Are you calm, Damasco?"

Her dark eyes bored into his skull like black, buzzing insects. He had to physically restrain the urge to squirm.

"Yes, Mama."

"Excellent." She took another sip of tea. "What is it you wanted to speak to me about?"

Damasco took a deep breath and blurted, "Malcolm is still alive."

She dropped the tea cup and it bounced off the table to shatter on the hardwood floor. She stared at Damasco with fury sparking deep in her eyes.

"What did you say?"

He gulped. "It's true, Mama. I saw him in town. He threatened me and laughed at me. He looks just like Papa."

She clenched her jaw so hard, he was afraid it would shatter.

"What did he threaten you about?"

"Leigh and the Circle O. He knows we're behind the problems they're having, Mama! He knows."

She pursed her lips so tightly he thought her teeth were going to bite through them.

"He knows nothing. I don't even believe he is Malcolm. Unless his bitch of a mother lied to us and they buried stones in his coffin. How do you know it was him? You were twelve years old when he died."

Damasco was adamant. "He looks just like Papa." He turned and pointed at the painting over the fireplace. "In that picture. He could have stepped right out of it."

He had never seen such hatred in her eyes before. Damasco was suddenly very afraid of his mother. More afraid than he was of his big brother coming back to life.

"We will stop him, Damasco. Malcolm Ross will not rise from the grave. I will put him back in it before I let him ruin all our plans."

Her voice sent shivers up Damasco's spine. He nearly felt sorry for Malcolm. Nearly.

ભ ભ ભ

Leigh rode into Rancho Zarza half an hour after forcing Malcolm to sleep in the guest room in the house. There was no need for him to be in a bunkhouse full of noisy, stinky men when he felt like a stampede victim.

She left Ghost at the hitching post in the front of the house and stomped up to the front door. Her pounding brought Lorena to the door.

"Where is he? Where is that son of a bitch?"

Lorena looked flustered and tried to speak, but it came out as stutters and squeaks. Leigh pushed past her and strode into the house.

"Never mind. I'll find him."

She walked straight to the library, confident she'd find him there drinking whiskey and smoking his father's favorite cigars. Lorena remained behind, chastising Leigh for her manners.

She reached the door of the library, a dark wood door, almost eight feet high, and ornate like everything else in the house. Without knocking, she pushed the door open.

Sure enough, there was Damasco sitting in his father's chair behind his father's desk, with a glass of something and a half-smoked cigar. Pretending to be a man like Alejandro.

Damasco looked at her with disinterest. Taking a long puff of the cigar, he tilted his head back and blew smoke rings at the ceiling.

"You know it doesn't matter if you sit in that chair, Damasco. You will never be him."

"No, I will be better than him."

She laughed at his bravado. "You only wish you could be better than Alex. Or even come close to being better than Malcolm."

His feet hit the floor with a thump. "You are not to have anything to do with him, *querida*. He is a bandito, an outlaw."

"So are the low sons of bitches who are taking potshots at me, stealing my cattle and poisoning my water supply," she retorted.

That barb hit home. His cheeks grew a little ruddy as he stood and pointed at her. "You will not have such a sassy mouth when you are my wife."

Leigh was a bit flummoxed by that statement. She had refused him at least a dozen times. Did he honestly think she'd wake up one day and figure out she was wrong all those other times? As if she'd say to herself, "What was I thinking? Damasco is a prince. He's shown me the light by sending my ranch to bankruptcy."

"Damasco, I came here to warn you."

He tilted the glass back and swallowed the rest of the amber liquid. That's when she noticed he had obviously had more than one drink. In fact, he had probably had a lot more than one. His normally perfect clothes were wrinkled, untucked and half-unbuttoned. His hair was mussed as if he'd run his fingers through it a hundred times. His eyes were bloodshot and she caught a whiff of his cologne. Eau de Whiskey.

"Warn me?" He snorted. "What you need to do is get down on your knees and suck me dry."

Well, that got her temper up. She wanted to knee him in the balls again.

"You're drunk."

He smiled and bowed. "Absolutely. And not as drunk as I plan on getting."

It took him three tries to grab the decanter of liquor on the corner of the desk. When he tried to pour it in the glass, he ended up spilling it.

"Shit!"

He stared sourly at the glass, then picked up the decanter and took a long pull directly from it. She needed to speak her piece and get the hell out of there.

"Don't use any more sneaky, underhanded shit on me or anyone from the Circle O, Damasco. Leave Malcolm alone. Leave my cows alone. Or we'll have a war they'll hear about all the way to Kansas."

Damasco threw back his head and laughed. "When you are my wife, *querida*, you will no longer be helping bastards. They will grovel at your feet and shovel your horseshit instead."

"You're the only bastard in the Zarza family."

He stalked toward her so quickly she didn't have time to react. Before she could even think about what he was going to do, he reached out and slapped her so hard her ears rang and her lip split.

Leigh wasn't about to let that slide. She returned the favor and slapped him back.

"I warned you, Damasco. If it's a war you want, just push me one more time."

She held up one finger in front of his face. So incredibly angry she could have pummeled him into the ground, she turned and stomped out of the room. She was furious with Malcolm for being right and furious with Damasco for being such an ass.

ଓ ଓ ଓ

Lorena waited until Isabella had gone into the bathing room for her nightly bath before she snuck in to see Alejandro. From what Diego had already told her, and from what she'd overheard today, it was time Alex found out his elder son was still alive.

CHAPTER TWELVE

Leigh opened the door to the house quietly. It was dark in the kitchen, so hopefully Mrs. Hanson had gone off to whatever cave she lived in and Malcolm was asleep upstairs. He'd taken quite a beating. The extent of his bruises had shocked her. She reached above the sink and found a candle and matches kept there. She struck the match on the bottom of the candleholder and lit the wick. A warm glow suffused the room.

"Where have you been?"

Malcolm's question in the silence of the room nearly made her jump clean out of her skin.

"What the hell are you doing? Trying to scare me to death?" Her heart was beating a mile a minute.

"You went to see him, didn't you?"

Leigh didn't answer. She tried to ignore his shadowy figure sitting at the kitchen table as she set the lit candle on the shelf.

"Don't ignore me, *amante*. Answer the question."

She worked the pump handle until cold water splashed out. Taking a rag from the side of the sink, she let the water rush over it. Then she wrung it out and pressed it to her throbbing lip.

"What right do you have to even ask me where I've been, Mal?"

The scrape of the chair as he stood should have made her nervous. But it didn't. She felt…excited. The hairs on her arms stood at attention and her nipples tightened like river pebbles.

"I have every right."

He hovered right behind her. His warm breath rustled the small hairs on her neck, making them rise.

"You are *mine.*"

"For how long?" she couldn't resist asking. The question burned in her mind like the Circle O branding iron—two circles going around and around, without beginning or end.

"*Amante.*" He caressed her shoulders then down her spine. She arched against him like a cat in heat as her blood began to thrum through her veins. His hands... Lord, his hands were incredible.

"We have always belonged to each other. We always will."

That was not the answer she was looking for and he knew it. He blew out the candle and the room sank into darkness. The sound of their breathing echoed through the room. She could smell her own arousal and Malcolm's unique scent in the air.

His hands slid around to cup her breasts, the long fingers reaching up to pinch and twist her nipples into aching peaks. He pressed his hardened cock against the cleft in her buttocks and rubbed in delicious circles. She pressed back, anticipating having him deep inside her. Soon.

His nimble fingers made short work of her shirt and chemise. Then breasts were bare in his hands, his callused skin leaving a trail of goose bumps in its wake.

"Like fruit from the gods."

"More like melons from the gods," she teased.

He chuckled. "I love the weight of them in my hands. The softness of the skin and the puckered nipples. I want to bite them."

Yes, oh, yes, Leigh wanted that too.

More.

It was as if she'd spoken aloud. Her trousers and drawers ended up around her ankles in moments. One hand dipped into her aching pussy, and moved back and forth slowly in her wetness. She trembled each time he stroked her clit, and moaned when his fingers fucked her.

"*Dios,* you are wet. I need to have you, *amante.*"

"Yesss..." she hissed, uncaring if anyone walked by or walked in. She needed him *now.* Her body wept with arousal and need.

His hands left her and her body nearly screamed with wanting. He removed his pants in only a few seconds, but it seemed longer.

"Hurry," Leigh moaned.

"Spread your legs. *Sí*, that's it. A little more. Make room for me, *carina*."

As she braced her hands on the sink, Malcolm entered her with a slow slide that nearly made her come.

"Oh, yes…you are like heaven."

His hands traveled back around to pinch and tease her breasts while he thrust into her from behind. And oh, did he ever. Steadily, in then out, in then out, to the rhythm of her pulse. Never any faster, never any slower, designed to drive her mad. If only she could touch him, kiss him, suck him. She needed more.

"Faster."

He chuckled by her ear. "Anxious, *mi vida?*"

One hand left her breast and ended up on her pussy, rubbing and caressing her hot button as his hard cock pushed in and out of her. His balls tickled her clit with each thrust. Her fingers clutched the sink as the sensations within her swirled and twisted. It was as incredible as the first time. The thrill of knowing they could be caught any second made it that much more intense.

She felt the rush of blood and zinging that signaled her release.

"I'm going to come," she gasped.

He put one damp hand over her mouth. "Shhhhh…"

She smelled her scent on his hand and her tongue slipped out to lick its muskiness. Another naughty thing she knew she shouldn't do, but couldn't help herself. Leigh was almost out of control.

"*Amante…*"

That's when he really started fucking her. Harder and harder. She bit down on his hand as her orgasm rolled through her like a thunder boom in a canyon. It became louder and stronger until she thought her heart would stop from the sheer pleasure pulsing through her again and again. Finally, it crashed and her body trembled with enough pleasure to nearly steal her breath.

"Leigh," Malcolm whispered in her ear as he pumped into her so deeply, he touched her heart.

Their ragged breaths mingled with the musky scent of sex. Leigh realized she still held the rag in her hand and nearly every drop of water had been squeezed out of it. Malcolm was buried inside her, hard and throbbing. He took a deep breath she felt all the way to her toes.

"*Dios.*"

"You can say that again."

He slowly withdrew and his warm seed trickled down her leg. She heard him pull his pants up behind her. She was shaking too much to do that yet. The sink was actually holding her up. If it hadn't been there, she'd probably be on the floor kissing the wood planks.

Malcolm took the rag from her hands and pumped fresh water on it. After he squeezed the excess water off, he cleaned her off with gentle strokes. She should be embarrassed, but she wasn't. It was another considerate gesture that seemed to come naturally to him. With one last pinch to her clit that sent a shiver down her back, he lay the rag on the sink, then pulled up her drawers and pants. She didn't move until he touched her shirt and she stopped him.

"I'll finish."

While she buttoned her shirt, he lit the candle again. She was not surprised to see her hands shaking and it took more than one attempt to get a damn button in a hole. It still completely astonished her that sex with Malcolm was enough to knock her off balance. Not much ever did. Leigh always had to be strong, unbending and unyielding. Malcolm turned her into a woman...a soft woman.

Leigh finished buttoning her shirt and picked up the rag from the side of the sink. She worked the pump again, and let the water gush for a minute. After the water got a little colder, she put both hands and the rag under the stream. She sure as hell needed it cold. The heat in her body was still stoked up as high as a winter fire.

"You went to see Damasco."

It wasn't a question. She was finally able to look him in the eye without dragging him upstairs to her bed. Her body was screaming for more. More of Malcolm.

"Yes, I did. It's not your business where I go or who I see, Mal. You don't control me."

Malcolm's expression turned to stone when his eyes fastened on her lip. He touched the swelling with one callused finger.

"I hope you said goodbye because I am going to cut off his balls and ram them down his throat."

He turned and walked toward the door as if he had just said he was going to curry his horse. Completely matter-of-fact and without emotion. She found it hard to believe he was the same man who was just buried inside her spilling himself.

"If you walk out that door and go kill your brother, you might as well take all your gear with you, because I won't let you back on the Circle O."

Enough was enough, she thought. A little smack on the face was not worth killing someone over. They needed to catch him red-handed in one of his dirty deeds and then haul his ass to the sheriff, not castrate and kill him.

He stopped with his hand on the knob. "You ask too much, *amante.*"

"No, I don't." She stepped forward to touch his arm. It was like touching the branch of an oak tree, so rigid she thought he might snap his arm if he pulled the door too hard. "I care about you, Malcolm. Hell, I probably love you. And I'm not going to have you hang from a cottonwood because of a slap. Help me stop him and I'll help you find your mother."

She held out her hand to shake. "Deal?"

He turned his head slightly and stared hard at her hand. When he looked into her eyes, she couldn't read their black expression. He leaned forward and gently kissed her lip.

"If he does it again, you won't stop me."

With that, he went through the door into the inky night.

ରେ ରେ ରେ

Hell, I probably love you.

Malcolm's head reeled as he walked across the yard. Leigh's casually spoken words had literally knocked the breath from him. She loved him? She loved him? It was so incredibly foreign he didn't know what to think. *Roja's* gift of food and supplies had completely turned his life upside down. He didn't know his ass from his elbow anymore.

She loved him.

CHAPTER THIRTEEN

Malcolm was stuck repairing tack the next day since he was too banged up to sit a horse. Repairing tack was a thankless, boring job that ended up cramping your hands from all the braiding you had to do with the leather. Not only that, the tack room stank like old sweat and somebody's two-day-old lunch. He was sitting on a stool fastening the last of the reins to the bridle for one of the hands' horses—couldn't remember which one—when Earl skittered in, resembling a weasel in search of a quick Mexican meal.

"Didn't you get finished yet, boy?"

Malcolm didn't respond. He never did when anyone called him "boy", not only because it was annoying, but also because it angered off whoever was trying to belittle him.

"You deaf? Ears don't work?"

Malcolm looked up and stared at Earl blankly until the older man sputtered and mumbled something about dinner being on soon. He turned his watery eyes to the tack laid out on the table. Malcolm could almost see Earl counting in his head like a little kid on his fingers who had trouble remembering two plus two.

"Where the hell is that stirrup for my horse?"

There had been no stirrup on the table this morning, and of course there still was no stirrup.

"You left no stirrup to be repaired."

"Liar. You stole it, didn't ya? You thieving Mexicans are all alike. Can't wait to take stuff and go sell it over the border."

The border was a hundred miles away. Oh, sure. Malcolm would steal a single stirrup and ride all that way to make a profit.

"This is something O'Reilly is going to have to listen to." He turned to stomp out the door then stopped short when he saw Leigh standing in the doorway. Malcolm felt a rush of pleasure and pain seeing her. She was dressed in a red gingham shirt and black vest with jeans. Her boots were covered in muck and horseshit. She had a smudge of dirt on her cheek, her lip was still swollen and cracked in one corner, and her glasses were slightly crooked. And somehow, she was more beautiful than any woman he had ever seen.

"What's going on, Earl?" she said evenly.

Earl looked surprised to see her, but immediately pounced on her presence to show her what a thief she'd hired.

"We need to search his things. He done stole a stirrup and God knows what else he's stuffed in them saddlebags." His nostrils flared and a bit of spittle flew from his lips to hang in the air between them for a moment.

She turned her gaze to Malcolm, maintaining a flat expression that did nothing to reveal what she was thinking.

"Earl says you stole a stirrup?"

In the depths of her hazel eyes, he thought he saw a glimpse of the old Leigh.

"I steal *nada*, Leigh. Although if you look now, you may find something that someone else put there."

"That's ridiculous. No one would do that." Earl's face told a different story.

Malcolm lifted his brow and stared at Earl with contempt. That sneaky old man had planted something in his things for sure. It was unnecessary to even defend himself, but he wanted Leigh to show her foreman she was still in charge.

"Did you see a stirrup?"

Malcolm shook his head.

She turned toward Earl and planted one hand on her hip. The other leaned up against the doorway.

"What the hell are you talking about, Earl?"

Earl looked a little shocked by her question. "You know these Mexes. They'll steal from their own grandmothers if you don't watch 'em. I'm telling ya, let's go take a gander at what he's got in his saddlebags."

Leigh's brows drew together. "We've had Mexicans working for us as long as I can remember. Probably since Sean bought this ranch. None of them ever stole anything from this ranch, much less a frigging stirrup."

"Are you calling me a liar?" Earl's eyes narrowed.

She stood and bracketed both hips with her arms, elbows sticking out, chin up in the air.

"No, but I can't figure out why you keep riding Malcolm like a horse that hasn't been broken."

Earl said, "Malcolm?"

Malcolm took great pleasure in rising from the stool to stand over the older man with a wicked grin on his face. "Me. I am Malcolm Ross y Zarza."

Earl nearly gasped. Malcolm had never heard a *man* make a sound like that, but it sure as well was as close to a gasp as he'd ever heard.

"Zarza?" Earl repeated.

Malcolm's eyes met Leigh's. "Another canyon in here."

He saw her biting back a small grin. "Earl, Malcolm is my friend. We've known each other all our lives. I trust him with this ranch, my tack, hell, even my life. You have nothing to worry about. I don't think there's anything in his saddlebags that doesn't belong to him."

At least that he had put there anyway.

Earl had recovered some of the color in his weathered cheeks. "I don't trust him. I don't care whose bastard he is."

"Careful, *abuelo*," Malcolm murmured. His hands inadvertently clenched into fists. He had to unclench them before he actually hurt this old man.

"One more thing goes missing and I'll get the sheriff myself." With that, Earl shoved Leigh back to stomp out of the tack room and into the barn.

Leigh watched him leave with a perplexed look on her face. "What was that all about?"

"I think he's trying to get rid of me," Malcolm said flatly.

She rolled her eyes and walked into the tack room. With an audible "humph", she sat on the stool. "I figured that out, Mal. But why?"

"I think he might be behind a lot of your problems, *amante*."

She snorted. "Not a chance."

His eyebrows rose. "Why not?"

"Well, he was…that is…he worked for Sean long before I was married to him."

"That is not a good reason."

"No, you're right. I never liked Earl, but I never had any reason not to trust him."

"I might be wrong, no? But I don't think so. Let us ride out tomorrow and count your cows."

"What'll that prove? That you learned how to use your fingers?"

He ran his finger down her incredibly soft cheek. "You know I can use my fingers." She sucked in a breath and stared hard at him. He could almost see the heat pulsing between them, shimmering in the air. When he removed his finger and leaned back, the spell was broken.

He cleared his throat. "We compare our count to Earl's records. They should match or at least be close. In fact, I think you should double-check everything he has a hand in around the Circle O. Someone is helping to ruin your ranch. Who better than someone who practically runs it?"

She blew out a breath and nodded. "I don't think we're going to find anything, but it's a good idea anyway. I didn't do the count for the spring round-up, Earl did. The fall round-up is two months away, but I can't wait that long."

He grasped her elbow and pulled her up, guiding her outside to walk toward the house. Her scent filled his nostrils—leather, horse and essence of Leigh. He breathed deeply of the heady smell.

"Supper time? Or bath time?" Malcolm spoke into her ear with a flick of his tongue on the soft pink shell.

She snapped her head around to glare at him. "Is that supposed to be funny?"

"No, *amante*, but all day long I thought of nothing but how beautiful you look when you are wet and naked."

She stumbled and he caught her elbow. "You know how to knock me on my ass, don't you?" Leigh's voice sounded strained.

He smiled at her. "Only if it lands you on my lap, *carina*."

൭ ൭ ൭

After a dinner of beans and biscuits, Leigh and Malcolm headed out to the front porch again. It had become a comfortable ritual—something an old married couple would do. Sean never did anything like that with her. They hadn't had much in common really, except a friendship. They never talked, rarely laughed.

And here she was with Malcolm, wishing they could sit like this every night for the rest of her life. It made her want to take the plunge and ask him to stay. She didn't care what people thought, whether or not they got married or simply enjoyed life together. She just didn't want him to ever leave again.

"Did you find anything in the saddlebags?"

Malcolm took a drag of his cigarillo and blew out a stream of bluish smoke into the twilight air. "*Sí*. The stirrup, two silver spoons, a silver tea pot and a ring."

She whistled softly. "What the hell? Why would…I don't understand."

"I warned Damasco to leave you alone. That you had me at your back to protect you. He is getting rid of the wolf to get to the lamb."

"I thought I was the wolf," she murmured.

He chuckled. "Mmm…you are my *lobo*. We are a pack, you and I. So, I say that wrong. He is getting rid of the male to get to the bitch."

She slapped him playfully on the arm. "Are you calling me names?"

He grabbed her hand and kissed the tips of her fingers. "*Nunca, amante.* Never would I call you names."

A shiver started working its way up her arm, making the hairs rise as it marched on. When it reached her shoulder, it turned south and headed straight for her nipples, which obligingly stood at attention. Next in line was her stomach, which fluttered and twittered like mad. And then it reached between her legs and the tingling zinged all the way down to her toes. How could that happen with just a few kisses on her fingers?

Magic. It had to be magic.

He took another drag off the cigarillo and laced his hands with hers.

"Someone will see."

He shrugged. "I do not care. What is between us only concerns us."

Leigh knew it wasn't true. What was between them threatened whoever was behind the last two years of trouble on the Circle O. And if Malcolm was right, it was Damasco.

She could almost see the tension in the air. As if everyone were holding their breath waiting for the storm to arrive. Something was coming, not the least of which was a battle for her ranch. There would also likely be a battle for her life. Someone had already tried to end it more than once. Leigh figured the stakes were raised and the ante higher.

"I must go to the bunkhouse, *amante*. I was invited to play poker. I thought I could listen and maybe hear something."

That was *not* disappointment hitting her.

Oh, hell, yes it was. She still felt a shiver way down deep as it vibrated through her. All she wanted to do was drag his ass upstairs and get naked. They could stay in bed until she forgot all her troubles and remembered what it felt like to be happy. Truly happy.

"*Buenas noches, amante*," he said as he stood.

He leaned down and grasped her chin to give her a soft kiss His tongue snaked out and licked the wound on her lip.

She thought she heard him mutter "*Dios*" under his breath.

As he walked away, Leigh took great pleasure in contemplating his graceful, predatory stride and his well-formed behind. Malcolm had turned into quite a man. She watched until he was out of the reach of the light and the shadows had swallowed him again.

CR CR CR

The next morning dawned hazy and sticky, a potent reminder of the blistering summer heat that threatened the day. The sun was almost hidden behind the scattered clouds crowding the odd-colored sky. The day felt strange already, as if there were natural forces at work gathering energy, ready to unleash themselves on wary travelers.

Today would be a day of traveling. Counting the herd was a daylong job that took her from one end of the Circle O to the other. Compared to some, it was not a large ranch, but it was at least ten thousand acres. Spread across those acres should be over two thousand longhorns. The count wouldn't be entirely accurate yet because the calves hadn't been tallied, nor had the entire herd been counted since the spring round-up.

When Leigh came downstairs, she had a strange feeling, more like an omen. The day would bring change, for good or for bad. Mrs. Hanson was nowhere to be found, but happily there was a hot pot of coffee on the stove. Leigh poured herself a cup and stood at the window staring out onto the range. A few longhorn were visible in the distance, munching their breakfast. She took a biscuit from the pan on the stove and walked outside to find Malcolm.

ભ ભ ભ

Leigh found Malcolm shaving in the back of the bunkhouse, shirtless. In his hands was a huge knife with which he slowly scraped his whiskers off. The sound of the blade on his skin was audible in the quiet morning air. He used a mirror nailed to a fence post, and a bowl full of soapy water hanging from a wire. Droplets ran down his skin and sprayed on the ground as he flicked the water off the knife.

As she came up behind him, he dipped the knife in the water and muscles rippled across his wide back. This time when she saw the horrible damage to his flesh, she saw the past. The past that haunted both of them, which needed to be overcome and put where it belonged—behind them. Leigh clenched her fists in frustration. Soon she would help him lay that past completely to rest, and he would help her into the future.

She stepped toward him, and beneath all the scars, she looked at the man. The beautiful bronzed skin, the tight muscles and the liquid movement as he raised his arms to shave. He caught her gaze in the mirror and a smile lit his eyes.

"*Buenos dias.*"

"Good morning, Mal. How are you feeling? You look like hell."

He had a swollen lip, a black eye, a cut cheek and multiple bruises all over him. Ah, but he was still beautiful enough to snatch her breath.

"You flatter me." He smiled. "I am a little sore, but I plan on sitting on my horse today. Did you sleep well?"

She pondered her answer before she spoke. "No. I missed you."

He cursed as he nicked himself with the blade. She regretted her honesty when he grabbed the towel tucked into his waistband to press it to his cheek.

"I'm sorry, Mal. Sometimes I need to keep my tongue in a bridle."

"No, *amante*, you would not be yourself if you were not honest. I would expect nothing less from you. My knife needs to be sharpened, it is dull."

"Next time we're in town you can get it sharpened at Mr. Hall's. He's the blacksmith," she suggested as her eyes continued to devour the man.

He staunched the bleeding, rinsed off his knife and completed his shave. Tossing out the dirty water, he refilled the bowl from the rain barrel and splashed cool water on his face. He dumped the rest of the water, then hung up the bowl for the next drover. Blotting his face dry on the towel, he approached her. Water droplets traveled down his chest and circled the whorls of hair like she wanted to do with her tongue.

Mary and all the Saints above! Was sex all she thought about? Her ranch was in serious jeopardy. She needed to keep her mind, and her hands, out of Malcolm's pants.

He reached her and threw the towel around her neck, effectively lassoing her and drawing her closer. Soon she was pressed up against his warm, hard body. Her body reacted with a pulse of heat and she leaned toward him. He smelled like soap, and sunshine, and man. The combined scent was more tantalizing than the most expensive perfume.

"I missed you, too."

He cupped the back of her head and brought his lips to hers. She still had a split lip and his was swollen so theirs was a relatively gentle kiss, when all she wanted to do was let loose and to hell with the cow count.

Malcolm stepped back and Leigh clearly saw the outline of an erection in his jeans. From a kiss. A small kiss. So he was as affected by her as she was by him. The current between them was strong, like a river. She had a feeling they were heading toward the white water, and it had only begun to get rough.

He grabbed a shirt from a nail by the door and shrugged into it with a small wince.

"Are you sure you're up to riding today?"

"If I have to repair tack again today, I'm going back to the snow in Wyoming."

She smiled. "That's serious. I guess we'd better saddle up and head out. Wouldn't want you to freeze any important body parts off."

He threw back his head and laughed, then slapped her on the ass with one big hand.

"*Vamanos, amante.* We've got some cows to count."

Leigh hoped the count would be good news. Any more bad news and she wouldn't have enough cows to sell to keep the ranch. The bad feeling still rode her shoulders and she hoped it was only a split lip that bothered her today.

CHAPTER FOURTEEN

Leigh stared down at the tally she'd calculated. Seven hundred fifty-two. Impossible. No, not impossible. Unbelievable. She flipped the small piece of paper over and diligently began to add their totals together again. Malcolm stood behind her, holding the horse steady while she used the saddle to brace the paper.

She finished adding and stared at the number again. Still seven hundred fifty-two. That meant more than twelve hundred head of cattle were missing. Or more. They usually had at least five hundred calves, and they'd only seen twelve. Someone had not only stolen from her, they'd ruined her. There was no way in hell she'd make the payments due on the ranch with only seven hundred fifty-two cattle. She had to keep at least four hundred cows, which left three hundred fifty-two. Ten of them were bulls she needed to keep—their bloodlines were too great to lose. That whittled the total down to three hundred forty-two.

Two years ago, she had driven the herd up to Abilene and made seventy-five dollars a head. With the railroad less than fifty miles away and still coming closer, these cattle were only worth about ten dollars a head. Quick calculations confirmed her worst fears. She wouldn't even come close to having enough to pay her yearly debts. What was in the bank from last year would only last until the fall round-up, to pay the drovers and buy feed and supplies.

After the fall round-up she'd sell her three hundred forty-two remaining cows—if there were that many left by then—and have one quarter of the money she needed to run the ranch and survive until the following spring. She had, by her count, four to six months before total bankruptcy.

She felt sick. Her stomach churned and started creeping up her throat. Turning, she ran for the nearest tree and threw up what remained of the biscuits and coffee from breakfast.

Holy Mother of God. She'd never been in such a crack. Oh, she'd been in corners before, but none this tight.

Malcolm gently touched the back of her neck.

"*Amante?*"

Leigh wiped her mouth on her sleeve and straightened. Her head whirled around mercilessly making her stomach lurch again. Malcolm's hand on her arm steadied her.

"Easy, now. Take a deep breath."

She did as he bade, then took a few more. Her head started to clear. The paper and pencil were still clutched in her hand. She opened her fist and stared down at the numbers, blurred by the sweat from her clammy palm.

"Someone stole my ranch, Malcolm."

He sighed and leaned against the tree, pulling her into his arms. She went willingly. He was so warm and hard, and his very scent was all she needed to calm her. His hands stroked her back.

"How bad is it?" he asked.

"At least twelve hundred head are missing, probably more. And nearly all the calves."

"*Mierda!* How could someone steal that many cattle and no one noticed?"

She grimaced against his shirt. "Someone noticed. You were right, Mal. Earl must be behind this. Maybe Damasco is giving him a cut."

He hugged her tightly.

"We'll get them back. Even if we have to kill a few to turn their hides out to see the Circle O brand."

Even if a cattle was re-branded, the original brand could still be seen from the inside out. It was a bloody way to prove cattle rustling, but effective.

"Are you sure we've counted all over the ranch?"

"Yes. There might be some that wandered onto Rancho Zarza, but I don't think it would be one thousand head. They're dumb beasts, Mal. They stay where the grass is green and the water is nearby. We've checked everywhere."

His ear was so close to her nose, she felt the unrelenting urge to lick it. So she did. He sucked in a breath.

"You are playing too close to the fire, *amante.*"

He was right, but she really wanted to burn. Right now. Right here. Life had just given her a swift kick in the ass and she needed. She needed him. She needed to lose herself in him.

"Please, Mal. I…I can't…"

She started kissing his neck frantically. He seemed to understand and grabbed her mouth with his own in a startling, deep kiss. His tongue delved and danced and caressed the inside of her mouth, her tongue, her teeth, her lips. Her pussy flooded with moisture, with need, with hunger.

More.

He unbuttoned her jeans and reached down inside them until he touched her pulsing core. Using his nimble fingers on a nipple and her hot button, he kissed her senseless while he brought her quickly to a climax that had her moaning and writhing in his arms. After a few minutes, he kissed her softly, then withdrew his hand and buttoned her pants back up.

She clung to him and he wrapped his arms around her. Not taking any pleasure from her, just giving her a release of emotion and the comfort she needed.

"Better?"

She nodded against his chest, embarrassed now by the way she let him give her pleasure in the middle of the day, under a tree in plain view of anyone.

"I sure as hell hope none of the drovers are nearby."

He chuckled and she felt the vibrations through his chest.

"If they are, they're probably back behind their own tree, imagining it was your hand wrapped around them."

She stepped back and looked at him incredulously. "You are absolutely blind if you think any one of them imagines me with my hands on their bodies."

He smiled and her heart was caught again. "Why not? I did. You are *muy bonita, amante.*"

She scoffed at his compliment and stepped back. The paper crinkled beneath her boot. She picked the list of her decimated herd up off the ground as a spurt of anger zipped through her body.

"Let's go find Earl."

He nodded and they headed back to the horses happily grazing on the tall Texas grass.

After they'd mounted, Leigh let her anger build further. Who the hell did Earl think he was? And for that matter, Damasco? What right did he have to ruin her or try to steal her ranch? And why did he want it? Rancho Zarza was already ten times the size of the Circle O. It wasn't for the stock, and it sure as hell wasn't for her. He'd been in that pasture already. So why?

ରଃ ରଃ ରଃ

By the time they arrived back at the ranch, her anger had turned to all-out rage. She wanted to tear into Earl like a bear at a chokeberry bush. Her proverbial claws were sharp and hungry.

Leigh leapt off Ghost and left him standing at the barn, taking long dirt-eating strides to the bunkhouse and Earl's office. She barely heard Malcolm behind her, calling her back. There wasn't going to be any stopping her now. Not a goddamn chance.

She was nearly running by the time she got to the door. Thrusting it open, she found a few of the drovers playing cards. The cards flew up in the air and coins tinged on the floor as they all jumped out of their seats.

She ignored their surprised looks and stalked toward the office at the end of the building. The door was ajar and light spilled from within. She slammed the door open so hard, it jarred her hand and put a few splinters in her fingers.

Earl sat at the desk with a bottle of whiskey in front of him and a Colt Peacemaker .45. Her anger stepped back and wariness replaced it.

"Earl, you've got some explaining to do."

The older man stared at her, eyes a little bloodshot. He'd obviously had a few hits of whiskey already. How many was anyone's guess. His expression was bleak, resigned.

"Ya counted the cows, didn't ya?"

Of course he knew why she was there.

"Where the hell are they?"

He didn't answer. He fingered the pistol and poured himself another whiskey. The amber liquid spilled on the desk, which was littered with papers and old cigar butts.

"Don't rightly know, Leigh. Don't rightly care."

She punched the desk. "I care, goddammit. Why, Earl, why the hell did you do it?"

"Didn't have no choice."

She laughed sardonically. "Oh, I believe that completely. The ranch that you've worked at for twenty frigging years and you've run it into the ground. No choice? I don't believe it." She punched the desk again. "You owe me an explanation, old man."

Earl's expression turned a bit mulish and he tightened his grip on the Colt. "Don't owe you a thing, girlie. Just 'cause Sean took you in like a lost puppy in the rain don't mean I owe you a thing. He shoulda left this ranch to me, but you came along and snatched it."

She stared at him, flabbergasted. "What? I didn't snatch anything, Earl. I didn't even know Sean had left it to me until after he'd died."

"I don't believe you. You seduced him until all he could think about was fucking you and making money to give you pretty gee-gaws."

That's when Leigh realized Earl was quite possibly mad. What in the hell was he talking about? She didn't own even one pretty gee-gaw, and she certainly never did anything remotely like "fucking" Sean. It was more like groping under the sheets in the dark for a quick poke.

"Easy, *abuelo*," came Malcolm's voice from behind her.

Earl blanched. "What are you gonna do, shoot me? Go ahead."

Malcolm must have drawn his pistol. The tension crackled between the two of them. The animosity had never pulsed so strongly.

"No. But if you don't take your hand off that Colt, old man, you will lose a finger."

Earl eased his hand back, obviously aware of how dangerous Malcolm really was. Earl showed his teeth in a feral snarl and snapped, "You're like a dog protecting his bitch."

Leigh realized they weren't going to get any information out of him, but she had to try one last time.

"Earl, tell us where the cattle are. I won't turn you in. Just tell us and you can go on your way."

"*Amante,*" Malcolm admonished from behind her.

Earl stood, grabbing the bottle of whiskey, then reached down and picked up a pair of saddlebags from the floor by his feet.

"I don't know where they are. And I don't care. You can all rot in hell."

He staggered a bit, then came out from behind the desk, walking right up to Malcolm's pistol. Leigh watched the old man press his chest against the nose of the gun.

"Shoot me or get the hell out of my way, Mex."

"I am not Mexican, *abuelo.* I am Spanish and Scottish."

Earl waved the hand with the bottle in it. "I don't give a shit. Just get out of the way."

Malcolm's eyes were black ice. They flickered to her, allowing her to make the decision.

"Let him go," Leigh said.

Malcolm moved in a circle to allow Earl to pass through the door. His eyes and the pistol never left him. The drovers at the table watched Earl with interest and a bit of disbelief.

Leigh let out a breath of frustration. "I can't believe it. That old man is crazier than a bug house. He stole my cattle and we're letting him go."

Malcolm said, "Yes, but I will follow him. And before you even say another word, you are not coming with me. Go to town and talk to the sheriff. He's a friend of...of Alex's. He might be able to get around his belly and do something."

"But—"

"No, Leigh."

His voice was so grave, so serious, she cocked her head and stared into his eyes. As usual, those black orbs told her nothing.

"Fine. But if you're not back here by morning, I'm coming after you."

೧ ೧ ೧

Leigh gathered the drovers together within an hour. They all stood around talking quietly, smoking or staring at her. She was sure they'd heard about the confrontation with Earl. Malcolm was itching to get started after him, but Leigh asked him to wait until after she'd spoken to the men. He stood behind her again, literally and figuratively. It had been a long time since she had experienced that feeling.

"Listen up, everyone," she began. "I'm sure you've all heard about Earl. I wanted to let you all know what I know so you can make your own choice. There are over twelve hundred head of cattle missing. If we don't find them, the Circle O will be bankrupt within four to six months, and all of you, and me, will be out of a job and a home."

A few curses and exclamations of disbelief met her words.

"It looks like Earl was in on it. He admitted it a little while ago before he left. If anyone here had anything to do with the rustling, I'll give you a choice. Take your sorry asses and leave before the sun comes up tomorrow. Because if I find out you're guilty, I'll geld you and leave you to the buzzards."

Murmurs rippled through the men.

"From here on out, the new foreman is going to be the man standing behind me. You may all know him as Hermano. His real name is Malcolm Ross y Zarza."

The ripples turned into a full blown wave.

"Zarza?" asked Andy. "As in Rancho Zarza?"

She didn't answer, waiting for Malcolm to step forward and speak. It was his choice whether or not he wanted to do so.

He did.

"Yes, as in Rancho Zarza. Alejandro is my father. Damasco is my half-brother."

She smiled inwardly. It was about time he stopped hiding in the shadows.

"I am going to be at Leigh's back until we find the cattle and catch the bastards red-handed. If you are loyal to the Circle O, then you are loyal to her. That means you have me at your back too. Together we can stop them and save the ranch."

The men were silent, digesting Malcolm's words.

Leigh's thoughts kept returning to him saying he would be with her until the cattle were found and the culprits caught. Then what would happen? Would he leave again? Disappear back into the shadows he'd been hiding in?

She had to set her personal demons aside and think about saving the ranch. Then she'd think about keeping Malcolm there with her.

Andy was the first to step forward. "Well, I'm with ya, Hermano...I mean, Malcolm."

His friendly grin was all that was needed for more of the men to express their agreement. Leigh released the breath she'd been holding. No doubt some of them would be gone by morning, but others would be there to fight by her side.

It was the first time in two years she really felt like she owned the Circle O and was ready to fight to the death to keep it.

ભ ભ ભ

Malcolm was cinching his saddle when he sensed Leigh hovering behind him. What he felt about her had sunk deep inside to take hold of him. Take hold and not let go. Even now, his body was rising to her nearness. This must be what *Roja* felt for that son of a bitch bounty-hunter husband of hers. The unrelenting connection and the unending need to be near.

"You ready?" she asked.

He turned. She had her hands in her back pockets, pulling her shirt tight across those magnificent breasts. Her brown shirt was a little crooked, and she had a smudge of dirt by her nose. This was Leigh. And he loved her.

The realization sank through him like a rock in a pond. Deeper, and deeper, sending ripples behind it.

He loved her.

When she'd said, "Hell, I probably love you" he'd run like an idiot. Now wasn't exactly the best time to profess his love to her, if there ever would be a good time. He had too many ghosts and not enough life.

"Yes. He already has a good head start. Even though I think he was as pickled as an egg, he has been gone more than an hour."

She nodded, then pulled something out of her back pocket. It looked like a watch.

"This is a compass. I got turned around my first month here and spent a cold night shivering in a tree. Sean bought this for me, ordered it from the Sears and Roebuck catalog and it came all the way from New York. I want you to take it with you so you can find your way back home easier."

When *Roja* had gone out of her way to make sure he had food and supplies, he was touched. Now here was another woman giving him a gift, and this one far more precious. It was one of her few possessions, he knew. Leigh was not the kind of woman to collect things. She only had what she needed, what was special to her. This compass was obviously one of them.

"It helped me find my way around. I don't really need it anymore, but I'd feel better if you took it."

He closed the distance between them and gathered her in his arms. "*Amante*, I'll be back in a few hours."

She didn't respond.

"Okay, I will take your compass."

"Thank you," she said against his shoulder.

She leaned back, cupped his face in her hand and kissed him hard.

"Be careful. *Cuidado*, Mal."

"*Sí*, I will be careful. Trust me, *amante*."

She stared into his black eyes. "I do." And he saw in her eyes that it was true. Somewhere along the way she had remembered how to trust someone, to trust him. He felt glad of it. Not many people trusted him because all they saw was the outside and never looked past the two-day-old stubble and the hardness that surrounded him.

She laid the compass in his hand. The silver metal was still warm from her body. He felt like she'd handed him a piece of herself. For some reason, his throat closed up a little and he felt something inside him crack.

Malcolm mounted Demon and rode away before he did something really stupid like ask her to marry him.

ೞ ೞ ೞ

Malcolm followed Earl's trail easily. The old fool was definitely three sheets to the wind. The horse he rode meandered along at a snail's pace, but it was clearly headed for Rancho Zarza.

Malcolm stayed in the shadows, watching as Earl approached the front gate. He couldn't hear what was said, but he saw the bottle waving in Earl's hand while he shouted at the sentries. A few minutes later, Damasco came out the front gate. They argued. Malcolm tried to get a little closer, but there was no cover within two hundred yards of the damn gate. It was intentional, of course, so he stayed flat on his belly at the crest of a hill, watching.

Damasco paced back and forth, his arm pinwheeling as he shouted. Earl stayed on the horse until the other man yanked him down. He fell on his head and apparently either passed out or died. Damasco tried to rouse him, but gave up and told the guards to do something, then went back inside.

The guards lifted Earl by his arms and dragged him through the gate. A moment later, one came back out and brought the horse in.

The gate closed and Malcolm swore. He knew now for sure Earl was working with or for Damasco, but he still didn't know why.

CHAPTER FIFTEEN

Leigh pulled Ghost to a halt in front of the sheriff's office early the next morning. She couldn't sleep, and worry over Malcolm kept her from sitting on her hands doing nothing. So she left Andy in charge and headed to town as the first pink rays of the dawn painted the sky.

She hoped Joe Monroe was sober this morning. As a sheriff, he wasn't too bad, but he wasn't too good either. Most of his job involved keeping drunks locked up until they sobered up. Twenty years ago, Joe was a fit man with a hell of a lot more vim and vigor. Today, he was a tired, aging man who needed to step down from his post and let someone who could actually run after an outlaw take the job.

She wore her most sober clothes this morning. Black shirt and vest, dark brown trousers and a pistol on her right hip. There was no way in hell she was going anywhere without protection. The rifle in her saddle also stood testament to that.

She tried the door and it wasn't locked, so she pushed and stepped into the gloom.

Surprisingly, Joe sat behind the desk with his nose buried in a pile of papers. He didn't even notice she walked in the room. Leigh had a suspicion his hearing wasn't the only thing losing steam.

"Mornin', Joe."

He looked up, startled. "Morning, Miz Leigh. What are you doing here so early?" He squinted through the window at the daylight. "Can't be much past seven."

"I've got a real problem, Joe. I need your help."

He gestured for her to sit in one of the chairs in front of his desk. Everything in the sheriff's office looked like it had seen better days and the chairs were no exception. She was no featherweight and one of them looked like the weight of a tortilla would break it. She chose the sturdier—although sturdy seemed too strong a word—chair and lowered herself slowly into it. It emitted a short creak, but stayed together.

Joe had a tin mug of steaming coffee and a half-eaten biscuit on the desk. He nibbled on the biscuit and picked up the coffee cup, leaning back in his chair to look at her. Behind the watery eyes and sagging jowls, she saw a sharpness that age hadn't dulled. Perhaps coming to see him was a good idea.

"I've got over twelve hundred head missing, Joe, including most of my spring calves. Rustled clean off my place. I don't know when or how, but I know Earl was behind it. And I think Damasco Zarza."

Joe's expression remained inscrutable. "What else?"

"I've told you about the water problems before, but there have been dozens of things going wrong over the past two years. Someone's trying to ruin the Circle O, and they're doing a damn fine job of it. Without those missing cattle, I can't last much past four months."

She felt a little despair speaking the words out loud, but only a little. Her anger and determination reared their two heads and bit her ass to keep her strong.

"What makes you think it was Earl?"

"We confronted him and he admitted to being a part of it. Said he had no choice, then he took off."

"Who is 'we'?"

"What do you mean?"

Joe took another sip of coffee. "You said 'we confronted him' so I was wondering who the other part of 'we' was."

He was still sharp. "Malcolm and I."

"Malcolm the stable boy from Rancho Zarza?"

She shook her head. "No, Joe. You may as well hear it from me because I'm sure you will hear it from someone else. Malcolm Ross. Alex's bastard son is back."

For some reason, Joe didn't look surprised. "I heard something about that. I thought he was dead."

"Looks like his mother arranged for that and helped him get out. Isabella wanted him dead and she did her damnedest to make that happen."

Even thinking about Malcolm's back made her fists clench. That heartless bitch.

"So you and Malcolm are...what? A team?"

She didn't like the insinuation. "He is my foreman for the time being. He's helping me out. Malcolm and I grew up together, Joe. We were best friends for most of our childhood."

Joe nodded, apparently digesting her words. After another gulp of coffee, he said, "Do you have proof? Against Earl or Damasco?"

That question made her stomach sink to her feet. "I'm sure we do. I haven't had a chance to check the ledgers yet."

"Proof perhaps against Earl, but what about Damasco? He's not the type of man to accuse without solid evidence, Leigh."

Leigh closed her eyes and took a deep breath. "Thanks for your time, Joe."

As she headed for the door, Joe spoke. "Leigh, wait."

She turned and looked back at Joe, plans for the coming battle brewing in her head already.

"Get me proof and we'll go after them."

Leigh nodded and left before she said something to him she would regret. He wasn't being lazy, but he was covering his ass. No one wanted to get on Damasco's bad side since it was as deep and menacing as any pit in hell.

As she untied Ghost's reins, hands grabbed her and yanked her back into the alley next to the sheriff's office. Her boot heels dug into the dirt in her struggle to break free.

She was slammed up against the wall and her breath gushed out, leaving her gasping for air. One hand held her throat and the other groped at her breast. Her gun was out of reach.

"So, *querida*, you change your mind yet about marrying me?"

Damasco. That low-down bastard.

"Let go of me."

She pushed and tried to kick at him, but he had her legs trapped with his own. The hard ridge of his arousal pressed against her hip and she fought a wave of nausea. There was no way in the world she was going to let him do this. No goddamn way. Leigh's anger rushed through her and her courage stood tall.

She jerked one hand free and reached down to squeeze his balls. His hold loosened on her throat and she was able to twist until most of Damasco's body weight was off her. With a little kick to the knee, taught to her courtesy of Malcolm, she freed herself completely. She cleared leather and pointed the pistol at his chest.

Damasco stood, one hand braced against the wall of the sheriff's office, alternately touching his balls and his knee.

"Goddamn bitch!" he snarled. "You know you want it. You begged me for it the first time. And now you act like you are an untouched virgin."

"I was until you raped me, you bastard."

She felt the overpowering rage of every woman who has ever been trapped and assaulted by a man against her will.

"I never raped you. You wanted it."

Although she shook with fear, hot anger pulsed through her. She hated weakness and tried to shake off the fear completely, but it was damn hard. Being under him again brought back horrible memories of running from Rancho Zarza with nowhere to go. Of being held in Sean's arms as she cried her eyes out.

"Don't you ever touch me again, Damasco. I swear to all that's holy if you do, I will kill you myself."

He looked into her eyes and apparently saw she meant it. Damn straight. She meant every goddamn word.

She backed away from him to the sunlit wooden planks of the sidewalk, then side-stepped to Ghost, her eyes never leaving Damasco. She hopped on the horse and holstered her weapon.

"I'm not giving up my ranch, Damasco. If you wanted a war, you've got one."

Beth Williamson

Leigh wheeled the horse around and galloped down the street, willing herself not to shake. Goddamn him! When she reached Burt Green's office, she stopped, hoping the attorney had good news.

Following a brief conversation with the sleepy-eyed man, she walked to the General Store next door and sent a telegram. All the while, she kept an eye out for Damasco and his grasping hands.

After she was done with her errands, she kneed Ghost into a gallop and headed for the Circle O. She prayed Malcolm was back. They needed to make plans and fortify for the coming storm.

ભ ભ ભ

By the time Leigh arrived at the Circle O, she was much calmer. The incident with Damasco just served to fortify her resolve to fight him until he had to kill her to get her ranch.

When Andy met her at the barn, she knew Malcolm wasn't there yet. It wasn't so much disappointment as the goddamn worry about him. He said he'd return in a couple of hours, and dammit, he wasn't here. She hated worrying.

"I'm glad you're back, Miz Leigh." He tipped his hat back to squint at her.

She dismounted and faced him. "Tell me what's going on."

From the expression on his normally chipper mug, she wasn't going to like what she heard. He scrunched up his face and heaved a great sigh. "Well, we had six men leave last night."

That was not good news. There were only fifteen drovers in all, so that left only nine. Ten including her. Not much of an army.

She looked at Andy. "What else? I can see there is something else gnawing at you."

He scratched his cheek. "Yeah, Hermano, I mean Malcolm, came back after you left and told me to let you know he was okay. He left after getting some supplies and a bedroll."

She frowned. "Where was he going?"

"He didn't rightly say, Miz Leigh. But I expect he's found where Earl is holed up and is waiting on him to make a move."

Andy was probably right, but it didn't mean she had to like it.

"Which way did he go? And how much did he take with him?"

"North and probably a couple days' worth of grub."

North. Toward Rancho Zarza.

"Did he say anything else?"

"No, ma'am."

She definitely didn't like that. The Circle O was her ranch and she deserved to know what Malcolm was doing to get her cows back. To know if he was safe. To know if he was putting himself in danger. Damn, loving somebody put you in a pickle if it meant wanting to know anything and everything at the same time. She was tempted to get back on Ghost and find Malcolm, but resisted the urge.

Trust me, amante.

He'd asked her to put her faith in him. She had to believe in him.

She led Ghost into the barn. "Come on, Andy, it's time to batten down the hatches."

"Batten the what?"

She smiled grimly. "Never mind. Let's go check the weapons. I picked up some shells and bullets at the store. And we need to gather up some boards for the windows in the house."

Andy looked at her like she was crazy, but a hint of fear flashed in his eyes.

"What's gonna happen, Miz Leigh?"

"I don't know, but we're going to be ready for them, come hell or high water. They'll know the Circle O won't give up the ghost that easily."

CHAPTER SIXTEEN

Malcolm chewed on the jerky and tried to imagine it was beef stew and biscuits. And that he was staring at Leigh across the table.

But it was still cold jerky, and the ground was hard, and the rabbit staring at him sure didn't resemble Leigh. He should have dragged her off to her bedroom and made love to her before he left. That would have been a novelty—actually having her in a bed instead of standing up.

Night had fallen and Rancho Zarza was quiet again. He had checked around the perimeter last night and made notes of all the sentries and possible entry points. There was a low wall in the back by the kitchen garden he could get over with a little luck and a lot of grunting. He needed to get inside without being seen.

As soon as the last light winked out in the house, Malcolm left his hiding place and slithered across the tall grass toward the back of the hacienda. When he reached the lowest point in the wall—which was at least ten feet high—he stopped and waited, still as a whisper. Five minutes passed, then ten. After fifteen, he knew he hadn't been spotted.

After shucking his boots and socks, he tucked them into the back of his jeans upside down. Not the first time he'd had to be sneaky barefoot—he'd learned that trick in Tijuana one night. He slid on his gloves and started climbing the adobe wall, using the natural indentations to hoist his body up. The strain on his arms was incredible, but his bare toes hung on like claws, allowing him the time to haul himself up higher inch by inch. A river of sweat ran down his body by the time his hands connected with the top of the wall.

He pulled himself up and laid down flat on the two-foot-wide wall. He only had about ten more minutes before the sentries did their hourly walk around the entire wall of the hacienda. But he had to catch his breath and regain some of his strength. He controlled his breathing although what he really wanted to do was suck in air like a bellows.

When Malcolm could take a normal breath, he slipped his socks and boots back on. He lowered himself until he was hanging on with his fingertips, then dropped the last few feet to the ground.

Keeping to a crouch, he scuttled over to Diego and Lorena's small cottage at the back corner of the hacienda. He went to the window he knew was the bedroom and scratched lightly for a minute, then stepped back and waited.

Diego came out, shirtless, with a rifle in his hands.

"Diego," he whispered.

"Who the hell is that?"

"Malcolm."

He lowered the weapon and puffed out a breath. "Dammit, *chico*, what are you doing? Trying to scare ten years off my life?"

"Shhhh. *Por favor, amigo*, come into the shadows. I need your help."

Diego walked toward him and they crouched together behind the cottage, out of sight of any sentry.

The older man's eyes studied him in the darkness. His eyes were virtually unreadable.

"Speak, *hijo*."

And so Malcolm told him the whole story. How there were twelve hundred head missing, how Earl had admitted his guilt and come here, and how they suspected Damasco was behind it. After he finished explaining everything, Diego dropped to his behind on the sandy ground and put his head in his hands.

"*Dios*, I knew something was going on. But I did not know how bad it was."

"What do you know?"

Diego sighed. "I've seen some of the cattle being driven through Rancho Zarza. I didn't ask where they came from. I cannot believe there were so many taken."

"It was over a two-year period, Diego. You probably saw fifty head or so at a time. They did not want it to be obvious. Do you know where they brought them?"

"There is a canyon, down in the south corner of the ranch. Do you know where I mean?"

Malcolm did. He had often gone there when he wanted to be alone. It was like a box canyon. One way in, one way out. Anyone coming in without good reason was easily picked off by sentries.

"*Sí*, I know the canyon. We can worry about getting the cattle back later. Now I need you to do something for me."

"What can I do, Malcolm? I do not want Lorena in danger."

"Keep your eyes and ears open and send a message to me when you see them coming."

"You think they are going to attack the Circle O?"

Malcolm grimaced. "I am sure of it. They can blame it on banditos or Indians or whatever else they can think of. Either way, we'll all be dead and will not say anything different. No one will question the powerful Zarzas."

"I will do as you ask, *hijo*."

Diego calling him son had a strange effect on him. It made him realize that no man had ever called him son, but Diego was the closest thing he'd had to a father. He didn't want the older man to put himself in a position where he could be hurt or killed either. No one must ever know of his involvement.

"When you send the message, send the boy Malcolm."

Diego sighed. "You know about him?"

"*Sí*, and I think Damasco may use him to punish me. I do not want that boy hurt."

Diego's hand fell on Malcolm's shoulder and squeezed. "You are a good man, Malcolm. Your mother would be proud."

Mention of his mother reminded him that he had not thought about her for the past few days. He would think about her when Leigh was safe and the war was over.

"*Gracias, amigo.* That means a lot to me." Malcolm's voice was hoarse.

"Poor little Leigh. Is she okay?"

Malcolm smiled in the gloom. "*Sí,* she is okay. Leigh is a fighter."

He saw a slash of white when Diego smiled back. "She is like a little wolf, no? All fangs and fierceness."

Yes, she was a wolf. And he was her mate. Like all wolves, they were mates for life. He had to save her ranch or they would both die trying.

ตา ตา ตา

After thanking Diego and bidding him good night, Malcolm crept toward the house itself. This was his one opportunity to speak to Alejandro and he wasn't going to let it pass. From what Leigh said, he was dying and would not last much longer. Malcolm tried to feel grief at the thought, but could not summon that emotion from the depths of his childhood. Alejandro had stopped being a father to him when he was six years old and Damasco was born.

Perhaps it was Isabella's influence, or perhaps it was all Alejandro. Either way, Malcolm was tossed aside like stale bread and left to rot in the stables until he turned eighteen. He wasn't angry anymore, but he needed to speak his mind and say his piece to his father. There was a great deal of things he needed to lay to rest before the rest of his life could begin.

After reaching the house, he stayed in the shadows of a pecan tree for ten minutes near the double glass doors of the library. There was no one about. He slid his knife out of its scabbard on his back and maneuvered it in the lock, popping it easily. The knife went back in its place and Malcolm eased the door open, wary for any noise to give him away.

Malcolm entered the dark room and closed the door behind him. The smell of the room hit his nostrils and he was suddenly awash in memories. The scent of leather, of fine cigar smoke, of expensive bourbon. The last time he stood in this room was so long ago…it had been the day Damasco was born. Alejandro had told Malcolm his new room was to be in the stables, that he was such a responsible boy at the age of six he needed to contribute and earn his living. It sounded like such a grown-up adventure and he happily moved

Beth Williamson

into the stable. Eager to please, eager to be thought of as a man. He had been a boy, a fool, and realized within a day he wasn't sent to the stables to earn his living. He didn't even get a wage. He was sent there because Papa's wife had a baby boy, someone who took his place and was destined to inherit Rancho Zarza. He ate with the servants and his clothing was never so fine again. When he outgrew his clothing, it was replaced with the coarse material worn by the rest of the servants' children.

He had cried himself to sleep for six months. Each time he tried to talk to his Papa, he was told they would talk later. Later never came. Here it was, so much later, a lifetime had passed—a lifetime full of hate and resentment, of unhappiness and loneliness. He actually felt the prick of tears to be back in this room. The room where his entire life had changed.

Swallowing his memories, he crept to the door and opened it as slowly as he could. The doors in the house were monstrous things, eight feet high and ornate like chapel doors. Alejandro's room was in the west wing of the house. Diego had confirmed it for him.

Malcolm crept through the darkened hallway on his toes, not letting the heels of his boots hit the stone floors. When he reached the end of the hallway, he turned right and saw the glow of light coming from under Alejandro's door.

His heart started beating faster. He was about to see his father, a man he hadn't laid eyes on in over fifteen years. A man he hated, resented, but somehow, deep down where little Malcolm lived, still loved.

He stood outside the door, listening. All he heard was an occasional sound, like the turning of a page and someone coughing. Alejandro was reading and he was alone.

Malcolm pushed the door open and stepped inside.

The man lying on the bed in a voluminous white nightshirt was not Alejandro. It was a shriveled old man Malcolm had never seen before who didn't look surprised at all to find a strange man in his room in the middle of the night.

"Malcolm. I thought you would come to see me. *Dios mio, hijo,* but you have grown into such a fierce-looking man."

Malcolm nearly stumbled when he heard the man speak. That was Alejandro's voice coming from a wizened old stranger. No, not a stranger.

Madre de Dios!

This was Alejandro. His father. Yellow and wrinkled with age, liver spots marching up his face and hands. His hair was wispy and sparse and his cheeks were sunken in his face, making his eyes look like an owl's.

"Papa?" It was out of his mouth like a croak before he could call it back.

"I don't look so good, no? They all lie to me and tell me that I don't look too bad, but I know the truth. They can hide the mirrors, but when little Leigh comes to see me, she tells me the truth. I am worried for her, Malcolm. I think Damasco and Isabella are planning to do her harm."

Malcolm simply stared. Here was the monster of his bad dreams, reduced to the size of a child. He was welcoming him, expressing concern for Leigh, and acting as if fifteen years of hatred had not sat on his father's shoulders like an unwelcome guest.

"Sit, sit. *Por favor*, Malcolm. You give me a neck ache, you are so tall."

Without thinking, he walked to the bed and sat on the edge. When Alejandro clasped his hands together and smiled, he saw the father of his youth. The father who taught him how to ride, how to shoot, how to dance. The papa who gave him rides on his shoulders and peeled apples with him.

Was it all that simple? Would it just be washed away because Alejandro willed it?

"I have hated you for so long, Alejandro."

He sighed. "Yes, *hijo*, I know. I turned away from you and listened to Isabella, forgetting about my firstborn son. I have no excuse, but I can still beg you to forgive me."

"People say many things when they know they are dying."

Alejandro laughed rustily. "*Sí*, you are right. And I am no exception. Can you take off your hat so I can see you, *hijo*?"

Malcolm pulled off his hat, knowing his hair was still stuck to his skull with dried sweat from his midnight hike up the wall.

Alejandro looked him over and smiled. "I see myself thirty years ago. I also see my sweet Leslie in your eyes."

"Do not think I will allow you to mention my mother."

He held up a hand in surrender. "This is your time, *hijo*. Say what you came to say."

Suddenly, he didn't know what to say. So many words crowded in his mouth like little demons of hate, jumping up and down, waiting to be spewed forth. Did he want his last time with his father to be all about hate? Or was he ready to forgive?

"Why?" was all he said.

Alejandro sighed. "There is no simple reason. I was already engaged to Isabella when your mother came to me and told me she was pregnant with you. Leslie was such a beautiful, strong woman. I loved her. I think I still do. But my papa had plans for my marriage and they didn't involve a Scottish immigrant orphan with no family and no money, and certainly no pedigree. I could not marry Leslie, but I kept her as close to me as I could. Isabella never forgave me for that and Leslie didn't either."

He looked into the shadows and his eyes focused on the past. "When you were born, I was so happy. I wanted to shout it to the world that I had a son. I loved you from the moment I laid eyes on you, *hijo*. Kicking and screaming into the world. Since Isabella didn't conceive for so long, I selfishly kept you fed and clothed and taught you everything a father could teach a boy. I took whatever time I had and guarded it. The day was coming when she would have a child, only it took longer than I thought."

His eyes misted. "Isabella told me she would see to it that you would have an accident and not live to see your next birthday if I didn't send you out of the house. Her family was powerful and I was weak with worry for you. The guilt ate away at me as I saw you suffer and struggle. So I took the coward's way out and stopped looking."

Malcolm listened with his ears and his heart. He heard the truth coming from Alejandro. And he was glad he hadn't let the demons loose out of his mouth.

"Then Isabella had you whipped while I was gone to Houston for two weeks. I think she even planned it, had Damasco push you and push you until you snapped. She knew you had my temper and played on it. She wanted to kill you and devised a way to do it. By the time I got back, you were dead. Or so I was told. Leslie would not speak to me and within six months she was gone. Little Leigh moped around like a shadow of herself. Isabella and Damasco had never looked happier."

"Yet you were not surprised to see me step in the room."

Alejandro turned his gaze back to Malcolm and he was shocked to see tears streaming down his father's face.

"Lorena told me two days ago. She has always loved you like a nephew. A good woman, that Lorena. She was right to tell me. I could not get a message to you, but I hoped, no I prayed, you would come to see me so I could meet the man you had become."

Malcolm was afraid to ask. "And what do you see?"

Alejandro cocked his head and studied Malcolm's face. "I see a man who has had a hard life. A man who has honor and dignity. A man who knows what's right and may have lost his way a time or two, but found his way back to who he really is. I see a man I am proud to call my son."

The tears clogging his throat were raw and salty. He had waited so long, so damn long, to hear those words from Alejandro. Did he really mean them and could Malcolm accept them? Probably not entirely, but they meant something. The crack in the wall around his heart grew wider.

"Alejandro, Isabella and Damasco are up to something. They have set out to ruin the Circle O and take it from Leigh. Do you know anything about it?"

Alejandro's brows drew together in a frown. "No, I know nothing about it. But I am not surprised. Since I cannot take care of my business, Damasco is taking care of it. There is talk of the railroad coming to Millerton and the route it takes will make the landowners wealthy."

The railroad. Son of a bitch! That was it.

"The Circle O must be in the path the railroad will take and Damasco wants a big piece of that pie. He's rustled more than half the cattle, killed some, even tried to kill her. *Bandejo*. She must have an angel on her shoulder to have survived the last two years."

Malcolm was angry; no, he was absolutely furious. It was all about money and greed. Forget human life, or kindness, or respect. Or family.

Alejandro's light touch on his hand drew him back from his inevitable explosion.

"You must stop them. I am not strong enough to help you, but I can at least distract Isabella to keep them apart. Damasco alone is not as strong without his mother behind him."

"I will stop them. They will not take the Circle O or succeed in killing Leigh. You have my promise on that."

Alejandro squeezed his hand. "I am glad to hear that, *hijo*. Now can you stay a little longer and talk to your papa?"

His eyes were full of pain and the shadow of death, but also a hint of hope. That hope made the final decision for Malcolm.

"Yes, Papa. I will stay a little longer."

෴ ෴ ෴

It was the middle of the night, long past midnight, but Leigh couldn't sleep. She sat on the front porch steps with a rifle across her lap, staring at the stars. Malcolm had been gone for more than a day. She was not only worried about him, she missed him. It was a lonely supper again without him. Not to mention the absolute yearning to feel his hands on her, to feel him inside her.

She needed Malcolm to erase the shadows of Damasco's hands on her body. Goddamn him for reawakening her demons long since put away. She had been young and more than stupid to follow Damasco into the stables to see the new foal. More than stupid to stare at him when he locked her in the stall and forced himself on her. He had been fifteen years old for God's sake. Yes, but he had been big, like Malcolm, and so much stronger than she. And she had been shocked that he would force himself on her. She didn't even cry "no" until after he'd penetrated her and spilled his seed almost immediately. It was like it had happened to someone else. But years later it still had the power to hurt her. *He* still had the power to hurt her.

She shivered and wrapped her arms around herself.

"*Amante*," came a whisper near her ear.

She whirled around, dropped the rifle with a clatter and launched herself at a crouching Malcolm, knocking him flat on the porch. Her lips found his and she dove into him for all she was worth.

"Malcolm," she said in between kisses. "I'm so glad you're here."

"I can see that." He chuckled. "Do you think we can go upstairs and actually use a bed?"

He was hard against her already and she responded by rubbing herself up and down on him. She sat up so she straddled him.

"Can I go on top? Like this?"

He groaned lightly. "*Sí, por favor.* I would love to have you ride me."

She rose after one last ferocious kiss and held out a hand to pull him to his feet. Then he did the most amazing thing. He scooped her up in his arms.

"Can you open the door?"

She reached down and opened the door. He turned sideways and carried her in, then stopped while she closed and locked the door again.

"Put me down. I'm too heavy for you," she whispered.

"No," he said, giving her a nibbling bite on one breast. "I am not letting you go again."

She nearly giggled. *Giggled,* for Pete's sake. What was she…a silly girl?

"Let's go upstairs then."

He carried her up the stairs like she weighed nothing. When they entered her bedroom, he set her on her feet, slowly sliding her down his hard, erect body.

"Lock the door." His voice was rough, seemingly at the edge of his control.

She did as he bade and returned to his arms.

"*Amante,* I need you naked, beneath me. I need to be inside you. Now."

He started pulling at her shirt until she stopped his trembling hands. "I'll do that."

He took a great, gasping breath and stepped back. In the weak moonlight filtering through the curtains, she saw him taking his clothes off as fast as she was. She needed him, too. Oh, God, how she needed him.

"Hurry." He reached for her. She was just shucking off her pants and drawers. In a blink, they were both naked and he walked her toward the bed as his kisses ravaged her mouth. When her knees hit the mattress, she fell back and he landed on top of her.

He was so damn hot and incredibly hard. His chest hair rubbed on her nipples, which were already like rocks, tantalizing and teasing them mercilessly.

"I can't wait, *amante*. Please let me in."

She felt as frantic as he was. She spread her legs and he drove into her wet pussy in one stroke. It was a wild joining. More of a mating, like the wolves he had said they were. She clawed at his back as he pumped into her again and again. Stroking her, biting her nipples and neck. Licking and kissing over and over.

"Oh, God, Malcolm. Oh, God, oh, God, oh, God," she chanted as he pulled her legs up to circle his waist and drove deeper and harder. He was touching her soul, guiding her along to the place where they were one.

Yes. More. More. Just a few more strokes. Please.

"I'm coming, Mal. I'm coming." As she tried not to scream the words, he plunged into her until her heart stopped beating. It was a moment that hung in the air like a full moon. Bright, shiny, perfect.

"*Amante!*" he said hoarsely into her ear. She felt him shudder as she clenched around him again and again. His seed spilled into her, giving his life into hers. Joining them.

He laid his forehead against hers. "This is where I am. Home. I am finally home."

Yes, home. Together they were home.

CHAPTER SEVENTEEN

Leigh woke up in the middle of the night in a man's arms for the first time in her life. The feeling of belonging, of being safe, was indescribable. It was like nothing she had ever experienced. His shoulder was hard beneath her head, yet it was the most comfortable place she had ever slept. Her nose was pressed up against the crook of his neck and she breathed in his scent. His essence.

She kissed his neck, tasting the salty tang of his skin.

"*Amante?*" His voice was husky from sleep.

"I'm here."

He chuckled a bit hoarsely. "*Sí*, you are definitely that."

"Where were you, Malcolm?"

His fingers grazed her neck. "I followed Earl. He ended up at Rancho Zarza. With Damasco."

She didn't have doubts about Damasco's guilt, but to know for certain she'd been harboring a snake in the grass was hard to swallow. She'd thought herself smarter than that. To be fooled for so long, to have so much taken from her, proved to the world she was the stupid woman they all thought her to be.

Malcolm must have sensed her mood.

"It was not you, *chica*. I think he moved the cows in small herds. Over the course of two years, small amounts are less noticeable, no? Diego remembers seeing the smaller herds. He thinks he knows where they are."

Nonetheless, she still felt like an idiot. "Can he help?"

"He is going to keep watch for us. I asked him to send little Malcolm when it begins."

Her hands roamed his chest, feeling the crisp curling hairs sliding through her fingers.

"When 'it' begins?"

"They are coming, *amante*. Make no mistake about that. They are coming to pick off what is left of the Circle O. Damasco wants the land."

She propped herself up on one elbow and glared at him.

"Why? What does he want with something that's one-tenth the size of his inheritance?

His black eyes regarded her steadily. "The railroad."

She sucked in a breath. "It's coming through my land."

His silence was all the answer she needed. She leapt out of bed and paced the room. "Son of a bitch! Why didn't he just offer to buy it?"

"Would you have sold?"

"No."

She grimaced at her quick answer. She would have told him no and kicked dirt on him to boot for even asking. But this. This was cruel, illegal, and would soon become murderous.

"That's not all."

She regretted the impulse, but asked anyway. "What?"

"I think he killed Sean."

That just made her madder than hell. What did Sean ever do to hurt anyone? He was one of the kindest people she had ever known. That Damasco would murder him for money was enough to make her sick. Then she had another nasty thought.

"You think he's going to kill us?"

Malcolm's gaze never wavered. "I think he's going to try."

Leigh knew in that moment he was fully prepared to take on Damasco's army of fifty men or more with her measly crew of ten and expected to survive. No, not survive. Triumph.

"Can we win?"

"Yes."

He sounded so certain. Her confidence in his abilities could not be any higher. It was the abilities of herself and her crew she wasn't too sure of.

"We're not gunfighters, Mal. Me and what's left of my crew—six of those bastards ran by the way—are cowhands. I've never fired a gun at a man in my life."

"I will help you learn."

She stopped pacing and realized she was stalking around her bedroom buck naked. And didn't feel embarrassed about it. Perhaps it was the appreciative gaze directed at her.

"Come back to bed, *carina*." His softly spoken command penetrated her self-perusal.

Malcolm held open the covers with a smile. Oh, that smile of his could turn her knees to jam in an instant. She crawled up from the bottom of the bed and tucked herself back under the covers. Before she even stopped moving, he pulled her close to him spoon-style. Now that was worth waking up to every day. His hard, warm body was like a living piece of sculpture, perfectly defined, hard, hot and smooth to the touch.

"What else did you find out?"

She felt a tightening in his muscles, a minute change she would not have noticed if she wasn't pressed up against him from head to toe

"I saw my father."

Leigh wanted to blurt a hundred questions, but decided not to. Whatever he had to say, she needed to hear it, and she had to be patient. She loved Alejandro like an uncle, but she loved Malcolm like he was her life. If father and son could not make peace, she would have to choose between them. And miss Alex because her choice was already made.

"He is the one who told me about the railroad. We...we talked."

The silence was excruciating. Her natural inclination to shake him didn't seem like a wise thing to do.

"I made my peace with him, *amante*. He promised to help us with Isabella."

Now that was surprising.

"I don't know if I trust him, but I believed him."

His arm had tightened a bit against her stomach while he spoke of his father.

"Good… How long do you think we have?"

She felt him shrug one shoulder. "Could be two hours. Could be two days. Could be two weeks. All we can do is be ready to face those *cabrons*."

She turned and wrapped her arms around his neck, pulling him as close as he could get. She wasn't used to being nervous or afraid without doing something about it.

⋅⋅⋅

Malcolm woke up again just before dawn. The gray light filtering through the curtains shed a gloomy pall over the room. He lay in a soft bed with a woman beside him, spooned together. A tall, sleek woman who fit next to him like she was made to be there.

His very own Eve. Too bad the Circle O Ranch wasn't the Garden of Eden.

He began nibbling her shoulder and neck lightly. Tiny little bites meant to titillate and tease. She moved against him, arching, pressing her rump against his rapidly expanding cock.

More.

He circled her breast with his fingers. Around and around, not touching the nipple, but caressing the petal soft skin.

He grew hot as his blood pumped faster. A pink flush crept over her skin and he knew she was awake.

"Are you going to torture me all morning or latch on?" came her sweet sleep-laden voice.

"Mmmm…I think I like to torture you."

She pressed herself against his hardness and wiggled her ass. "Me, too. Only because I know how much I want it. How much I want you. God, Malcolm, please, touch them…"

He ignored her pleas and continued to circle her breast over and over.

She opened her legs and he slipped his engorged staff between them. She was wet and slick. He slid back and forth against her throbbing pussy. Hot, wet skin against hard, taut skin, pulsing and moving as one.

"Jesus, yes, please," she breathed as she caught his rhythm and moved in sync.

He was tempted to thrust into her, but wanted to savor the anticipation a few minutes longer.

His fingertip finally reached her nipple and he tweaked lightly. She jerked and gasped, shoving herself toward him hard, forcing the head of his cock into her an inch.

Oh, sweet Heaven. She was so hot and wet.

He pulled himself out with a groan.

"You aren't going anywhere," Leigh said huskily.

She lifted her leg and grabbed him, leading him back to where she hungered the most.

"In, *in.*"

Leigh took his cock in her hand and rubbed it against her pussy, spreading her juices all over him and her hand. She moaned each time the head made contact with her clit.

"Yes, *amante*, please yourself. Please me."

Her nimble fingers pushed him inside her hot cavern again. She rocked slightly and the movement set his teeth to tingling.

"Deeper."

He pulled away from her when she tried to impale herself. Instead, the head slipped in and out of her pussy to her rhythm, teasing, tantalizing both of them. His body screamed to bury himself inside her yet he held back. Anticipation ran through his veins. She slid her hand down and started caressing herself. He jerked in surprise and his arousal notched up even higher Malcolm had never had a woman do that with him inside before and he grew another inch. He bit her shoulder, holding back the initial deep thrust he was desperate to make. He tweaked and twisted her hardened nipple while she teased herself, teased him.

"*Deeper.*"

Her command grew frantic as her hand moved faster.

"Please, Malcolm."

He couldn't stand it another moment. With a thrust he was embedded in her hot, wet core. Deep, deep inside where she clenched and pulsed around him. Incredibly he found himself ready to climax immediately. He stopped where he was, savoring the feeling of being so deeply connected to her.

Leigh couldn't be still though. She moved, caressing herself, slick with her own juices.

As soon as he had himself under control, he started his rhythm. One he had learned from a Chinese whore down in San Antonio.

Nine long strokes, one short stroke, Eight long strokes, two short strokes. Seven long strokes, three short strokes. Alternately building until he was at one long stroke, and nine short strokes. By the time he reached the end, Leigh was panting. She grabbed his leg and pinched.

"My turn. I want that ride now." Leigh's voice was whisper soft, yet determined.

When she pulled away from him, Malcolm felt the loss of her heat and he groaned. With a shake of her head and a grin, she pushed him onto his back. Oh, she was going to ride all right. As her long legs straddled him, her eyes wild and her pupils dilated with such passion, Malcolm felt a moment of pure heavenly anticipation. He quivered with the need to grab her and throw her back on the bed. Leaning down, Leigh kissed him open-mouthed while she took his cock and guided it into her hungry self. Slowly, inch by inch, she swallowed him up.

"Jesus, I didn't know it would feel this good."

He tried to laugh, but found his voice had deserted him momentarily. He was buried to the hilt inside her, with his balls pressed up tight against her ass. Skin to skin.

It could not feel any better than this. He reached up and continued to twist and tweak her nipples, wishing they were closer to his mouth so he could bite them. Leigh sat up and started rocking like a woman used to riding. The natural sway of her hips allowed her to find her rhythm quickly.

"Like riding a stallion," she murmured as she picked up her pace. She rode him fast and hard like a wild bronc, with abandon and passion he'd never seen before. Each time she came all the way down and impaled herself, pleasure ricocheted through him.

Malcolm didn't think his balls could get any tighter, and the orgasm building inside him felt like a volcano. He couldn't hold back anymore, and he wanted her to come with him. She was panting and moaning, still rubbing her clit and swallowing him into her moist, tight cunt.

"Now, *amante*, now!"

She slammed down on him, gripping him so hard it was nearly painful. He buried himself deep into her pussy and felt pleasure so intense he thought he heard bells in his head. His ears rang and even his toes tingled

She jerked as the ripples of her orgasm faded and his still echoed through his body.

He thought he might have died, it surely felt like angels were singing around them.

"Damn, Malcolm."

Leigh lay down on top of him, pressing her breasts into his sweat-coated chest. Her heart beat like a rabbit's against him. She even shook a bit.

That's when he realized what he felt on his shoulder was not sweat. It was tears.

হ হ হ

Leigh was crying. She tried to stop it, tried to bite her lip to send the tears back, but dammit, it wasn't working. She was crying for God's sake. She hadn't cried in so long, she had forgotten what it felt like. Her nose filled up and her eyes hurt; her throat clogged.

"*Amante?*"

She shook her head slightly against his hot skin, signaling she wasn't ready for him yet. Not yet. Not until she stopped the horrible leaking.

Their love making was, and she could say that with certainty, so intense an experience it had made her cry. So much. There was just so much that had zinged through her. Like a tornado or something. More than her cobwebby soul could handle.

Malcolm stroked her back slowly with his big callused hands. Soothing her battered emotions. After a few minutes, she felt more in control of herself. She wiped her eyes with both hands, then straightened.

That's when she remembered he was still nestled deep inside her, and he was still hard. Not only that, he was smiling at her like she was the only other person in the entire world. Lord, how she loved him.

CR CR CR

They slept late, then made love again. But their idyllic peace came to a crashing halt when a fist pounded on the bedroom door. In less time than it took Leigh to realize what the noise was, Malcolm was crouched, pistol drawn and pointed at the closed door.

"Miz Leigh! Ya gotta get up."

It was Andy Parker. He did not sound like his usual chipper self, but then again, he hadn't for days. This time he sounded a little frantic.

"Give me two minutes, Andy," she answered.

Malcolm lowered his weapon and his chin dropped to his chest. She heard him muttering in Spanish. She didn't ask or push him to talk. Figured he'd get around to it if he wanted to.

She jumped out of bed and went to the washbasin. Using the cold water in the pitcher, she gave herself what was called a "whore's bath" by washing between her legs and under her arms. She dried off then yanked clean clothes off their hooks and dressed as quickly as she could. Even so, when she turned around, Malcolm was completely dressed with his guns strapped on and an impatient expression on his face. Then he looked at her neck and his expression turned furious.

"Who touched you?"

She didn't understand at first. "Only you, Mal."

He crossed the room and gently wrapped his hand around her neck.

"I am only going to ask you one more time. *Who touched you?*"

His voice was cold and hard. The fury in his eyes was nothing she had ever seen before and hoped to never see again. It sent a chill dancing down her spine and goose bumps rising on her arms.

Leigh hadn't realized Damasco had left behind any bruises when he'd pinned her against the wall yesterday.

"It's nothing."

His grip tightened so slightly she hardly felt it, but she could not move.

"It is not *nothing, carina.* Tell me so I can hear his fucking name."

For a moment she felt sorry for Damasco, but it was only a moment.

"Damasco."

He cursed heartily in Spanish as he glared at the offending marks. As if his anger would will them away.

"How? Was he here?"

"No. I went to town to talk to the Sheriff, remember? I...I ran into Damasco and I got away before he hurt me."

"No, you didn't. You have his fingerprints on your neck, *amante.*" His voice was like a hot knife, slicing through everything. "There is something you're not telling me."

"Miz Leigh!" came Andy's voice again. "Please hurry up."

"We can't talk about this now." *Please, please, let it go.*

He finally took his hand away from her neck. He stared at the bruises once more then did the one thing that guaranteed she would love him for the rest of her life. He bent down and pressed feather-light kisses on each and every mark. His lips were soft and his breath fluttered on her skin.

Stupidly enough, she felt the prick of tears again in her eyes. What the hell was wrong with her anyway?

"I will never let anyone hurt you again."

She saw a promise in his black eyes. A promise that warmed her from her head to her toes.

"Miz Leigh!"

Andy's shout broke the spell.

"Coming," she said as they headed for the bedroom door.

လ လ လ

Alejandro Zarza had made many mistakes in his life. Mistakes he'd come to regret as the years passed. His first was giving in to his father's machinations to marry Isabella when he was in love with Leslie Ross.

His second was allowing Isabella to treat Malcolm like dirt beneath her feet and throwing him out to the stables when he was a young boy. Alex thought perhaps if he hadn't showered so much attention on Malcolm, Isabella might have left him alone.

It didn't work. Instead, he spent little or no time with his firstborn son after Damasco was born. Then Malcolm began to resent him and the chasm between them grew wider and wider until it seemed they would never again see eye to eye.

When Alejandro thought Malcolm had died, his heart nearly burst from grief. To know that his wife caused his son's death—a cruel, tortured death— was the day he began to hate Isabella as much as he hated himself.

He had not made love with her since, nor shared any affection whatsoever. Her fussing over him now he was dying was for show, although he wasn't sure who she was trying to impress. Lorena and the rest of the household knew who slept in whose bed. It was no secret. Perhaps she thought he would cut her out of the will if she didn't mend a few fences.

Little did she know that Isabella and Damasco were no longer in his will. He sent Diego into town before the sun rose to fetch Burt Green. A little bleary-eyed, but happy to help, Burt revised Alejandro's will. Everything on Rancho Zarza would be Malcolm's. It would not make up for all the years he'd lost with his son, but it would ensure Damasco and Isabella no longer had any power over Malcolm or Leigh O'Reilly.

He couldn't wait to tell Isabella the news. He had even had Burt send a copy of the will to Houston immediately so there could be no disputing the legality of the document.

Lorena came bustling in with his morning tea and smiled at him. He was sitting in his chair by the window with his ever-present quilt on his damn frail legs. She was dressed in her normal flower print dress and blue apron with her black hair in a long braid down her back.

"*Buenas dias, Patron.* How are you feeling today?"

She knew who had been there already and why. He smiled back at her.

"Much better, Lorena. Much better."

"What are you two grinning about? The *patron* is dying, Lorena. Have you no respect?" Isabella's shrill voice cut through his good mood like a broken glass.

Lorena set the tea on the table and, with one last wink at Alex, exited the room.

"I shall pour." Though strict in enforcing manners in others, Isabella held herself above those standards. Her bluntness was never dulled by any sort of manners. She simply did what she wanted. Today she was dressed in dove gray, apparently anticipating wearing black soon. He could almost hear the wheels of greed grinding in her head.

"I saw Malcolm last night."

The teacup she was handing to him jerked, splashing boiling hot tea on his stockinged feet. The pain was minimal compared to the satisfaction he found looking at her expression. She was shocked. It had been a long time since anything he'd done had shocked her.

"What do you mean, you saw Malcolm? He's dead, Alejandro. He did not suddenly come back to life."

She looked down at the mess on the floor and he stared at the top of her head, the silky black hair caught up in a perfect knot at the base of her skull. She was an incredibly gorgeous woman. Too bad her beauty hid a core of hate and venom.

"Do not pretend with me, Isabella. You know he's not dead. He left here very much alive and came back the same way."

She tried to look surprised, but failed. "I don't know what you're talking about. You must be having hallucinations."

Alex shook his head and waggled a bony finger at her. "You are lying, Isabella. You know he is alive, both you and Damasco. And I know what you've been doing with the Circle O. You want the land for the railroad. Well, you're not going to get it."

Isabella's eyes grew hard. "And how are you going to stop me, *viejo*?"

Calling him old was supposed to hurt, but it didn't. He knew he was old, but he was still kicking.

"I already have. Rancho Zarza will be Malcolm's when I die."

She threw the soiled napkin across the room where it splattered against the closed door.

"You lie."

"No, it's true. And Malcolm will stop you from hurting Leigh or the Circle O anymore."

Her lips curled back into a snarl. "Rancho Zarza will never belong to that *bastardo*. We will have it and the Circle O. You cannot stop us."

In a blur of movement, she grabbed a pillow from the chair beside her and pressed it into his face. He couldn't breathe; he couldn't push her away. He knew he was going to die and everyone would assume it would be from natural causes. As he tried desperately not to black out, to will Lorena to come back in, he knew it was too late. His last thought was that he was so happy to have made peace with his beloved son.

 Q Q Q

Isabella was sweating. It was something she did not do. Ever. But Alejandro had forced her hand. He had made her angry and tried to ruin her plans. But she stopped him. She pressed and pressed the pillow against his hated face until he stopped struggling and still she kept it there. Finally, after what seemed like enough time, she stepped back from him and pulled the pillow away. His head lolled against the chair. She threw the pillow onto the other chair and approached him warily.

She held her hand under his nose for a moment. Nothing. The old bastard was finally dead. For years she had hoped for this. None of the accidents she'd rigged had ever worked right. Somehow God had answered her prayers and given him a wasting sickness. She had done a jig the night after the doctor gave them the news.

He'd forced her hand before his illness could take him, and now she was free at last. She had to find Damasco and put their plans for the raid on Circle O into motion. It had to be tonight before any legal paperwork muddied up the waters.

But first she would take another bath. She hated to spend the rest of the day sweaty. Before her bath though, she should tell everyone the *patron* was dead.

With one last smile at her husband's dead body, she picked up her skirts and ran for the door.

"Lorena! Lorena! Come quickly. The *patron* has collapsed!" she screamed after she opened the door.

CHAPTER EIGHTEEN

Andy was standing in the hallway, wringing his hands when Leigh opened the door. His narrow face was flushed, his blond hair sticking up like he'd been pulling at it.

"Oh, thank Gawd. Miz Leigh, there's a whole bunch of people here. A woman dressed in trousers like you, and five other men that look a lot like her, and then a big sumbitch. Bigger than Herm—I mean Malcolm. Black hair and the coldest, meanest eyes I ever did see. He's a gunslinger. Mark my words. I could see it. I don't know who they are, but they wanted Herm—I mean Malcolm. Miz Leigh, ya gotta—"

"Okay, Andy, okay. Malcolm and I will sort this out. Don't fret."

She patted his shoulder and he shuddered under her hand.

"Thank you, Miz Leigh. I was gettin' powerful worried, what with you and Malcolm in there so long."

He seemed to realize what he said because his cheeks turned an even deeper shade of crimson.

"I mean, oh, hell, why do I even open my mouth?" He sounded so miserable with himself.

"Andy, just shut up and let's go downstairs. Okay?"

He nodded. When she turned, suppressing a grin at Andy's antics, she realized Malcolm was long gone. He must have gone outside without her. Curious.

Leigh walked down the hallway and the stairs as quickly as she could. She opened the door from the kitchen to see Malcolm with his arms wrapped around the woman Andy had mentioned.

Her stomach dropped to her feet and her heart squeezed so tightly, she had trouble getting a breath in. What the hell was that? Jealousy?

She surveyed the circle of men behind the hugging couple. All big men, except the one who was huge. Topped her by more than six inches and probably a hundred pounds. A muscle in his jaw ticked as his gaze fastened completely on Malcolm.

The other men were dusty, but otherwise looked clean and reputable. Each one carried pistols slung low on their hips. Leigh didn't know who the hell they were, although Malcolm obviously did.

ଔ ଔ ଔ

Malcolm hugged Nicky until he felt more in control of himself. To walk outside and see Nicky, Tyler and all her brothers gathered there. For him. Because he needed help. It moved him so much he actually felt like crying.

"You okay?" Nicky whispered to him.

"*Sí*," he whispered right before stepping back. He held both her hands in his own and looked at her. She was still as slender as she ever was, wearing her jeans and blue chambray shirt, her favorite dusty boots and brown flat-crowned hat. Her green eyes were happy, glad to see him.

"How did you get here?"

"The railroad. It stops only about fifty miles north of here."

Mention of the railroad made his gut tighten, but he kept a careful rein on that story until they could talk and plan.

"You look *muy bonita*. Are the babies good?" Nicky had given birth to twins three months earlier when he was at their ranch in Wyoming.

"Yes, they're fine. I left them with Mama and Papa."

He heard a catch in her voice and cocked his head. "You did not want to leave them, no? Then why did you travel all the way to Texas?"

She sighed and looked at him with what he thought was exasperation. "I told you before, you are my adopted brother. My family. When you are in trouble, I am there for you."

Beth Williamson

"And I couldn't keep her home unless I glued her ass to a chair. And even then, she'd probably climb up in a wagon, rip out the seat and drive herself here," came Tyler's voice from behind him.

Malcolm smiled at Nicky although Tyler couldn't see him. "Good to see you too, bounty hunter."

"I notice the accent's completely gone now, eh, *amigo?*"

He turned to look at Nicky's husband. "*Sí,* I am back home. Everyone now knows me by my real name."

Nicky frowned. "And what exactly is your name? Tyler thought he was being funny by not telling me. Much less how he knew to even come here to this little town in Texas. All he said was, it has to do with Hermano."

Malcolm felt like a mule had kicked him this time. *Tyler* had known? *Tyler* had arranged for all of them to be here? For him?

The big man finally smiled, his black mustache spreading out over his lip.

"Sheriff Joe knew my Pa, so I've been in contact with him for weeks. He told me about some trouble at the Circle O, mentioned some strange Mexican that was working for its boss, Leigh. He wired me to say it was coming to a head and that I'd better come if I was coming."

Malcolm had no idea what to say to Tyler. They'd been at odds with each other since they had met more than a year ago in a bandito hideout in west Texas. Malcolm had tried to get the bounty hunter to give up his information using his knife, which hadn't worked. Several months ago, when he'd helped track down and save Nicky's brother Jack and the sweet *chica* Rebecca, Tyler had not even been remotely friendly.

But Tyler had kept track of him, and came when he most needed help. Nicky was right. It was family. Something he hadn't remembered, or forgot on purpose. Family.

One of Nicky's brothers cleared his throat. "Uh, Hermano, do you think you can introduce us?"

"Yes, Malcolm, please do." Leigh's voice came from behind him.

Santa Maria!

He had forgotten about Leigh. He turned and found her standing at the foot of the steps, hands on her hips, hat pulled down low, her mouth a little pinched. Those hazel eyes were guarded and gazed steadily at him. Her hastily donned clothes were still a bit untucked, but he didn't care. She was his.

He walked over to stand at her side and slid his arm around her taut shoulders.

"Malcolm? Is that your real name?" Nicky asked.

"*Sí*, Malcolm Ross. Everyone, this is Leigh O'Reilly, owner of the Circle O, and…my oldest friend. My best friend. Leigh, this is Nicky Calhoun and her husband Tyler."

Tyler nodded and Nicky walked over to pump Leigh's hand. "I am so happy to meet you. Oldest friend? You knew him as a child? I think we need to find some biscuits and coffee."

Leigh's expression softened a bit at Nicky's enthusiastic greeting, but she still regarded everyone with a suspicious eye.

"These are Nicky's brothers. Ray, Trevor, Brett, Ethan and Jack."

Each man in turn tipped his hat to Leigh. All of the Malloy brothers had brownish hair and green or blue eyes. Wide, expressive faces and big builds ran in the family too. Nicky only got the height, however. In fact, Nicky and Leigh were about the same height. He'd never noticed before. Where Nicky was reed slender, though, Leigh was curvy and round.

Just the thought of Leigh's curves had his mind wandering. He had to clamp down on it real fast before it became obvious what he was thinking about.

"Let's make some coffee so we can talk about what's going on," Nicky said as she ushered Leigh back into the house.

Malcolm watched helplessly as Nicky took Leigh inside. His emotions were too raw, too exposed for him to immediately follow. He sensed someone beside him.

"So is she your woman?"

He turned to look at Ray. The oldest of Nicky's brothers, he'd been dealt a few raw deals in his life, took a lot on his shoulders, and was the most serious of all her brothers. His intense green eyes were very much like his sister's. They looked at him steadily from beneath his wide-brimmed black hat.

"*Sí*. She is mine." Malcolm was surprised by the sheer certainty in his voice.

Ray shrugged. "Just asking. She looks like a good, strong, steady woman."

His description was what most people saw. Leigh was all of that and so much more. She was smart, brave and beautiful. The childhood version of that "steady" woman was hiding in there, too. The reckless, fun-loving Leigh who never shied away from having a good time or a challenge. Life had kicked her so many times, she'd put up a wall to keep people out.

Just like he had done. *Dios!* They were two of a kind. Two castles made of stone, standing side by side. Did he dare raise the portcullis and lower the drawbridge?

"Hey, Hermano, I mean Malcolm, can you show us where to put the horses? I think mine's about to start gnawing on Brett's." Jack was always the funny brother, full of mirth and laughter. Malcolm had helped Jack a few months ago with some outlaws who wanted to hurt Rebecca.

He turned and smiled at Jack, whose laughing blue eyes set him apart from his brothers. Brett and Ethan resembled Ray a great deal. They were a bit more serious than Jack, but not quite as serious as Ray. Trevor was another story—the charmer who did his best to get into every woman's drawers with his own brand of honey.

"Just don't stable him near my roan or he will get his own ass bitten," Malcolm warned.

"You still have that mean son of a bitch? He already took a bite of me."

Tyler and the five Malloys followed him to the barn after grabbing their horses' reins. It gave Malcolm a few minutes' reprieve to catch his breath. The last twenty-four hours had been so intense, and the next forty-eight promised to be even worse. The storm clouds were gathering over the Circle O.

ભ ભ ભ

Leigh was nervous, and she was never nervous. Well, apparently there was an exception to that rule. She wouldn't have believed it herself if there weren't butterflies dancing around in her stomach like a stampede. Nervous! This was Malcolm's friend Nicky, the one friend he told her he'd made in fifteen years. The friend who reminded him what family was all about. And she certainly was a woman. A very beautiful woman with thick, curly reddish brown hair shot with gold, gorgeous green eyes, perfect skin, and she was tall. What did Malcolm think when he compared them? A deer versus a buffalo?

She had stirred up the coals in the stove, pumped some fresh water for coffee and put the pot on the stove. That was one thing she could do pretty well. She wondered where Mrs. Hanson was. The biscuits on the stove were cold but edible. Grabbing a plate, she put the six remaining biscuits on it and brought it to the table. As she sat, Nicky framed her face with her hands and leaned on her elbows, staring at Leigh.

"I thought Malcolm sprang from a cactus patch."

Leigh was momentarily at a loss for words. "Um…what?"

Nicky smiled. "He never told me a thing about his past. He's been a very private man the whole time I've known him. Can you tell me a little bit about his growing-up years?"

Leigh hesitated. "Some of it's not pretty enough to tell."

Nicky frowned. "I kind of sensed that from the beginning."

"Well, let's see. His father is Alejandro Zarza who owns the neighboring ranch. His mother is Leslie Ross, who was the cook at Alex's ranch. Malcolm was a bit of a surprise, but very much loved by Leslie. She was a wonderful mother for him to have growing up."

Nicky looked surprised. "His mother is *Scottish?*"

Leigh laughed and nodded. "Yup. And from the hills of Scotland, too. Her brogue was thicker than coffee on a cattle drive."

Nicky laughed and slapped the table with her hand. "Damn. I never would have guessed…so his father is Spanish?"

She nodded. "One of the old Spanish hacienda owners who helped Texas during the war with Mexico. They've been loyal citizens for two generations now."

"What was his favorite thing to do growing up?"

Leigh thought back to when they were children and couldn't suppress the grin. "Play pretend."

That got Nicky snorting and slapping her thigh. In a minute, tears were going to roll from her eyes.

"Oh my God, that's too funny. I can't imagine it."

"Oh, it's true. We'd get the leftover clothes from the household and sneak it to our tree house in the orchard. We'd play knights or soldiers or pretend we were Indians."

Nicky's smile was pure satisfaction. "I'm gonna tuck that little bit of information away and save it for a rainy day."

Leigh didn't want to know why or how Nicky was going to use it.

"Has he mentioned me to you?" Nicky asked.

Leigh's stomach cramped up again. "Yes, he told me about you. He said you were the reason he came back home."

She couldn't help it, her voice caught on the last two words and she had the crazy notion to cry again. To remember that he had not come home for her, to find her, see her, was enough to rip the scab off a wound and let it bleed again.

Nicky put her hand on hers. "Leigh, Malcolm loves you. I could see it in his eyes. He may have lost his way for a while, but he found it again, right?"

Leigh nodded, not particularly reassured. "But along the way, he met you. And, you'll pardon me, but compared to you, I'm not exactly a gold mine."

Surprise shone in Nicky's eyes. "You can't think that he compared you to me."

Leigh's silence was her answer.

"He never compared *you* to *me*. Leigh, he compared *me* to *you*." The earnestness in Nicky's expression was unmistakable.

Leigh wanted so badly to believe Nicky she actually felt her eyes prick with tears, again. "I don't know if I believe it."

Nicky slapped her forehead with one hand. "It's amazing to me that the human race has even made a new generation based on the stupidity of ours."

She took Leigh's hands in her own and locked their gazes. "The expression on Herm—I mean Malcolm's face, it's going to take me a bit to get used to that, when he introduced you. There was *joy* and *love*. Two things I have never seen on him in the four years I've known him. He was proud to introduce you. He...he could barely keep his eyes off you to look at us."

The lantern of hope, long since snuffed out, flared to life in Leigh's heart. Could it be true? Could Malcolm really love her?

The tin coffee pot top rattled as the water began boiling. She stood to get the coffee and catch her breath. The old Leigh would have run out the door and found some chore to hide behind. The new Leigh was ready to face the possibility she could get her heart broken, or find the reward of a lifetime.

ᘯ ᘯ ᘯ

There wasn't enough room for all of them in the house, so they ate dinner in the bunkhouse with the hands. Old Moses strutted around like the cock of the walk when the Malloys politely complimented him on his beef stew. Andy Parker kept his distance from Tyler and eyed the rest of them from beneath the brim of his hat, poised to run as soon as any of them tried anything.

Malcolm sat beside Leigh, while Tyler and Nicky sat across from them. Malcolm could hardly keep from touching Leigh. Just the heat from her leg was enough to make the hairs on his leg stand at attention. Not to mention other parts of his body. *Dios!* Even his damn nipples were erect.

Leigh was recounting the last two years' worth of trouble on the Circle O. Each time Malcolm heard it, he grew angrier. When he'd heard how many times Leigh had been shot at, which he *didn't* know about, he grew absolutely furious.

"You did not tell me about someone shooting at you," he said through clenched teeth.

She turned to look at him, one eyebrow raised. "I didn't think I owed you a day-by-day explanation of my life for the last fifteen years. Were you going to do the same for me?"

Her barb hit home. He hadn't told her anything really, but the thought that someone had tried to blatantly blow her head off her body was painful. Loving someone as hardheaded, stubborn and secretive as he was going to make her life more interesting, more challenging and certainly never boring.

Was that what he was concerned about? Being bored with life? Or was it sharing every day with the same person? Something he never, in his wildest imagining, thought would happen. Not for a bastard like him. A dark man who lived in the darker shadows of life.

"Malcolm!"

Leigh shouting his name was enough to stop his meanderings. But then he realized she wasn't calling him, she was calling little Malcolm.

She scrambled off the bench and went to the door of the bunkhouse to greet the boy. He was dressed the same as when he'd first met him, down to the dirty feet and no shoes. His bright eyes devoured all the people seated around the bunkhouse. When he got to Tyler, Malcolm saw some apprehension flicker, but the boy looked at everyone in turn. Weighing them, making his own judgments. Clearly a smart boy.

Leigh reached his side and put her arm around his shoulder.

"What are you doing here?"

"I come to see him," the boy answered, pointing one grubby finger at Malcolm.

Leigh turned surprised eyes on him. Her surprise became something else entirely when she saw the look in his eye.

"*Vaya aqui, hijo,*" he called to the boy.

He screwed up his face and said, "I told you I don't know no Spanish." Although he did approach Malcolm, pulling a piece of paper out of his pocket.

"Diego gave me this. And told me to take one of the horses. I didn't like it too much. Don't want to be no horse thief or nothing." The boy looked affronted to be even thinking such a thing.

Malcolm took the paper and unfolded it. One glance at Leigh's face told him he'd better read it out loud.

"I have sent Malcolm as you asked. They are coming tonight after the moon sets. I will try to help you if I can. Protect Leigh for us," he read. When the last line of the letter came into focus, the paper fell from his hands and fluttered to the ground.

His vision began to gray around the edges as his stomach danced and jigged, trying to expel his dinner with a vengeance.

Leigh ran to his side and bent to pick up the paper. He vaguely noted she actually gasped when she read it.

"Oh, Malcolm, I'm so sorry."

She sat beside him on the bench and wrapped her arms around him. The others in the room quickly disappeared. He heard little Malcolm protesting loudly as Nicky practically shoved him out the door. Then they were alone.

And he finally took a breath. Which was more like a sob. His papa was dead. After so long he'd made peace with him, only to have him snatched away. There was so much more he had wanted to say, so much more he had wanted to hear.

A surge of red hot rage poured through him, displacing the shock and grief.

"Why the hell did I come back here?" he snarled. "To find my family? Hah! What's left of it has already tried to kill me. And now this. What am I still doing here? I hate this place."

He grabbed the end of the table and twisted it, spilling all the plates, cups, forks and knives to the floor with a loud clatter of tin.

It wasn't enough. He started upturning the benches, the chairs, then the beds, throwing everything in front of him. It wasn't enough. He wanted to hurt something. To hurt someone. Goddammit! It wasn't enough.

His hands clenched into fists, he turned and found someone.

CHAPTER NINETEEN

Leigh should have been frightened by the hatred in Malcolm's black eyes. They glittered with anger so bright, she was surprised she hadn't caught on fire yet. He looked like he wanted to kill someone and she was in the direct line of his gaze. His hands clenched and unclenched and he was breathing hard. His chest heaved with each breath. He resembled a bull getting ready to charge.

And when he did, he moved so fast she barely had time between blinks and she was in his grasp. Gripping her shoulders painfully and staring in her eyes.

What she saw in those black orbs was all of the pain, the immense mountain of agony, that lived inside this man. The anger was a shield; the little boy who had suffered so much all his life was hiding behind it. So much pain. An ocean full of it.

Leigh didn't fight him off. She didn't protest. She just looked into his eyes and willed him to see she wasn't trying to hurt him. She was trying to help him. By loving him. By not causing him any more pain through rejection, humiliation and neglect.

"Little Leigh?" His voice sounded unsure and wavery, like he'd just woken up from a long nap and was disoriented.

"I'm here. I was always here. And I will always be here."

The murderous tension in his shoulders began to ease and the pressure on her arms did the same. The look of hatred and venom in his eyes was replaced with what she expected. Mind-numbing, soul-stealing grief.

"I love you, Mal. I never stopped."

He released her arms and pulled Leigh to him tightly. She held on, crooning comforting nonsense to him.

"It's okay. I loved Alex, too. We can cry like babies together."

For a long while, they stood there, hanging on to each other, absorbing the strength from each other. Grieving for a man they had both loved.

ೞ ೞ ೞ

When Malcolm and Leigh walked outside the bunkhouse, the group gathered around the door was grim-faced and determined. Time was short—they had less than twelve hours to get ready. The battle was about to begin.

Tyler was the first to speak. "This is your show. Do you have a plan?"

He looked back and forth between Malcolm and Leigh like he couldn't decide who to ask or who would answer.

Leigh immediately liked the dangerous-looking man. She already liked his wife. Nicky's gaze never left hers.

"I do. I'll try to lay it out for you. And I have to say," she grabbed Malcolm's hand and threaded her fingers through his, "thank you to the Malloys and Calhouns for coming and helping me and the Circle O. I know you came because of Malcolm, because he's family, but he's my family, too. So, I guess that means you are my brothers and sister."

Malcolm squeezed her hand. "*Sí, gracias* to *Roja* and her band of able brothers. And to the bounty hunter I now call *mi amigo*."

Tyler inclined his head to Malcolm and Leigh. His cold blue eyes never changed expression, but she could tell he was pleased by their words. Especially Malcolm's.

"Together there are eighteen of us to cover ten thousand acres and about seven hundred and fifty head of cattle. On a good day that would be impossible. So what we need to do is move the cattle to a place we can guard them and us. There is a valley up in the northwest corner that will fit all of them. There's only one way in and one way out."

She paused to take a deep breath, grateful to see heads nodding as she laid out her plan.

"They're also going to go for the house and the crew. We'll need to split up. Twelve with the cattle and six here."

She pointed at her drovers. "The nine of you go with three of the Malloys and start rounding up the cattle. Most of them are in the west pasture."

They all nodded and turned to head for the barn. The Malloy brothers had a brief conference and Brett, Trevor and Ethan followed the drovers.

"Make sure you bring supplies for at least two or three days. We'll send a rider when it's over."

"And plenty of ammunition," Malcolm added.

The six left were Leigh, Malcolm, Nicky, Tyler, Jack and Ray.

"Hey, how come you didn't count me?"

Leigh turned to look at little Malcolm. He wore a mutinous expression.

"You've got the most important job, *hijo*."

Little Malcolm turned his distrustful eyes on Malcolm. "Don't call me son. I told you I don't speak no Spanish."

She fought hard not to grin, as did all the other adults. Except Malcolm. He squatted down to look the boy in the eye.

"Your job is to go back to Rancho Zarza and tell Diego we are ready. You will do this for Leigh, no?

The boy's chest puffed up with pride as he squared his shoulders. "Yup, I can do that. Leigh is my friend. I would do anythin' for her."

"*Bueno*. Leigh is my friend too. I would not ask someone to help her who did not love her. *Comprende?*"

The boy nodded. "Yeah, I got it."

Malcolm squeezed his shoulder. "*Sí*, I think you do."

When Malcolm rose to his full height, Leigh barely resisted the urge to run over and plant one on his lips. Lord, she loved that man.

"What do you want us to do?" Nicky asked.

"We can start by boarding up the windows and leaving rifle holes to shoot those varmints when they come calling. Andy and I stacked the boards in the back of the barn a few days ago," Leigh said.

She and Nicky headed for the barn, followed by Ray and Jack.

"I gotta ride back now?" little Malcolm asked in a whine.

"No, you can stay a little while, but you must be back home before dark," Malcolm said firmly.

The boy grumbled under his breath and followed the rest of them to the barn with one last baleful look at Malcolm.

ཙ ཙ ཙ

Tyler was staring at Malcolm. Malcolm stared right back.

"Were you going to paint my picture?" Malcolm asked.

Tyler raised one eyebrow.

"You're staring, gringo," Malcolm snapped.

One corner of Tyler's mouth lifted. "You're not the same man who left my ranch three months ago. You're looking at Leigh like she's a prize-winning peach pie, and at that boy like you want to hug him, for Chrissake. Hermano seems to be gone."

Was it true? Had he finally and completely emerged from the shadows he'd been living in for so long?

He definitely loved Leigh. And he wanted to love little Malcolm. It didn't seem his own father did. A life with them, here on the Circle O, provided the boy's mother came to live here, too. It was almost too much to wish for.

"Nothing to say?"

For the first time he could remember, he smiled at Tyler—a genuine smile without his usual sarcasm or cynicism. "No, I was thinking I agreed with you."

He was glad to see a bit of surprise on the bounty hunter's face.

"Maybe we will have a miracle today."

Malcolm grimaced as he thought about what faced them. "We're going to need one."

"How many men will he bring?"

Malcolm shrugged. "Fifty, perhaps sixty. He has a small army at Rancho Zarza, but some of them are, I mean, were loyal to Alejandro." His voice broke a bit on his father's name, but he swallowed and continued. "I also have a man on the inside. He's the one who sent the boy."

Tyler nodded. "Good. Can we count on your friend to help?"

"He will try. I'm sure Diego will ride with them. He will do what he can to stop them."

Eighteen against fifty were shitty odds, but it's all they had. Perhaps the cattle would survive, but the remaining six people at the Circle O were not likely to see the dawn.

ભ ભ ભ

As Leigh nailed the last board into place on the window upstairs in her bedroom, she glanced longingly at the bed and wished for one last time with Malcolm. She wanted to believe they would survive the night, but doubts kept creeping in like unwanted visitors, crowding her brain and refusing to leave.

"Done?" came Nicky's voice. Leigh turned to look at the other woman. Nicky stood in the doorway with a hammer in hand.

"That was the last one. Little Malcolm is downstairs counting the shells and bullets, dividing them into equal piles. Smart little sucker. Reminds me a bit of my Noah."

Nicky had talked at length about her adopted fifteen-year-old son, Noah, and her twins who were only three months old. Leigh's stomach got jittery thinking about being a mother, but her heart longingly listened to the pride and love in Nicky's voice.

"He's a good boy. No credit to his father though," Leigh said, although it was an understatement.

"Who's his father?"

Leigh grimaced. "Damasco. Malcolm seems to think he created the boy just to taunt him. His mother is the cook."

Nicky's green eyes hardened. "If he did that, then he deserves whatever he gets when he arrives. Bastard. What kind of sick mind would do that to a child?"

Leigh walked toward Nicky, scooping up the extra nail bucket and boards from the floor.

"Good question. I think it's more his mother's doing. Isabella is a grade-A bitch. Colder than a well digger's ass on a January morning."

Nicky snorted with laughter. "You and I are going to be good friends, I can tell."

For as long as we're alive.

Leigh didn't voice the traitorous thought, but she couldn't help thinking it. She would do her best to make sure her new friend survived to return to her babies and adopted son. Family was more important than anything. She knew that now. It didn't matter if she survived because little Malcolm had his mother to raise him. But a family needed to stay together, to love and laugh, to just live.

CB CB CB

Isabella reviewed the plans with Damasco. She made him repeat them over and over until she was sure he would not forget. She loved her son more than anything, but he was not the sharpest tack in the box. This had to be perfect. It had to look like outlaws attacked the Circle O and the Rancho Zarza hands rode to help. A few sacrifices were necessary, like that sneaky Diego, but the end result was what was important.

As long as Leigh O'Reilly and that *bastardo* Malcolm were dead, all of the land, and all the money that came with it, would be theirs. Tonight would be their crowning glory. Tomorrow would be the coronation ball.

CHAPTER TWENTY

Little Malcolm came running up the stairs.

"Miz Leigh, there's some crazy woman downstairs yelling at me. She messed up my count and grabbed me by my collar and shook me like a dog."

Leigh had an idea of who it was. Mrs. Hanson. That crotchety old woman could scare the fleas off a dog. Leigh followed the boy back down the stairs, knowing this was probably going to be the last time she fought with Mrs. Hanson. Once she put her hands on the boy, she had sealed her fate in Leigh's mind.

"I cain't believe that filthy boy was counting bullets in my kitchen. In all my born days, I never saw such a thing."

Mrs. Hanson's voice was like nails on slate. When Leigh rounded the corner, she was surprised, yet relieved, to see the older woman had her bags packed.

"There you are," she shouted when she spotted Leigh. "That little hooligan was in here with bullets all over the table. I know him. He's that dirty stable boy from Rancho Zarza. What is he—"

"Take your bag and get the hell off my land, lady."

Mrs. Hanson's mouth gaped open, the folds in her chin waggling along with her head.

"How dare you?"

Leigh set down the boards and started swinging the bucket of nails. "Oh, I dare a lot. You have about five seconds to do what I told you to do."

"I've got a better job. I'm going to replace that awful Lorena at Rancho Zarza. You just watch me."

"Four seconds." She swung the pail harder, her gaze never leaving Mrs. Hanson's eyes.

"You just try and get along without me."

"Three."

She scrambled to grab her bag, but it was too heavy and she dropped it. A tinkling crash inside the bag echoed across the room. Leigh reached for the bag. Mrs. Hanson made a snatch for it at the same time but Leigh moved faster.

"Two."

"Hey, that's mine. Give it back."

Leigh took the bag and threw it out the open door. It landed on the ground with a dusty thud, the tinkling sound following. No doubt the old witch had stolen half of the silver in the house. Leigh didn't care. She just wanted her gone.

"Why, you!"

Mrs. Hanson raised her arm with her reticule, intending on hitting Leigh with it. A strong brown hand stopped her.

"Get out, *bruja*. Before you make me regret letting you live."

Mrs. Hanson harrumphed loudly then stomped out the door, down the stairs to her bag. She half-carried, half-dragged it to a waiting curricle parked near the house. A young man hopped down, picked up the bag, heaved it in the back, and jumped into the driver's seat. With one last venomous look, she climbed into the curricle. In a moment, they were off, headed in the direction of town.

"Do you think she's really going to replace Lorena?" came little Malcolm's voice. "'Cause I really like her. Maybe she could come here? With my mama?"

"Maybe, Malcolm. We'll have to see what happens, okay?

Leigh's response was something he'd apparently heard before.

"Why do grown-ups always say that? It don't make no sense."

He sat himself at the kitchen table and crossed his arms, looking for a moment exactly like the man for whom he was named. Nicky plopped in the chair across from him and started counting the bullets.

"Do you think she was telling the truth? About Lorena?" Leigh whispered to Malcolm.

His hot breath fanned across her cheek. "I paid the driver twenty dollars to drive her all the way to Houston. She won't be getting to Rancho Zarza anytime soon."

Leigh almost laughed. "Thank you. I would hate to think that woman could hurt Lorena."

"I love Lorena too. I would never let anyone harm her."

She felt a bit better, but also wondered how she had let a vicious woman like Mrs. Hanson stay beneath her roof for so long. More than likely another spy for the Zarzas. Her own self-respect was flagging.

"Malcolm, you need to go home now. It will be dark in a couple of hours. Can you saddle your horse yourself?"

He snorted and rolled his eyes. "I cain't believe you'd ask me that, Miz Leigh. How many times have I saddled your horse?"

The boy was right. Her brains were like overcooked eggs right now.

"Sorry, you're right. I guess I was thinking like a girl for a minute."

He nodded, obviously agreeing with her assessment. "Yup, I see that happen now and then to you. Luckily it don't happen too much."

"Home. Now."

He stood slowly, dragging his feet, reluctant to leave.

"I want to make sure you have time to make it back to Rancho Zarza, Malcolm. And you need to deliver the message to Diego for me. You said you would, remember?"

"I will. I said I will. Okay, I'll go. But I can come back right? I like it here."

His young face was so hopeful, she couldn't tell him they might not be here after tonight. It tore at her that the boy had so little waiting for him, aside from his overworked mother. She wanted to tell him he could come over any time he wanted. Instead, she took the coward's way out again.

"We'll see. Now it is time for you to go. *Andale, chico.*"

"I'm going. And I told you and him enough times, I don't speak no Spanish. And don't call me boy."

To her utter shock, he gave her a quick hug then banged out the back door, headed for the barn at a dead run.

She stared after him, completely poleaxed by little Malcolm's affection. It was going to be so hard for her to get used to being touched all the time. The boy held a firm place in her heart.

"Will he be okay?"

"Diego will make sure he's okay. Don't worry, *amante*. That boy has lived through a lot in his life. He's a tough little man."

Leigh was surprised to realize she was worried about the boy. That she missed him already. Having a family, even one that wasn't related to you, was definitely going to take some getting used to.

"Are the windows boarded?" Malcolm asked as his hand rested on the small of her back.

"Yes, Nicky and I finished."

"Then perhaps you can put the nail bucket down?"

Sheepishly, she grinned and set the bucket down outside the door.

"*Bueno*." Malcolm drew her into his arms and hugged her tightly.

"The others are scouting around to make sure no one is watching the house." Leigh spoke into his shoulder, breathing his scent into her body.

"Good idea."

She started to melt in his arms, forgetting everyone and everything. It was an indescribable feeling, being in love. Like warm sunshine on your face after a long, cold, rainy spell. His big hands rubbed circles on her spine.

Nicky cleared her throat. "I, ah, think I need to find Tyler."

Malcolm and Leigh didn't acknowledge her exit. They continued to touch and caress as if no one else in the world existed.

"Mmmm…you feel so good," Leigh said.

"So do you."

The unmistakable feel of him growing hard and pressing into her softness was enough to drive her temperature up five degrees.

"*Amante*." His whispered endearment tickled across her ear, raising goose bumps and her nipples. "I need you."

"Yes."

They headed for the door at the same time, hands entwined like lovers going for a walk on a Sunday afternoon.

ଦ୍ୱ ଦ୍ୱ ଦ୍ୱ

There was so little time. The sun was setting and night was crawling in like a snake on its belly.

She needed him. She needed to feel life, to feel alive, to know for this bit of time in her life she loved him and had someone to call her own.

They reached her bedroom in record time. She started pulling at his clothes, yanking and nearly tearing his shirt off. She needed to feel his skin against hers, to have him buried deep inside her. He stopped her by grabbing her hands.

"Easy, *amante*," he whispered against her temple.

"I can't. I need you. Please, Malcolm, please." She was surprised to hear her own voice pleading with him. She never pleaded, but her need was so great it controlled her.

"I know, I know. I need you too," he said as he held her. "This must be…perfect for us. *Comprende?* I want it to be a memory to hold."

Oh, yes, she understood. It might be the last time for them together. The night was bringing not only darkness, but death and blood. Someone was going to die, and it could be either one of them. Now was a time to savor.

Leigh pushed aside the frantic clawing need for him and concentrated on savoring this time together. With her pulse beating a strong rhythm, she pressed herself against him and reveled in the feel of his hardness touching her softness. He growled from deep in his throat, sending a shiver through her. His hands slid down and kneaded her ass, pulling her close enough to rub his cock on her mons. Combined with her own body's movements, it was enough to heat her blood to a near boil. Her nipples scraped against her clothes, eager to be touched and licked.

"I think we've got too many clothes on."

Malcolm chuckled hoarsely and let go of her. "Let me."

He slid off her glasses and set them on the dresser. Button by button, he slowly opened her shirt. By the time he popped the last button, Leigh was panting. He bared one shoulder, then kissed and licked the exposed skin. He repeated it with the other shoulder. As he pulled her shirt down her arms, he bit each nipple lightly through her chemise. A shudder of desire wracked her body.

"Did you like that?"

"Mmmm…yes," she responded. "More. Bite them."

"My wolf. You like teeth, eh?"

He threw her shirt on the chair. As he straightened back up, he gave one more quick bite to each nipple. His eyes glittered like black diamonds. The leashed passion in their depths was enough to set her knees knocking. He held back so much.

He peeled her chemise up inch by inch, alternately licking, kissing and biting the flesh as it came into view. When he got to her breasts, the chemise was up around her face and her arms were raised. She was effectively trapped as he feasted on her. And, oh sweet Jesus, he was a starving man.

His tongue circled each nipple, then he gave it a bite. He kissed every square inch of one breast followed by the other. His hot lips and wet tongue stroked and licked until she thought she'd go mad from not being able to touch him. She tried to free her arms, but he held her in place. When he closed his mouth over one nipple, she almost screamed. He pulled and tugged with his mouth, deeper and deeper, swirling the nipple with his tongue. Leigh moaned and struggled again to get free. She needed to touch him.

He let the nipple loose with an audible pop. When he sucked in the other nipple, the intense tugs and talented tongue drove her over the edge. Unbelievably, Leigh felt herself heading toward an orgasm. Before he even touched her pussy. She couldn't see, she couldn't touch. All she could do was feel.

"Oh, God, Malcolm. Please…" Now she was begging. Hell, she didn't care.

He pushed his hand down her pants and cupped her pussy. When he spread the lips with his thumb and fingers, she shook with anticipation of his touch. When his thumb flicked her once, twice, three times on her clit, she came like a tornado in June. Hard and fast.

While she tried to stay upright, Malcolm pulled the chemise the rest of the way off, then he kissed her. Fierce and deep. She wrapped her arms around his neck and hung on. Her bare nipples, so incredibly aroused, rubbed on his shirt, inciting them once more. His tongue danced with and caressed hers until she knew the depths of his mouth better than her own.

With one last bite on her lip, he pulled back and smiled at her.

"That was the first time."

"First time?"

"The first time you will come. Now comes number two. Are you ready?"

She wasn't sure if she was ready but there wasn't anything in the world that would stop her. Malcolm walked her backwards to the bed, kissing her, stroking her hot skin. He knelt in front of her and unbuttoned her jeans, kissing and biting her belly as he shimmied the fabric down. Her throbbing pussy ached for his touch. She was dressed only in a pair of cotton drawers, a pair of *wet* cotton drawers.

"Hurry up, Mal. I need you," she pleaded. She'd never felt such an aching want.

He looked up at her and his expression was, as usual, unreadable.

"You take my breath away, *amante.*"

Before she could respond, he pushed her drawers down. When she was finally naked, he kissed all around her pussy without touching where it pulsed and burned. Now she was completely naked and he was completely clothed. It was enough to make her even wetter.

Oh God, oh God.

"Please," she heard herself gasp.

He kissed his way back up her legs and again circled her aching mound without touching it.

"Please."

"Do you want me to lick you? To kiss you?" He nipped at her trembling inner thigh. "To bite you?"

"Malcolm. Please. If you don't touch me soon I'm going to shoot you."

"My wolf…" she thought she heard him say as he eased her thighs open. He started with one long lick from bottom to the top. She almost stopped breathing. "Mmmm…you taste like honey."

He reached up and spread her lips. His tongue snaked out and licked her clit over and over while his thumbs slowly sank in and out of her pussy. Then he pulled her clit into his mouth and started sucking it as he had her nipples. She rocked on her feet, nearly falling, her legs like jelly. His strong hands held her up as his tongue plundered her hot box.

"Oh, God, Malcolm!" She tried not to scream but that was impossible. The orgasm started in her toes and her head, traveling down and up her body to converge in her pussy. He sucked harder and fucked her with his thumbs as she pulsed with incredible pleasure.

She felt the prick of tears in her eyes. Every experience with Malcolm was as amazing as the last and this as no exception. She never knew how much pleasure a person could give or receive with someone they loved. Until now. Until Malcolm. With one last lick, he stood and cupped her face with his big hands.

"You are so beautiful."

He kissed her and she tasted the muskiness of her pleasure. The sensation was too much for her knees because they let loose. As she sank toward the bed, he caught her and laid her down gently. Letting her mouth go, he licked each puckered nipple again. Her body responded with a shiver of desire that traveled from her head to her toes.

"That was the second time. Now comes number three. Are you ready?"

Leigh wasn't sure she would be conscious for the third time, but she was ready. She scooted back on the bed to watch him undress.

"Show me," she commanded.

Malcolm was a beautiful man. A bronzed god with black hair and black eyes. As he removed his shirt, she marveled again at the fact he was here now with her. With *her*. Leigh Wynne O'Reilly. When he removed his trousers and his cock sprang free, her hunger for him ran rampant anew. Lord have mercy. He looked bigger every time she saw him.

He crawled on the bed like a big cat, a panther circling her. She felt a chill of goose bumps march up her spine at the predatory look in his eye.

"*Amante*. Are you ready?"

"Oh, yes. Bring it to me, Mal."

He rubbed and caressed her body with his own. From his hard, hair-covered chest to his enormous erection, he traveled up her body slowly. By the time he got to her lips, she was just as ready and panting for him as she had been before her first two orgasms.

He stared into her eyes and she saw something in them she hadn't seen before. Not just passion and desire, but something that almost looked like love.

When he spread her legs and slid into her, her body took control. Her mind was gone. He was so big, so perfect, so *right*. He trembled as he held his position for a minute. She clutched his shoulders as he filled her.

"Malcolm?"

"Momentito."

He squeezed his eyes shut and seemed to force himself back under control. Then he started moving in and out using deep, long strokes, pulling completely out of her every time before plunging back in. Her hungry pussy wanted more. It was incredible, it was bliss, it was…heaven.

Sweat beaded on his upper lip and forehead as his pace increased. The sounds, the scents of their lovemaking, filled the room. She spread her legs wider, making him go even deeper.

"All of you. I need all of you," she commanded.

And so he gave it. Stroke after stroke. Again and again. Faster and faster. So close. Oh, Jesus, so close again.

"Malcolm!"

"Sí, mi vida, mi corazon. Te amo. Te amo."

My life, my heart. I love you. I love you.

He sat up on his knees and shoved a pillow beneath her ass. Completely exposed, Leigh waited for Malcolm to complete their circle. He grabbed her hips and plunged in so deep, she actually saw his soul.

She came with a thunderous sound that stole her voice and her breath. Wave after wave crashed down on her as she pulsed and clenched around him. Over the roaring in her ears, she vaguely heard him call her name as he pumped into her. This time, she did see stars. She saw Leigh and Malcolm—two souls merging into one.

৩ ৩ ৩

Malcolm felt the wall around his heart give way. There was no going back now. Leigh was in his life to stay and he'd told her he loved her. Twice.

He was shaking like a baby. *Dios mio!* He had never, ever had an experience like that. It was enough to kick him out of the shadows into the sunlight. He knew now he would never be happy without her.

He eased himself out of her and lay down on the sheets. He was covered in sticky sweat and felt like he'd run to the Gulf and back. The hairs on his legs were wet and there wasn't even a hint of a breeze to cool him off. Leigh was as warm as a brick oven next to him. She still breathed a bit heavily, but she hadn't moved an inch.

"*Amante?*"

She didn't answer. He hauled himself up on one elbow to peer down at her. She stared straight up at the ceiling, her hazel eyes focused on the cracks. Her fists clenched at her sides and her skin was covered in a sheen of sweat.

"Leigh?"

That's when he saw the tear. One solitary tear trickling out of her eye. Before this week, he had never, *ever* seen Leigh cry, and here it was again. Even when she was a little girl, she'd get hurt, then get mad. There were never any tears. Until now. The second time in as many weeks.

"Are you all right?"

With a wail he was sure they probably heard at Rancho Zarza, she launched herself at him and hung on for dear life. Her fists dug into his back as she held him so tightly, he heard his spine creak.

Malcolm cupped the back of her head, letting her hang on. Her heart thudded against his chest. He felt her nipples, still rock hard, pushing against him. He didn't dare move. Whatever Leigh was going through was enough to squeeze tears from her normally dry eyes. Malcolm was determined to hang on and help her through it. He didn't even want to think about being the cause of it. His arm anchored her to him as he tried to figure out what else to do.

"*Amante*, please tell me."

She took a deep, shuddering breath and pushed her nose into his neck. When she spoke, her voice was wavery and even huskier than usual.

"You told me you loved me."

"*Sí.*"

"No…no one has ever told me that before."

Malcolm forgot how lucky he was. His mother had told him every day when he woke up in the morning. She had told him when she kissed him goodnight every night. She had hugged him and kissed him and never let him forget he was loved.

Leigh had never had that. Her father practically ignored her except to make a comment about how he wished he'd had a son. She never knew her mother. All she ever had was her "family" at Rancho Zarza. It was hard to imagine growing up without someone loving you. He had always loved her, now he was *in* love with her. And it had taken him thirty years to say it.

"I love you, I love you, *te amo, mi corazón.* I will tell you every morning and every night."

He kissed her shoulder and neck until she let him loose and he was able to start kissing her in earnest. And kiss her he did. A long, slow kiss with dueling tongues and a lot of moaning. When he came up for air, she stared at him with her heart in her eyes.

"Malcolm, I think I was born loving you. I never stopped. All those years you were gone, you were still in my heart. I will die loving you. Only you."

He hadn't realized the depth of her love before. He should have known. Leigh never did anything halfway. She was an all or nothing kind of girl.

"Will you leave again?"

The question popped out of her mouth like a bullet and slammed into him. He jerked and she immediately scooted out of his arms. She jumped out of bed and glared down at him with her hands on her hips, a challenge in her eyes.

"Will you leave again?"

He opened his mouth to answer, but didn't. Was he ready to stay with her forever? To never leave her? To wake up in her arms every day?

"I guess that's my answer."

She picked up her clothes and stalked across the room to her washstand. He hadn't moved from the bed or answered her. She nearly dropped the pitcher of water trying to pour it into the basin, sloshing half the water on the floor. He saw her hands tremble.

"Shit!"

He hopped out of bed and crossed to her in two strides.

"Don't you touch me now, Malcolm. I'll get my goddamn gun and shoot you."

He grabbed her arms as she started to run and forced her up against the wall. He tried to kiss her, but she turned her head.

"Let me go."

When her knee headed for his balls, he moved his leg so she got him in the thigh instead, leaving him with a painful charley horse.

"Let me go."

"Never, *amante*. I will never let you go. I will never leave you."

She bucked against him, and unwillingly his cock began to grow again as her curves slammed into him.

"I love you. I won't leave you. Do you hear me?"

She stopped fighting him and looked at him in surprise, the anger and hurt fading from her eyes.

"What?"

He smiled and kissed her lightly on the lips.

"No, I won't leave again. I will always be yours."

"Really?"

He let her arms loose and stepped back a half-step. He spread his arms wide.

"I am all yours, *amante*. For as long as you want me."

This time when she launched herself at him, he was ready. His arms closed around her tight as hers did on him.

"Oh, God, Malcolm, I love you."

Malcolm's response was cut off by loud banging on the bedroom door.

"Get your asses out here. The sun's gone down and we need to take up position." Tyler's voice came through the door.

Leigh let go of Malcolm enough to look him in the eye. "Is he always this friendly?"

"And put some clothes on first."

They heard him stomping away.

Malcolm smiled. "No, he's usually meaner."

She laughed and hugged him again. When she pulled back, her expression was more serious. "It's time."

"Yes, it is time. We need to be done with Damasco tonight so we can have tomorrow."

CHAPTER TWENTY-ONE

When Leigh and Malcolm made it downstairs ten minutes later, everyone was gathered in the kitchen. Ray stood in the corner, big arms crossed, silent. Jack sat at the table with Nicky. They were like two peas in a pod with their expressions and mannerisms as they discussed the merits of the Colt pistol versus the Winchester repeating rifle. Tyler stood near the door, ready, it seemed, for anything.

Leigh wasn't sure what to make of Malcolm's friends, but they looked like they knew their way around guns.

"I wanted to say thank you again for being here. This isn't your fight. You don't even know me. I will never forget this and if you ever need anything from me, you only need to ask."

Malcolm reached out and squeezed her hand.

Nicky smiled. "Nothing to it, Leigh. You're family now."

You're family now.

Nicky's response was enough to bring back the damn tear to her eye. She'd never really had a family. Now here they were, announcing to all and sundry that she was a part of the family.

"What's the plan, boss?" Jack asked her.

She squared her shoulders and took hold of her rampant girlie side. "I was thinking me and Nicky here in the house. I'll take the front, she can watch the back. Jack and Ray in the barn, one in the loft, one by the back. Tyler and Malcolm in the bunkhouse at either end. Anybody sees anything, hoot like an owl three times in a row, one hoot response."

Murmurs of agreement met her plan.

Nicky looked up at her husband. "Anything you want to add, bounty hunter?"

When he smiled at her, Leigh saw why Nicky loved him. He was simply gorgeous and the love shining from his ice-blue eyes was clear for all to see.

"No, magpie, I think she's got it all planned out."

Nicky stood and handed pouches made from potato sacks with bullets and shells to each of them.

"Everyone has a Colt and a rifle. This is all we have. Make every shot count because we don't know how many will be coming."

Jack had lunch buckets made up. "We cut up the bread, sliced some ham and put some water in jars. Didn't know how long this would last."

He handed a bucket to Tyler and Malcolm, one to Ray and one to Nicky.

"Thanks, Jack. I didn't even think about food and water." Leigh hated to admit she was forgetting things.

"No problem." He smiled.

"Okay, then, we should split up. Remember the signal for help is two shots fired close together," Tyler said.

Nicky went to her husband, wrapping her arms around his neck in a natural movement that spoke of deep closeness. His arms circled her and they whispered softly.

Jack looked at Ray and batted his lashes. "Since Becky's not here, will you give me a hug, big brother?"

"Go hump a tree, Jack," Ray responded.

Jack laughed and stood. "Shall we go then?"

Ray grunted and the two of them headed for the door.

"Be careful," Leigh said.

Jack saluted her with a blue-eyed twinkle and Ray nodded. How could two totally different people be brothers?

Malcolm's hands landed on her shoulders and he pushed his cheek against her hair.

"*Amante. Cuidado, por favor.* I do not want to lose the woman I just promised to be with forever."

"I'll be careful. But you have to promise that you won't do anything stupid like run out with your guns blazing." She had to have that comfort.

She felt him smile. "I promise."

Her throat grew very tight and fear skittered through her. Turning, she hugged him tightly.

"I love you," she said into his shoulder.

"*Sí, te amo, amante.*"

"Don't leave me."

"I promised, didn't I?"

She nodded, then lifted her head and gave him a hard kiss. She stepped out of his arms. His black eyes started to harden as she watched. He was preparing for battle, getting ready to face his lifelong enemy. There was so much at stake now. So much. Lives were depending on them, on everything they did tonight. Leigh hoped her little army would still be standing when the dawn broke and painted the ground red. It had been a long time since she prayed to God. But if He was listening, she was praying now.

Please keep him safe. Keep them all safe. Don't let them die because they wanted to help a lonely, over-the-hill widow.

Malcolm pulled his hat low on his forehead and approached Tyler and Nicky.

"*Roja*, I need to take your man for a while. I'll bring him back in one piece."

Nicky stepped back and raised one eyebrow at Malcolm. "As long as you bring him back."

"*Sí*, I will. Because for some reason, you want to keep him."

"Yup, I do." With one last kiss for her husband, Nicky joined Leigh.

"How the hell did I get stuck with you again?" Tyler groused at Malcolm as they walked out the door.

"I told you before, *buena suerte*, bounty hunter."

Leigh looked at Nicky and saw the worry written plainly in her green eyes.

"How bad is this Damasco?"

Leigh repressed a shudder. "Bad. He...he was twisted up inside by his mother. She is the queen of bitches. I'm surprised she doesn't howl at the moon and shed like the dog that she is. I never believed in evil until I met Isabella."

Nicky nodded grimly. "Call me if you need me. I'll do the same."

She grabbed the bucket from the table where she'd left it and headed to the back of the house. Leigh picked up the rifle from the table, then turned out the lamp.

Darkness spread around the room. She let her eyes adjust before taking up her position by the sink near the rifle hole.

It was almost time.

ଓ ଓ ଓ

It seemed like days had passed, when it had probably only been hours. Leigh was anxious. Crazy anxious. Like waiting for a whooping when she was a child. It was the anticipation that was killing her. Her palms were sweaty so she kept wiping them on her jeans. All she could hear was her own ragged breathing and the chirp and twitter of the night outside.

Waiting was never her strong suit. Leigh always simply took or asked for what she wanted without waiting. She couldn't do that tonight. They had to catch that bastard and his cohorts on her ranch. That way if they killed them, it would be self-defense. And if, God forbid, one of her new family got killed, it would be murder.

Leigh felt a trickle of sweat meander down her forehead, then take a left turn to head for the side of her nose, making her glasses slide. She really wanted to take them off, but she couldn't see six feet past her face without them. There was a six inch by six inch rifle hole for her in the boarded up window. Ray and Jack had removed one pane from each window to allow for it.

It was one of those things if you thought about for too long you'd go crazy. But if you did it, like scratching your nose or taking off your glasses, that's when whatever it was you were waiting on finally happened. And you weren't ready.

Leigh was afraid that would be her. So she just wiped the sweat off her nose as best she could with her damn sweaty hands, and pushed her glasses back up.

That's when she saw a shadow move by the corral. She squinted and focused tightly on the area right behind the fence.

It moved again—a figure, crouched down, walking on its haunches. Her heart began to beat faster. Its steady rhythm echoed through her ears as her pulse picked up as well. She concentrated on the shadow as it slowly made its way toward the barn.

She leaned her mouth toward the rifle hole and hooted three times. An answering hoot came from the barn. They'd heard her. Thank God. Perhaps they had even seen the shadow, too.

She cocked the rifle and peered outside again. The shadow had stopped moving. Leigh held her breath, never losing sight of the corral, and waited. Her shoulder and arm began to cramp, and the sweat trickled down her nose and her spine. And yet she stood, waiting, watching.

ৎ ৎ ৎ

Malcolm heard the three hoots from the house and realized it must have been Leigh. He heard an answering hoot from the barn. Ray and Jack were on point. He felt the weight of Leigh's compass in his pocket. Carrying a piece of his woman beside him.

"You see anything?" came Tyler's hiss from across the room.

"No," Malcolm snapped.

"That was Leigh, right?"

"*Sí*, that was her."

Silence again. Malcolm shifted his position so he could peer in the other direction out the rifle hole. Nothing. Not a goddamn thing. What did Leigh see?

He was wracked with the urge to go running to the house to make sure she was okay. That urge battled against his common sense and experience. He had to keep his ass glued in place and stick to the plan. Leigh had a good plan; she was a smart, capable woman, but still…

Malcolm worried about her.

It was a completely new experience, along with loving her, which he just had not gotten used to. Hell, the whole thing was hard. Harder than running and hiding for fifteen years.

Something moved by the corner of the house.

He wasn't really paying attention, dammit, but his night vision was keen enough he caught it out of the corner of his eye.

"North side of the house," he whispered to Tyler.

"I see 'em," Tyler whispered back.

No, there were two, no, *three* somethings moving. They headed for the front of the house down the porch. And Leigh.

And she couldn't see them because they were coming up under her line of sight.

Malcolm wasn't worried anymore—he was scared shitless. He leaned his mouth close to the rifle hole and hooted three times. If he didn't hear her answering hoot, to hell with the plan, he was going out there.

ଔ ଔ ଔ

Leigh heard three hoots from the bunkhouse. Malcolm or Tyler must have seen something near the house or barn. She hoped it was the barn, but her gut told her it wasn't. Someone was near the house.

It was nearly time. She tasted fear, excitement and anxiety on her tongue. This would be it. Live or die. The rest of her life would be decided tonight.

Leigh cupped her mouth and hooted back, then eased herself into position to wait for the attack. She wiped her hands again on her pants and her forehead across her sleeve. She had just taken her glasses off to wipe her eyes when she saw the barrel of a pistol poking through the rifle hole. At her.

ଔ ଔ ଔ

From the loft, Jack tracked three men as they approached the barn. He didn't want to take his eyes off them or he'd lose sight of them in the darkness.

Starlight shone in the lonely night and the blackness was as deep as a well without the moon for company.

There were probably more of Damasco's men in the back, but Ray was positioned with his rifle and pistols. He was damn deadly with both weapons.

Jack was so focused on his three shadows he almost missed the ones by the house. They were creeping up on the southeast side, where Nicky waited. A quick look showed at least three, perhaps four or five.

He hooted three times in the direction of the house and hoped his sister heard him.

CR CR CR

Nicky heard the hoots from the barn, the house and the bunkhouse and figured they were being surrounded. She checked her ammunition supply again, made sure it was within reach, and cocked both guns. She hooted once then settled herself.

Waiting was always the hardest part. She hoped Tyler and Malcolm were okay. They were both seasoned fighters, smart, deadly men. They wouldn't be taken down unless someone got a lucky shot.

But both she and Leigh were in the house alone, and she had a feeling they would be a big target. Nothing motivated a man more than having his woman in danger.

She hoped those two fools wouldn't take it in their heads to come charging to the rescue.

CR CR CR

Malcolm couldn't see the porch because the shadows were too deep there. That meant he couldn't see the *bandejos* who were sneaking up on the house.

His palms itched and his heart thumped. He was going to lose his mind waiting.

"They're on the porch," he whispered to Tyler.

"I know."

"I can't see them, dammit."

"I know."

He stood and ran over to Tyler who crouched on the other side by his rifle hole.

"I can't stay here and let those women fight three men alone."

Tyler turned to him in the gloom, his blue eyes pools of shadows.

"Do you think I would let my wife die?"

"No."

Tyler rose so he was eye to eye with Malcolm.

"You ready to die for your woman, *amigo*?"

"Yes."

A gleam of white in the darkness told Malcolm that Tyler smiled at his response.

"Let's go."

ঙ ঙ ঙ

Leigh cursed herself. She knew if she wasn't ready, the attack would come. Only she didn't think it would be so soon. She didn't move a single smidge. It was dark enough in the kitchen she didn't think whoever owned the pistol would be able to see her. Unless she moved.

Her glasses were hidden in her right hand so hopefully they wouldn't reflect anything. The damn sweat slid down her nose. It itched something fierce, but she dared not move.

The barrel of the pistol moved slowly inch by inch right to left, then back again. The nearer it came to her, the more rapidly her heart beat, the itchier her nose got.

That's when the knob to the door next to her started to turn.

Oh, damn. It wasn't locked.

If she moved, she was a target for the owner of the pistol. If she didn't move, the door was going to hit her when it opened.

Leigh figured she had about five seconds to decide.

ঙ ঙ ঙ

Malcolm and Tyler eased the bunkhouse door open. Malcolm crouched, pistols cocked and ready. Tyler sat beside him like a panther ready to spring. Both of them surveyed the immediate area and saw no one. Obviously the bunkhouse was not the attack point.

"Malcolm," a man whispered.

"Diego?"

"*Sí*, I am here. There are eight at the house, and another six at the barn. The rest are looking for the cattle. You hide them good, *hijo*."

"You two are making enough noise for four people so shut the hell up," Tyler hissed. "If there's eight goddamn men gunning for my wife, let's haul our asses over there and stop them."

Malcolm couldn't agree more. He ran at a crouch for the porch, so glad he'd slipped on his moccasins from his saddlebags. He was as silent as the stars.

When he reached the hitching post and the horse trough, he stopped and listened. He heard a scrape of a boot on the wood-plank porch and pinpointed the noise. He crept closer with his pistol steady.

His heart thudded in his ears as he finally got close enough to the *cabron* about to open the door.

With an ear-splitting war cry, Malcolm launched himself at the man while firing at the other man by the window. The door swung open and a rifle pointed in his face as he grappled with the son of a bitch.

"Move, Malcolm. I can't tell which one you are." Leigh's terse command was easier said than done.

With a mighty push, he broke free and rolled to the right.

"In front of you," he shouted.

A rifle shot and a cry of pain followed.

"Malcolm?"

He saw it out of the corner of his eye. Another *cabron* hiding behind the horse trough.

"Get down!"

In the blink of an eye she lay flat on her belly, out of the line of fire. He whirled to find the man, but no one was there.

Leigh didn't call out again. She knew Malcolm was hunting.

They heard gunfire from the barn and the other side of the house. Malcolm figured Tyler had reached where he was going and found the other bastards. Answering fire from the corral pinged and dinged off the side of the barn. The whine of bullets echoed through the pre-dawn air.

Malcolm paused, unmoving and silent. Still nothing. That *bandejo* was waiting. As soon as one of them moved, he'd pick them off like buzzards on a carcass.

ଓ ଓ ଓ

Leigh stretched out flat on the porch, breathing dust and dirt into her nose. Her eyes watered and dammit, she felt like she was going to sneeze. She wanted to itch, to move, to shoot something. Instead she was trapped until Malcolm told her otherwise.

That thought was enough to change her mind. No man *told* her anything. She made her own decisions.

She sprang to her feet, rifle ready, and jumped down from the porch onto the ground. She headed for the other side of the trough to where she thought Malcolm was.

"No, *amante!*" he shouted from somewhere behind her. "Diego, cover her."

Before she could turn and find him in the dark, something slammed into her back and suddenly the ground was heading for her face.

"Hah! Got you, you worthless bitch," she heard Damasco say.

And then the pain hit. Oh, shit. She'd been shot. In the back.

Malcolm's cry of rage burned her ears.

ଓ ଓ ଓ

Malcolm stood, both guns aimed at Damasco. His younger brother was dressed all in black with his pistol aimed at Leigh's prone head.

"Will you kill me, *hermano?*" he taunted. "She's an easy mark. If you even twitch on that trigger, I'll blow off that ugly head of hers."

"No, you son of a bitch. You're mine. Face me like a man," Malcolm shouted, helpless, furious and sick to his stomach. Leigh was lying on the ground bleeding, with a gun pointed at her head. He wanted to kill Damasco so badly his mouth filled with the taste of hate.

He sensed Diego coming up from the right, a solid presence. Malcolm needed to stay strong.

Damasco laughed. "You can't make the choice, can you? You want to shoot me, but you don't want her to die."

He laughed again, the noise like a saw scraping across an anvil. Damasco sounded crazed. Malcolm started backing up as the echo of gunfire began to lessen near the barn and the back of the house. It appeared as if it was almost over.

"If I go home and you're not dead, she'll kill me, *hermano*. I can't let that happen," Damasco shouted.

"Let her go, Damasco," said Diego from Malcolm's right.

"What the hell are you doing here, you old fool? You're supposed to be dead."

Diego's rusty chuckle floated across the darkness. "That *cabron* is sleeping with the devils in hell, *Señor* Zarza."

"That's where this bitch is gonna be in about ten seconds."

Malcolm's finger shook on the trigger. "If you shoot her again, I will not only shoot you, I'll cut you into pieces and let you watch as I feed you to the coyotes. Then I'll leave what's left for them to gnaw on."

"Do you think I care? Nothing you could do to me is worse than her."

Malcolm heard fear, real out-and-out terror, in Damasco's voice. He was truly more afraid of his mother than of facing a painful death at Malcolm's hands. That made him one dangerous hombre, more dangerous than someone who was simply angry. Leigh's life just slipped a notch lower.

"I'm going now, *hermano*, and neither one of you is going to stop me. It's either kill me or save her. I know which choice you're going to make."

The moment Damasco was gone, Malcolm dropped his pistols and ran to Leigh. She was still breathing, but her back was covered with blood on the right side. Diego crouched beside him.

"Malcolm?" Leigh whispered.

"Shhh, *amante*, don't talk. Save your strength."

Dios, ayúdame—I need to be strong.

He took off her neckerchief and felt along her back until she hissed. The wound was low, beneath her shoulder blade. He pressed the neckerchief into the wound to staunch the bleeding.

"Is he gone?" Leigh asked.

"*Sí*, he is gone. Back to the bitch's lair," Malcolm spat.

"You should have killed him."

He chuckled painfully at Leigh. She would never change.

"Bastard shot me in the back. He deserved whatever you give him. Goddamn! That hurts."

Her voice was choked with tears and Malcolm felt the sting of them in the back of his eyes. He wasn't even going to think about her dying. He would not let that happen. If he had to die himself just to go Heaven and kick God's ass, he would *not* let Leigh die.

"We need to get her inside, *hijo*," Diego said quietly.

"Malcolm?" Nicky's voice came from behind him.

"Here, *Roja*."

"What happened? Who is that?"

Malcolm swallowed hard as Nicky crouched on the other side of him. He started to realize Tyler was already there in front of him. He was so focused on Leigh he hadn't even *noticed* a two-hundred-twenty pound man sneak up on him.

"This is my friend Diego I told you about. Damasco shot Leigh in the back."

Tyler sucked in a hiss through his teeth and cursed colorfully. "Can we move her?"

"We're going to have to. I'm not going to let her bleed to death in the dirt."

"I'm still here, you know." Leigh's voice was weaker. "Don't make my decisions for me."

"Leigh, we need to get you in the house so I can look at you," Nicky said.

"Okay, fine," Leigh responded, sounding reluctant.

"Nicky? Tyler?" came Jack's voice from the dark. The sky was starting to turn gray as dawn approached. Malcolm saw the outline of two men walking toward them from the barn.

"Here, Jack," replied Nicky. Jack and Ray crouched down near them.

"What happened?"

While Nicky filled in her brothers, Malcolm leaned down and whispered in Leigh's ear.

"This is going to hurt, *amante*, but it has to be done. I can't carry you upside down. You can bite my arm if you want."

She tried to laugh, but it ended on a short sob instead.

"Ready."

He grabbed her left arm and slowly turned her over. Nicky examined Leigh quickly.

"The bullet didn't go through. It's still inside her. We'll have to get it out, Malcolm."

He felt sick, almost enough to return the bread he'd eaten two hours ago. He could not, simply could not, cut into Leigh's flesh. Nicky's hand on his arm steadied him.

"I'll do it. I just need you to carry her in."

Malcolm nodded.

"Malcolm, I will go check on the cattle and the other men. Little Leigh, you keep yourself alive, *comprende?*" Diego said as he stood.

"I'll do my best, Diego. Thank you for everything, *amigo.*"

"*De nada,*" he replied before turning to run into the darkness to his horse.

Malcolm leaned toward her ear. "*Te amo, amante,*" he said as he lifted her up. Her scream of pain was cut short as she lost consciousness.

"Thank God," said Nicky. "It will make it easier to get the bullet out. Hurry, let's get her into the house. Jack, get some firewood so we can stoke up the stove. Ray, see if you can find the medical kit in the house. Tyler, check to make sure all the bastards have high-tailed it out of here."

Malcolm would have smiled if his hands weren't stained with Leigh's blood as it seeped out. Leigh and *Roja* were very much alike—used to giving orders to men and being obeyed. And, chances are, they were usually right.

He carried Leigh into the house, trying desperately not to jar her too much. His soft-soled moccasins made it a little easier. Ray ran ahead and opened the door. Nicky walked in first.

"Hang on. Let me light a lantern." She took the matches from the shelf above the sink and walked to the table. After she lit the wick on the lantern, she turned up the flame. Malcolm stepped sideways through the door with Leigh in his arms.

"Take her to her bed."

Malcolm nodded grimly. He heard Jack come in the doorway with the wood and Nicky give him strict orders to build up the fire and put on water to boil. Ray was already searching the shelves for the medical kit.

Malcolm had to force himself to walk slowly up the stairs when his heart told him to run. He wanted this to be over and Leigh to be healed. This was so *hard*. He reached her room and Nicky opened the door for him. He walked to the bed. The bed they had made love in earlier.

A shudder wracked his body that had nothing to do with being cold. If Leigh died, he would do the same inside. Nothing, *nothing*, would matter anymore.

"Hang on. Just hang on. She'll be okay, but we need to work together." Nicky's voice and her hand on his arm brought him back.

He laid Leigh gently down on her side, then rolled her to her stomach, careful to lay her head to the side so she could breathe. She was so goddamn pale her freckles looked like paint spots on a white porch rail. Her compass practically burned his skin from inside his pocket.

His knees felt like jelly and he landed on them next to the bed. He brushed her hair away from her face as Nicky took her knife and began cutting away Leigh's shirt and chemise.

The sight of her white flesh, stained with blood, and the blackened hole in her back brought up his gorge again.

"Why don't you go check and see if Jack has that hot water? And find some bandages."

Malcolm heard Nicky, but he didn't move.

"*Roja*. I...I can't..."

She pressed the ruined shirt into the wound and glared at him.

"I don't have time to babysit you, Malcolm. Pull yourself together and get it done. You don't have to operate on her, but you do need to remember that you have a pair of balls. Use them."

He leaned down to kiss Leigh's cheek. "Don't let her die."

Nicky nodded grimly.

Malcolm walked out of the room and went in search of bandages.

ଓ ଓ ଓ

Nicky was amazing. With practiced skill and steady hands, she removed the bullet and sewed Leigh's wound neat and tight. She wrapped her up with clean white bandages made from sheets and towels. By the time she was done, the sun had risen.

She felt Leigh's forehead, then stood. Nicky had blood all over her clothes, and her hair was a frizzy cloud of red and brown.

"I think she's going to be okay. No fever yet and the bullet missed a lot because it ricocheted off a bone. She had a lot of bone fragments in there, and is going to be pretty sore when she wakes up, but it wasn't too bad."

Malcolm wrapped Nicky in a hug. She hugged him back, accepting his silent thanks.

"I'm going to go wash up and check on Tyler."

"*Gracias...hermana.*"

"*De nada,*" she replied as she closed the door behind her.

Malcolm turned to look at Leigh. She lay on her stomach, so still, so pale, she almost appeared dead. But her back rose steadily with each breath she took.

He dropped down on his knees next to the bed and clasped his hands in prayer. While trying to remember how to speak to a God he hadn't bothered to know in too many years, she spoke.

"Malcolm, I sure as hell hope I'm not dead. That would likely be the only reason I'd see you praying."

"*Amante!*" His heart took flight as her pain-filled hazel eyes focused on him. He reached out, cursing the fact his hand actually shook, and cupped her cheek.

Beth Williamson

"Did you get the bullet out?"

"*Sí, Roja* did it. She is a very good nurse."

She closed her eyes and groaned. "Feels like I've been kicked in the back by a team of mules."

"Leigh, I...I wanted to...that is..."

She opened her eyes again. "Don't wait here for me, Malcolm. Go find that son of a bitch and finish this because I'll be damned if I'm getting shot again."

If there was any doubt in his mind Leigh was the woman for him, that statement would have been enough to sway him.

He leaned down and gave her a quick kiss.

"I love you."

She managed a lopsided smile. "I love you, too."

"If I come back without too many holes in me, do you think you might marry me?"

"Depends on where the holes are. There are some areas I don't think I'd like you to have any."

He chuckled and kissed her again.

"Is that a yes?"

"It's a yes, although I don't know why you would want to marry a dried-up widow."

This time the kiss was hard. "You are not dried up, *amante.* You burn hot and wet for me."

Her face flushed a bit. "You play dirty."

"When it comes to you, I will do anything I need to."

She closed her eyes. "Be careful."

He pressed his lips to her cheek, her forehead and her lips.

"Come back to me," Leigh commanded.

"Always."

CHAPTER TWENTY-TWO

On the way to Rancho Zarza, Malcolm realized he was being followed. While he stopped and waited for them to catch up, he counted three. Jack, Tyler and Ray were right behind him.

"Shouldn't you be back at the Circle O protecting the women?"

Jack snorted. "Hah! Either one of them could kick my ass coming and going."

"The rest of the hands came back with your pal Diego. They had about a dozen men try to take the cattle, but it was no contest. Brett, Ethan and Trevor can watch the ranch without us. You need someone at your back to make sure that brother of yours doesn't shoot you when you're not looking." Tyler's jaw was like granite. He practically spit the words. "Nobody backshoots a woman. That lowdown son of a bitch is going to get a lesson from me."

"I'm first," Jack interjected.

"Both of you shut up. I'm going to be the one to kill Damasco. It's my fight. Not yours," Malcolm snarled.

Ray pushed his hat back on his head. "All of you stop yelling. Let's just ride over there and take care of this."

Malcolm wanted to argue, but his thirst for revenge was stronger. He reluctantly accepted the fact he wasn't going to get rid of them any time soon.

"*Vamanos, amigos.*"

He kneed Demon into a fast gallop and headed for Rancho Zarza and the final battle.

CR CR CR

The gate to the hacienda was open, with no guards in sight. That made the hackles on the back of Malcolm's neck rise. He did not like that. Not one bit.

Tyler's voice broke the uncomfortable silence. "They're waiting on you."

"And here I am."

"Last night, we killed at least twelve, and the others at least fifteen. His army is smaller, but he's definitely not alone. Don't forget, *amigo*, we are at your back. You are not alone either."

Strange how he considered these three men to be his family, his friends. They were willing to walk with him into the mouth of hell, knowing a madman and his crazy *bruja* of a mother waited to cut them to ribbons.

Loyalty, respect and sacrifice. A family was all that and more. He was never so glad of the fact.

As they got closer to the gates, he heard crying. It was faint, but there. It sounded like…it sounded like a child or a woman.

His gut tightened at the thought. Damasco wouldn't…

When they got to the courtyard, he almost had to close his eyes to lessen the pain. Damasco had young Malcolm tied to posts, naked from the waist up. His small back already had at least six lashes, bleeding, ugly bites in his tender flesh. A woman was being held back by two of the rat brothers. She was gagged with her arms secured, her eyes wild with fury and fear. She appeared around Leigh's age, much plumper and short, with curly light brown hair. Although two enormous men held her tight, she still bucked enough to make their job tough. He assumed she was Malcolm's mother, the cook. She screamed and cried behind the gag. Hers was the voice they heard.

Young Malcolm remained silent.

Damasco was still dressed in black, with his knee high, shiny leather boots, and his spurs clinking loudly against the cobblestones as he paced back and forth in front of the boy. His hair was mussed and sticking in different directions. He was not his usual, polished self. There was even dirt on his clothes. Malcolm did not see Isabella anywhere.

"Brother. I knew you'd come. As you can see, I have another choice for you. You liked the last one, didn't you? I hope the bitch died."

Malcolm flinched inwardly, but let no expression cross his face.

"Leigh is dead. Soon you will be too." Malcolm didn't want Damasco going near her ever again.

Tyler, Jack and Ray stood strong beside him with their pistols drawn, taut and ready for the battle.

At least a dozen or so armed men were stationed around the courtyard. None made a move toward them. They had been waiting for him, too.

"Big words, *hermano*. Here is your choice. You or him. I will kill one of you today. I will let you make the choice."

Jack sucked in a breath beside him.

Damasco walked to little Malcolm and draped the whip over the boy's ravaged back. He slithered it down the skin. The boy's body tightened, but he did not make a sound. Oh, God, the memories were nearly suffocating him. He'd been almost a man when he was whipped. This was a *boy*. A twelve-year-old boy who had the misfortune of being an instrument of revenge against his uncle.

"He's very much like you. I remember how you bit a hole through your lip that day rather than cry for mercy. Do you think he will do the same?"

The air crackled with tension. Malcolm waited for the opportunity he needed.

"What's your choice? Come on now, we don't have all day. *Rápido!*"

Malcolm dismounted. He heard Tyler hiss at him, but ignored him. This was his fight. He headed toward Damasco, his clothes stained with Leigh's blood and her compass in his pocket. She would ride with him in this battle— she deserved to be here with him when he ended it. His moccasins had been traded for boots that clunked on the cobblestones as he walked the twenty yards to Malcolm. The fountain gurgled happily next to them, incongruous next to the horrific scene of a man whipping his own son to death.

He saw fear and madness in Damasco's eyes as he approached.

"Did you know that old bastard left you the ranch?"

That he wasn't ready for. He almost missed a step. To think Alejandro would leave all of this to him instead of his legal son was incredible. He must have done it to finally show Malcolm that he loved him, that he was sorry. Malcolm's eyes misted briefly, but he reasserted his thirst for revenge by remembering whose blood stained his clothes.

"So get out. If I am the *patron*, get your sorry ass and your bitch of a mother out of here."

Damasco laughed crazily. "Hah! If it were only that simple, big brother. I cannot leave and she will not go. Don't you understand? She's going to kill you."

It all happened so fast, if he had blinked, he wouldn't have been ready. Isabella rose from behind the fountain with a rifle cocked and pointed at his head. Damasco cleared leather with his pistol when Malcolm's aim was true and the bullet landed straight in Damasco's black heart. Malcolm jumped toward the boy as Isabella screamed and pulled the trigger. The hiss of a bullet skimmed across his shoulder as he shielded the boy.

Bullets flew like bees in the spring as Tyler, Jack and Ray fought the rest of Damasco's men. Grunts of pain and screams assaulted his ears as Malcolm frantically sawed through the boy's bonds with his knife. As he stuck it into the scabbard on his back, he felt the boy trembling.

"Be strong, *hijo*. I need you to make yourself as small as possible under the edge of the fountain. Go!"

The boy scuttled across the cobblestones. Malcolm was amazed at his strength and courage. When he looked up, Isabella was trying to get a shot off at the boy from the other side of the fountain.

"Here, you worthless *puta*. Here," he shouted at her.

With her eyes and her rifle pointed at him, he saw the madness in their black depths eating away at her soul.

"You killed him. You killed him," she screamed as she began firing.

One bullet slammed into his arm near his elbow, but he ran toward her before she had a chance to fire again. As he ran, he zigzagged back and forth, giving her a harder target. The rest of the courtyard was quiet, the battle obviously over.

"Stay still, you *cabron*. You must die. This ranch is mine. Mine! Mine!" she screamed as spittle flew from her mouth and her eyes rolled like a crazed animal's.

Malcolm raised his pistol to shoot her when her body jerked backwards and a blossom of red appeared on her chest. The red mixed with the yellow of her dress, creating an orange reminiscent of the setting sun.

He looked to see who had shot Isabella and found Tyler with his gun still smoking.

"Any woman who would do that to a child don't deserve the air she breathes. Besides, Nicky would probably kill me if I let anything happen to you."

Malcolm stood, brushing the dirt off his clothes, and holstered his pistol. His arm stung where the bullet went through, and the steady drip of warm blood told him he needed to bandage it soon.

"Gracias, amigo."

Tyler smiled, his blue eyes actually matching the grin. "Anytime."

Malcolm ran over to the boy and crouched next to him. He was crammed under the edge of the fountain like one of those little sardines in a can.

"Malcolm? It's over. They're dead, *hijo*. Come on out now."

The boy glanced up at him and Malcolm saw fear and hate, like a trapped animal.

"Your mama needs you, *chico*."

The fear and hate began to fade and he started to look like a boy again. A boy who needed help and a lot of bandages. He started to scoot out inch by inch. Malcolm didn't offer to help, except to leave his hand out in case the boy wanted to grab it.

"Malcolm," came a voice from the other side of the courtyard. Jack had apparently knocked out the rat brothers, or killed them, and freed Malcolm's mother. She came running as fast as she could. Malcolm stood and stepped back to allow her access to her son.

She reached the boy in record time and cupped his face in her hands.

"Oh, sweetheart, I'm so sorry they hurt you."

"It's okay, Mama. Uncle Malcolm came and rescued me."

She turned her brown eyes on him with questions, but simply accepted her son's words at face value.

"Thank you, *Señor* Zarza. I don't know what to say."

"You're welcome. And it's Malcolm, *por favor.*"

"Of course. My name is Louise."

"*Con mucho gusto.*" He smiled at her.

Tyler's voice interrupted the reunion. "Riders."

Malcolm looked at Louise and Malcolm. "Into the house now. Find Lorena and stay with her."

Louise nodded and hustled the boy off to the front door where they disappeared inside.

A group of at least twenty riders came through the gates of Rancho Zarza. Malcolm, Jack, Ray and Tyler stood at least ten feet apart in a semi-circle with a dozen bodies around them. Waiting.

The battle was over, but the war raged on.

ଓ ଓ ଓ

Nicky looked out the curtains in the bedroom window for at least the tenth time in the past half hour.

"It's been almost three hours," Leigh said from the bed. "It only takes an hour to get there, an hour to get back. That means they were at the ranch at least an hour."

"Should I be more worried than I am?"

Leigh tried to laugh, but gasped in pain instead. "No, I don't think I could be."

"Me neither."

Trevor came running into the room. He was only a year older than Jack, although of all the brothers, he had the youngest-looking face. His wavy brown hair poked out from beneath his brown hat like that of a young boy's escaping a haircut. He was more slender than his brothers, although very strong and quick, perhaps even as quick as Malcolm.

He nearly skidded into the room, but stopped himself on the doorjamb. His green eyes were bright.

"They're coming."

There was nothing Leigh wanted more than to follow Nicky out the door when she took off at a dead run after her brother. She could barely move without excruciating pain. Nicky told her the bullet had nicked the bone, and that, more than anything, was causing her pain.

She refused laudanum. Couldn't stand the stuff. Made her nauseous and woozy. One time she even saw pink horses after taking a hefty dose. So she endured the pain as best she could. And waited for Malcolm.

Please come to me.

She heard horses outside and shouts, and some laughs and squeals. Her heart lightened a bit to hear it. That meant everyone had come back in one piece.

CR CR CR

Leigh heard the scrape of a boot heel on the floor, then she smelled his scent.

Malcolm.

"*Amante*," he whispered as he kissed her cheek.

Dammit all to hell, she started to bawl like a baby. She couldn't help it. She was tired, sore, and had been so damn scared. Scared he was going to be gone before she had a chance to really have a life with him.

"Shhh...it's okay. I'm here. I only have a scratch. *Roja* has already tended it."

His whiskered cheek scratched against hers. The relief coursing through her was incredible.

He came back to her.

"Are they dead?"

"*Sí*, they are both dead."

"And?"

"Diego rounded up the rest of them and gave them the choice of either dying or working for the bastard Zarza. They arrived after everything was over and in time to clean everything up." He sighed. "I will tell you more later. I am so tired, *amante*. It is so much... I..."

"Lie next to me."

He stood and stripped down to nothing. Leigh didn't even have the strength to get excited by his beautiful naked self. She saw the bandage on his left arm, white against the darkness of his skin.

He climbed in on her left side and kissed her forehead.

"Sleep, *amante*. Wake up in my arms."

With the sound of Malcolm's soft breathing next to her, she drifted off. Leigh had never felt safer.

ଔ ଔ ଔ

Ray Malloy sighed and stared out at the Texas prairie. He tucked his hands in his pockets and started walking. He hadn't had an easy time the past year, and here he was sniffing at a widow in Texas to marry up with to give his daughter a home. He snorted in self-derision.

He was scraping the bottom of his own barrel. His five-month-old daughter—who was obviously not his considering her straight black hair was neither inherited from him or her mother—owned his heart. He would do anything for the little mite. Even if it meant marrying a woman he didn't know.

Of course it would be a stupid thing to do. He scuffed the hard ground with his boot, sending a grasshopper flying in a hurry.

Why did Melody need a mother anyway? Running Deer, the Indian woman who was wet nursing her, was a good woman. She could stay for a while, at least until Melody was old enough to go to school. Then he would think about getting her a mother.

Of course that meant he would have a wife. A shudder went down his spine as a coyote howled in the distance. A wife. He spat on the ground. That was the last thing he ever wanted again. His first wife, Melody's mother, was a heartless, faithless bitch who had high-tailed it for parts unknown right after Melody was born.

Someday he'd find a woman like Leigh who was strong, sturdy and dependable. Someone who wouldn't take off for California to seek fame and fortune.

Someday the stars might fall from the sky, too.

ର ର ର

Trevor Malloy sat on the front porch steps of the Circle O and contemplated his life. He was twenty-seven years old, a rancher's son, a cow puncher and lonely as all hell. It wasn't that there was a shortage of women back in Wyoming, but most of them were like his sisters. And those that weren't, were already married by now.

He wanted excitement. Being here, helping with this range war between these folks, was the most exciting thing that had happened to him. A hunger rose inside him, ravenous for more. Ravenous for something other than cows and beans.

He didn't want to go back to Wyoming with his brothers and sister. He wanted to ask Leigh and Malcolm if he could stay here and work for a spell. Then find another place, another town to feed his hunger. But loyalty to his family came first. He would never ask.

He saw the strange wagon coming down the road toward the ranch and immediately got up to find his brother-in-law Tyler. Looked like trouble was coming to call again.

CHAPTER TWENTY-THREE

Malcolm was dreaming about riding across a bridge and Leigh was on the other side, mounted on Ghost. Waiting for him and smiling. He had just reached her when her face turned into Tyler's.

"Dammit, wake up. I'm tired of trying to shake your ugly ass up."

Tyler's impatient voice penetrated his dream.

He was so surprised to have to be woken up from a dead sleep he just blinked up at the former bounty hunter. Tyler's blue eyes were annoyed, but not truly angry.

He glanced down at Leigh, who still slept. He squinted at the window. It looked like nearly sundown.

"What is it?" he whispered.

"There are some people here, asking for you. For Malcolm Ross."

Malcolm didn't know who they could possibly be, but he was damn sure going to find out.

"Give me a minute unless you want an eyeful of what I've got."

Tyler grimaced and walked toward the door. "I'll meet you downstairs." He closed the door softly behind him.

People? What people? Maybe from Rancho Zarza. He had left Diego and Lorena in charge, but something could have happened. They would have sent a rider, not "some people"—so who could it be?

He dressed quickly but silently, and left the room sock-footed. After stopping to slip his boots on in the hallway, he went downstairs.

There was a tall man in the kitchen drinking coffee with Nicky. He had red hair, liberally laced with white, a craggy face, and kind blue eyes. He was dressed in the simple clothes of a farmer, with a homespun blue shirt and trousers. Three girls, ranging in age from probably nine to thirteen, sat on the floor playing jacks, wearing similar clothing. Each of them had the same bright red hair as the man and identical owlish blue eyes.

When Malcolm walked into the room, they all stopped talking and stared at him. He stared right back.

Who the hell were these people?

The man stood and held out his hand.

"Malcolm? I'm Donagh MacAdams."

Malcolm shook his callused hand. "Malcolm Ross."

The older man smiled. "I know who you are. And I can't tell you how happy she's going to be that you are alive."

His heart began to pound.

"She's outside by the wagon. Never could abide waiting inside—she paces too much. I want to thank your Leigh for contacting us. Without her, we wouldn't be here."

Madre de Dios. It couldn't be. It could not be.

Malcolm went out the door at a dead run, almost tearing the door off the hinges. In the light thrown by the lanterns inside, he found her. A little plumper, seemingly a lot shorter, with more than a few gray hairs, her wavy brown hair in its customary knot at the back of her head and wrinkles by her smiling brown eyes.

"Mama?"

She smiled and cried and held out her arms to him.

"Oh, Malcolm, me laddie."

He crossed to her in two strides and enfolded her in a hug that probably hurt. But he needed to hug her close. His heart had not felt whole without finding her. His mother.

Oh, Dios, his mother.

The tears mixed together on their faces as they hugged until he could hardly get a breath in. He set her back down and held her at arm's length. She hadn't really changed.

"Mama, I can't believe you're here."

"I'm here, sweetheart. I'm here. Donagh nearly ran the horses into the ground to get here. We got Leigh's telegram and came as quickly as we could."

Leigh. She had found his mother. She had brought his family to him. He would never, ever love anyone more than he loved her.

"I'm sorry, Mama. I'm sorry I never wrote to you. I'm sorry I—"

She put her small hand against his mouth.

"No need, me boy. All water under the bridge and all that. We're together now. And you need to meet your sisters. Never did have another boy after you."

Sisters. He had a family. A family.

He wiped the tears from his face with the heels of his hands.

"Where is Leigh? I want to talk with her."

"She was hurt, Mama, so she's sleeping. You can see her later."

She nodded. He hugged her one more time and breathed in the scent of love. He did not realize until that very moment how much he had missed her.

"I missed you, Mama."

"I missed you too, laddie. Now let's go inside then so you can meet the girls."

He hooked his arm through hers and headed back inside.

ભ ભ ભ

Leigh heard a commotion downstairs when she woke. It was dark in the room except for a candle on the dresser by the door. She wasn't alone although she could tell Malcolm was not in the bed anymore.

Gingerly, she tested her wound and found she could sit.

"Malcolm?"

"*Sí, amante.* I am here."

He had been sitting in a chair in the corner and rose in the darkness to approach the bed.

"What are you doing in the shadows?"

He smiled and kneeled down beside her. "I'm not in the shadows anymore. I am in your light. Always."

With more tenderness than she had ever felt, he kissed her.

"What's happened?"

"You. You happened, Leigh Wynne. I should have known when you were born and toddled around after me that you would turn my life upside down."

She looked in his black eyes and saw so much love, hope and happiness her heart began to do a jig. He was right, the shadows were gone.

"My mama is here."

She smiled. "Oh, Malcolm, I'm so glad. I didn't know if they'd come and I didn't want to get your hopes up."

He closed his eyes and shook his head. "You have given me the greatest gift ever. My life, my family, everything. You are everything to me."

Damn tears pricked her eyes again. She blinked them away.

"Does this mean you want to get hitched?"

He laughed and kissed her quickly. "*Sí, amante*, let's get hitched."

"Do I have to wear a dress at the wedding?"

He threw back his head and laughed. Then he wrapped her gently in his arms.

"I want you to meet my family and see my mama again, *mi vida*. I want them to meet the woman who holds my heart."

So full of the gifts that life had brought, Leigh could only nod. She held onto him and promised herself never to let go again.

BETH WILLIAMSON

You can't say cowboys without thinking of Beth Williamson. She likes 'em hard, tall and packing. Read her work and discover for yourself how hot and dangerous a cowboy can be.

Beth lives just outside of Raleigh, North Carolina, with her husband and two sons. Born and raised in New York, she holds a B.F.A. in writing from New York University. She spends her days as a technical writer, and her nights immersed in writing hot romances for her readers.

To learn more about Beth Williamson, please visit www.bethwilliamson.com. Send an email to Beth at beth@bethwilliamson.com, join her Yahoo! Group, http://groups.yahoo.com/group/cowboylovers, or sign up for Beth's monthly newsletter, Sexy Spurs, http://www.crocodesigns.com/cgi-bin/dada/mail.cgi/list/spurs/.

The Treasure
(c) 2006 Beth Williamson

The Malloy Family series continues. When a clumsy governess from New York meets a lonely, bitter rancher, more than her heart will fall. Available July 18, 2006 at Samhain Publishing…

Lily was hot. After the incident with Ray in the hallway, her entire body was flushed and she felt a bit feverish. Odd, really, that reaction to a man. She had never had it before, and honestly hadn't expected it.

After washing up, she went into her room and opened the window a bit to try to cool herself off. The moon was bright in the dark sky. She opened the window a bit more and leaned out to get a better look.

Then her natural grace took over, and she fell out the window into the snow.

She landed on her nose, which immediately made a popping noise, and a warm gush of blood bathed her face. The snow was absolutely freezing and her entire body was lying on that frozen mass, from tip to toes. She pushed up on her elbows and ended up shoving her hands deeper into the snow.

Yes, indeed, her fine graceful self just had to make itself known. Hopefully she could climb back into her window without anyone seeing her.

The sound of boots rapidly running through the snow toward her dashed that hope to the rocks.

"Lily!" Ray said. "My God, are you all right?"

She turned her head and peered at him in the darkness. Might as well be honest. "No, I think I may have broken my nose. And I can't seem to get out of this snow. I'm afraid frostbite will be a possibility if I don't figure out how."

Strong arms lifted her effortlessly and she found herself being carried by Ray before she could blink. It was dark enough she couldn't see his expression under the shadow of his hat, but she had no doubt it was not a happy face.

"Thank you."

Lily tilted her head back and pinched the bridge of her nose to stop the bleeding. Her nose was really the least of her concerns. Ray Malloy was the biggest.

He opened the door and carried her inside, kicking the door closed behind him. She had the insane notion of a groom carrying his bride over the threshold and she started laughing. The more she tried to stop, the harder she laughed.

"I'm not sure what's so damn funny, but if you don't hush up, I'm gonna throw you back into the snow."

Ray carried her over to the sofa in the living room and set her down. He glanced at her white nightgown and immediately his eyes changed. The pupils dilated and a hazy glow surrounded the green. His nostrils flared and his lips tightened.

Lily thought it was blood that he saw, but when she looked at her nightgown, she realized the snow had turned the white garment transparent. He could clearly see her breasts, and her nipples, which were puckered tighter than a stone, as well as a hint of the dark hair between her legs.

Lily was never so embarrassed in her life. She didn't know whether to stop her nosebleed or cover herself, so she tried both. One arm landed over her breasts, while the other continued to pinch her nose.

"Do you think you could get me a towel, and perhaps some of that snow for my nose?"

His gaze snapped to hers and what she saw in his eyes made her breath stop. Raw, blatant desire. For her. A plump, on the shelf spinster with a shady childhood and a penchant for tripping over her own two feet. Lily felt an answering yearning in herself, a need to find out if what she saw, what she felt from him, was more than lust.

"I—"

"Let me get that towel," he said and then he was gone before she could finish her sentence.

Lily started shivering. She didn't know if it was from the snow bath or from the look in Ray's eyes when he stared at her nearly naked body.

She was afraid it was from the latter. And she had no idea what to do about it.

Love can rescue a lonely heart…
Enjoy this excerpt from

Rescue Me

(c) 2006 Jaci Burton

Kyle Morgan doesn't want to be rescued, especially not by former beauty queen Sabrina Daniels. Sabrina fires up Kyle's long dormant libido, and it's like a match struck on dry tinder—an explosion of heat whenever she's around. Sabrina Daniels, newly divorced from her controlling millionaire husband, is out to build her independence and begin a new life. Both have firm goals for their future, but love has a way of interfering in the best laid plans. Now available in paperback and digital formats at Samhain Publishing…

"I'm here to rescue you."

Kyle Morgan was so intent on what he was doing he thought the female voice above him was his sister Jenna, bugging him about coming in for lunch.

"I don't need rescuing right now. Get lost." Another turn of the wrench and he might actually be able to get the blasted oil pan loosened.

"That's not what this paper says."

Definitely not his sister's voice. Those weren't Jenna's legs either. But then he couldn't see much while lying in the dirt under the truck. He tilted his head sideways and saw red-painted toenails and slim, tanned ankles. Jenna wouldn't be caught dead in skimpy sandals like that. Definitely *not* his sister.

He slid out from underneath the truck and squinted in the midday sun to see who thought he needed rescuing. All he could make out was a vague shadow attached to very shapely legs.

"Are you going to lie there and stare at me all day?" Her voice was deep and sexy, like skinny-dipping at midnight. Risky, forbidden, yet irresistibly appealing.

He so didn't have time for this. But he was damn curious and needed a break anyway, so he grabbed his shirt off the hood of the old blue Chevy truck, wiping his hands and sweat-soaked, dirty face. Blinking to clear the sunspots out of his eyes, Kyle got his first look at the woman attached to the voice.

Stunning, was his first thought as he gazed at her beautiful face. Golden blonde hair hung in cascading waves over her shoulders and rested just above her full, high breasts. Eyes the color of amber ale stared levelly at him as she licked her lips nervously.

"Are you Kyle Morgan?"

I don't know. Am I? He seemed unable to think about anything except the vision standing in front of him. "I guess I am." *Great answer, dumbass. Sunstroke, obviously. Normally he had a freakin' brain cell.*

"Then as I said before, I'm here to rescue you." A smile that could light up the entire state of Oklahoma graced her face as she held out her hand. "I'm Sabrina Daniels."

Kyle was dimly aware of her slim, warm hand in his as she shook it with fervor. Her skin was soft, like sliding his hand over silk sheets, making him wish he'd had a chance to wash the grime off his.

Suddenly the name sparked recognition. "You're Sabrina Daniels?" Shit. He sure hoped he heard that wrong.

She nodded enthusiastically. "Yes. I'm so glad to finally meet you, Kyle."

So this was the woman who was going to spend the next three months at the Rocking M Ranch. Three months, and he would have to work closely with her every day. He stifled a groan as his eyes washed over her cover-model looks and centerfold body, trying not to lick his lips at the way the blue silk dress hugged her womanly curves. Surely this woman was punishment for something bad he'd done in the past.

Maybe he should have asked for a picture first. She looked totally out of place and too damned distracting. Not good.

"I didn't expect you until tomorrow." Frankly he didn't expect her to show up at all. *Hoped* she wouldn't show was more like it.

"I know. I arrived this morning and thought about grabbing a hotel and waiting until tomorrow but I was so excited I decided to come out a day early. I didn't think you'd mind since we had an agreement and you were expecting me. You were expecting me right?"

The woman waved her hands around as fast as she was talking. He was already getting a headache and watching her swat invisible flies in the air was making him dizzy to boot.

"At first I planned to call, and then I thought if I called you might not let me come today and I really wanted to, so I decided to just show up and throw myself at you and here I am." She inhaled a huge breath of air.

Trying hard to recall if he'd had any whiskey for breakfast that could possibly be screwing with his clarity, he remembered he'd had coffee. So the reason for his confusion had to be the five-foot-six fast talking tornado standing in front of him.

"Yes I can see you're here." She might be here, but he'd be damned if he was going to be pleasant. No matter how good-looking she was, or how her voice reminded him of sex and sin, or how her face showed the enthusiasm of a child. This wasn't his idea in the first place. "So now what?"

She tilted her head, showing off a creamy expanse of slender neck. Kyle inhaled sharply, trying to avoid thinking of her as a beautiful, desirable woman. He wanted to think of her as a nuisance. Which she was going to be for the next three months.

"Well, now I guess we can get started."

"Get started with what?" He must have had whiskey *with* his coffee this morning.

Sabrina smiled shyly. "With my training."

His thoughts strayed to the kind of training he'd like to give Sabrina Daniels. Damned if all the blood in his brain hadn't migrated toward baser pastures. His long dormant sex drive sure picked a fine time to spring to life again. Great—now he could add lack of sex to his already long list of frustrations.

Maybe if he thought about all the negative things her presence represented he could get his mind off the fact Sabrina Daniels was a damned attractive woman.

It wasn't working. His mind continued on its wayward sexual course, heating his blood and tightening the crotch of his jeans. Maybe it was the weather. It was damn hot outside, way too hot for late April. He was dirty and sweaty and felt like a pig while she looked fresh and clean and smelled like peaches. He shuddered to think what he must smell like, but it was probably closer to rotted fruit.

He looked her over from head to toe. She crossed her arms across her chest, obviously uncomfortable with his scrutiny. Good. "I hardly think you're dressed to begin anything, other than maybe hosting a cocktail party. And gee, you just missed the one we hosted last night. All the Dreamwater elite were here."

Sarcasm obviously wasn't lost on her as she tapped her sandaled foot in annoyance. Maybe she'd be so irritated she'd leave. He should be so lucky.

"Kyle. I'm hot, I'm thirsty, and I've driven a long way today. It's my understanding we had an agreement and you were expecting me. But if there's a problem with our contract we can discuss it. Is there some place out of the sun we could sit and talk?"

Well hell. If his mother were still alive she'd kick his ass for lack of manners. He finally noticed sheens of perspiration moistened her face, and the shadow between her breasts that kept drawing his eye was damp. She looked about ready to pass out.

"Sorry. Let's go inside where it's cooler."

She nodded gratefully and Kyle directed her toward the large brick ranch house, following behind her. Watching her perfect backside swaying as she walked, it became quite clear this bargain he and his family had struck was a huge mistake.

Kyle didn't want to do business with Sabrina Daniels, but couldn't pinpoint exactly why. Maybe it was the instant attraction he felt for her, bringing to life feelings long held in check. More likely it was because she now held a financial interest in his family's ranch. That meant an outsider owned a part of the Rocking M.

When his parents died and he and his younger brother and sister took over the Rocking M, they vowed the Morgan's would retain ownership. And despite everything they'd been through, that's the way it had remained. Until now. Now Sabrina Daniels owned a portion of their ranch. At least temporarily.

If they didn't need the money so damn bad, if he hadn't been forced to pay his cheating ex-wife all that cash in the divorce settlement, they wouldn't be in this predicament now. This was his fault and an investor was the only way to dig the Rocking M out of the deep financial hole he'd put it in.

The sooner he finished his business with Sabrina Daniels and got her off the Rocking M, the happier he'd be. No one was ever going to own this ranch but a Morgan.